JIGS & REELS

Also by Joanne Harris

THE EVIL SEED

SLEEP, PALE SISTER

CHOCOLAT

BLACKBERRY WINE

FIVE QUARTERS OF THE ORANGE

COASTLINERS

HOLY FOOLS

THE FRENCH KITCHEN: A COOKBOOK

(with Fran Warde)

JIGS & REELS

Joanne Harris

Doubleday

LONDON · NEW YORK · TORONTO · SYDNEY · AUCKLAND

TRANSWORLD PUBLISHERS
61–63 Uxbridge Road, London W5 5SA
a division of The Random House Group Ltd

RANDOM HOUSE AUSTRALIA (PTY) LTD
20 Alfred Street, Milsons Point, Sydney,
New South Wales 2061, Australia

RANDOM HOUSE NEW ZEALAND LTD
18 Poland Road, Glenfield, Auckland 10, New Zealand

RANDOM HOUSE SOUTH AFRICA (PTY) LTD
Endulini, 5a Jubilee Road, Parktown 2193, South Africa

Published 2004 by Doubleday
a division of Transworld Publishers

For more information on Joanne Harris and her books,
see her website at www.joanne-harris.co.uk

'Faith and Hope Go Shopping' first appeared in *Woman's Weekly Fiction Special* in
April/May 2000; 'Gastronomicon' in *Woman and Home* in April 2001; 'Breakfast at
Tesco's' in *Good Housekeeping* in July 2002; 'Tea with the Birds' in *Sainsbury's Magazine* in
April 2001; 'The Ugly Sister' in the *Mail on Sunday*'s *You Magazine* in December 2000;
'Class of '81' in *Magic*, a collection of short stories by various authors, in June 2002;
'Free Spirit' in *A Day in the Life*, an anthology for Breast Cancer Awareness published by
Black Swan in September 2003; 'The Spectator' in *The Big Issue* in December 2002; and
'Fule's Gold' was read at the Hay on Wye festival for Radio 4 in May 2002.

A catalogue record for this book is available from the British Library.
ISBN 0385 606427

Typeset in 10½/14pt Goudy by Kestrel Data, Exeter, Devon.

Printed and bound in Australia by
Griffin Press.

1 3 5 7 9 10 8 6 4 2

Papers used by Transworld Publishers are natural, recyclable products made from
wood grown in sustainable forests. The manufacturing processes conform to the
environmental regulations of the country of origin.

Contents

Foreword

IT'S WONDERFUL TO SEE THAT, AFTER A PERIOD IN THE doldrums, the short story has finally made a comeback. A good short story – and there are some *very* good short stories out there – can stay with you for much longer than a novel. It can startle, ignite, illuminate and move in a way that the longer format cannot. It is often troubling, often frightening or subversive. It provokes questions, whereas most novels tend to try to answer them. Of all the books I have read and loved, I find that it is the short stories I remember most clearly, those vivid, anarchic glimpses into different worlds, different people.

Some of them trouble me, even now. I still worry about what happened to Ray Bradbury's Pedestrian. I still cry over Roger Zelazny's 'Rose for Ecclesiastes'. I still get the shivers when I remember Jerome Bixby's 'It's a Good Life'. And every time I catch the Tube, I feel a sense of unreasonable disquiet, which is largely due to a story called 'A Subway Named Moebius', even though I was twelve when I read it, and I cannot even remember the author's name.

Personally, I find short stories difficult and slow to write. To compress an idea into such a small space, to keep its proportions, to find the voice, is both demanding and frustrating. Four or five thousand words, which might take me a day to write as part of a novel, may take me two weeks to finish as a short story. Like my grandfather's home-brewed wine, my short stories are mostly experimental in nature. Success is never guaranteed; sometimes a story works, and sometimes it dies on the page, like a very long joke with no punch-line, for no reason that I can quite fathom. But I do enjoy them. I enjoy the possibilities; the variety; the challenge. I have been writing them – or trying to – for the past ten years. This is the first time they have been published as a collection.

JIGS & REELS

Faith and Hope Go Shopping

Four years ago, my grandmother went into an old people's home in Barnsley. Before her death I went there often, and a lot of stories came out of those visits. This is one of them.

IT'S MONDAY, SO IT MUST BE RICE PUDDING AGAIN. IT'S NOT so much the fact that they're careful of our teeth, here at the Meadowbank Home, rather a general lack of imagination. As I told Claire the other day, there are lots of things you can eat without having to chew. Oysters. Foie gras. Avocado vinaigrette. Strawberries and cream. Crème brûlée with vanilla and nutmeg. Why then this succession of bland puddings and gummy meats? Claire – the sulky blonde, always chewing a wad of gum – looked at me as if I were mad. Fancy food, they claim, upsets the stomach. God forbid our remaining tastebuds should be overstimulated. I saw Hope grinning round the last mouthful of ocean pie, and I knew she'd heard me. Hope may be blind, but she's no slouch.

1

Faith and Hope. With names like that we might be sisters. Kelly – that's the one with the exaggerated lip liner – thinks we're quaint. Chris sometimes sings to us when he's cleaning out the rooms. *Faith, Hope and Cha-ri-tee!* He's the best of them, I suppose. Cheery and irreverent, he's always in trouble for talking to us. He wears tight T-shirts and an earring. I tell him that the last thing we want is charity, and that makes him laugh. Hinge and Brackett, he calls us. Butch and Sundance.

I'm not saying it's a bad place here. It's just so *ordinary* – not the comfortable ordinariness of home, with its familiar grime and clutter, but that of waiting-rooms and hospitals, a pastel-detergent place with a smell of air freshener and distant bedpans. We don't get many visits, as a rule. I'm one of the lucky ones; my son Tom calls every fortnight with my magazines and a bunch of chrysanths – the last ones were yellow – and any news he thinks won't upset me. But he isn't much of a conversationalist. *Are you keeping well, then, Mam?* and a comment or two about the garden is about all he can manage, but he means well. As for Hope, she's been here five years – even longer than me – and she hasn't had a visitor yet. Last Christmas I gave her a box of my chocolates and told her they were from her daughter in California. She gave me one of her sardonic little smiles. 'If that's from Priscilla, sweetheart,' she said primly, 'then you're Ginger Rogers.' I laughed at that. I've been in a wheelchair for twenty years, and the last time I did any dancing was just before men stopped wearing hats.

We manage, though. Hope pushes me around in my

chair, and I direct her. Not that there's much directing to do in here; she can get around just by using the ramps. But the nurses like to see us using our resources. It fits in with their waste not, want not ethic. And, of course, I read to her. Hope loves stories. In fact, she's the one who started me reading in the first place. We've had *Wuthering Heights*, and *Pride and Prejudice*, and *Doctor Zhivago*. There aren't many books here, but the library van comes round every four weeks, and we send Lucy out to get us something nice. Lucy's a college student on Work Experience, so she knows what to choose. Hope was furious when she wouldn't let us have *Lolita*, though. Lucy thought it wouldn't suit us.

'One of the greatest writers of the twentieth century, and you thought he wouldn't *suit* us!' Hope used to be a professor at Cambridge, and still has that imperious twang in her voice sometimes. But I could tell Lucy wasn't really listening. They get that look – even the brighter ones – that nursery-nurse smile which says *I know better. I know better because you're old.* It's the rice pudding all over again, Hope tells me. Rice pudding for the soul.

If Hope taught me to appreciate literature, it was I who introduced her to magazines. They've been my passion for years, fashion glossies and society pages, restaurant reviews and film releases. I started her out on book reviews, slyly taking her off guard with an article here or a fashion page there. We found I had quite a talent for description, and now we wade deliciously together through the pages of bright ephemera, moaning over Cartier diamonds and Chanel lipsticks and lush, impossible clothes. It's strange, really. When I was young those things really didn't interest me. I think Hope was more elegant than I was – after all, there were college balls and academy parties and summer picnics on the Backs. Of course now we're both the same. Nursing-home chic. Things tend to be communal here – some people forget what belongs to them, so there's a lot of pilfering. I carry my nicest things with me, in the rack under my wheelchair. I have my money and what's left of my jewellery hidden in the seat cushion.

I'm not supposed to have money here. There's nothing to spend it on, and we're not allowed out unaccompanied. There's a combination lock on the door, and some people try to slip out with visitors as they leave. Mrs McAllister – ninety-two, spry, and mad as a hatter – keeps escaping. She thinks she's going home.

It must have been the shoes that began it. Slick, patent, candy-apple red with heels which went on for ever, I found them in one of my magazines and cut out the picture. Sometimes I would bring it out and look at it in private, feeling dizzy and a little foolish, I don't know why. It wasn't as if it were a picture of a man, or anything like that. They were only shoes. Hope and I wear the same kind of shoes: lumpy leatherette slip-ons in porridge beige, eminently, indisputably *suitable* – but in secret we moan over Manolo Blahniks with six-inch perspex heels, or Gina mules in fuchsia suede, or Jimmy Choos in hand-painted silk. It's absurd, of course. But I *wanted* those shoes with a fierceness that almost frightened me. I wanted, just once, to step out into the glossy, gleeful pages of one of my magazines. To taste the recipes; see the films; read the books. To me the shoes represented all of that; their cheery, brazen redness; their frankly impossible heels. Shoes made for anything – lolling, lounging, prowling, strutting, *flying* – anything but walking.

I kept the picture in my purse, occasionally taking it out and unfolding it like a map to secret treasure. It didn't take Hope long to find out I was hiding something.

'I know it's stupid,' I said. 'Maybe I'm going peculiar. I'll probably end up like Mrs Banerjee, wearing ten overcoats and stealing people's underwear.'

Hope laughed at that. 'I don't think so, Faith. I understand you perfectly well.' She felt on the table in front of her for her teacup. I knew better than to guide her hand. 'You want to do something unsuitable. I want a copy of *Lolita*. You want a pair of red shoes. Both are equally unsuitable for people like us.' She drew a little closer, lowering her voice. 'Is there an address on the page?' she asked.

There was. I told her. A Knightsbridge address. It might as well have been Australia.

'Hey! Butch and Sundance!' It was cheery Chris, who had come to clean the windows. 'Planning a heist?'

Hope smiled. 'No, Christopher,' she said slyly. 'An escape.'

We planned it with the furtive cunning of prisoners-of-war. We had one great advantage; the element of surprise. We were not habitual escapees, like Mrs McAllister, but trusties, nicely lucid and safely immobile. There would have to be a diversion, I suggested. Something that would bring the duty nurse away from the desk, leaving the entrance unguarded. Hope took to waiting by the door, listening to the sound of the numbers being pressed on the keypad until she was almost certain she could duplicate the combination. We timed it with the precision of old campaigners. At nine minutes to nine on Friday morning I picked up one of Mr Bannerman's cigarette butts from the common room and hid it in the paper-filled metal bin in my room. At eight minutes to, Hope and I were in the lobby on our way to the breakfast-room. Ten seconds later, as I'd expected, the sprinkler went off. On our corridor I could hear Mrs McAllister screaming, 'Fire! Fire!'

Kelly was on duty. Clever Lucy might have remembered to secure the doors. Thick Claire might not have left the desk at all. But Kelly grabbed the nearest fire extinguisher from the wall and ran towards the noise. Hope pushed me towards the door and felt for the keypad. It was seven minutes to nine.

'Hurry! She'll be back any moment!'

'Shh.' *Beep-beep-beep-beep.* 'Got it. I knew one day I'd find a use for those music lessons they gave me as a child.' The door slid open. We crunched out onto sunlit gravel.

This was where Hope would need my help. No ramps here, in the real world. I tried not to stare, mesmerized, at the sky, at the trees. Tom hadn't taken me out of the building for over six months.

'Straight ahead. Turn left. Stop. There's a pothole in

front of us. Take it easy. Left again.' I remembered a bus stop just in front of the gates. The buses were like clockwork. Five to and twenty-five past the hour. You could hear them from the common room, honking and ratcheting past like cranky pensioners. For a dreadful moment I was convinced the bus stop had gone. There were roadworks where it had once stood; bollards lined the kerb. Then I saw it, fifty yards further down, a temporary bus stop on a shortened metal post. The bus appeared at the brow of the hill.

'Quick! Full speed ahead!'

Hope reacted quickly. Her legs are long and still muscular; she did ballet as a child. I leaned forwards, clutching my purse tightly, and held out my hand. Behind us I heard a cry; glancing back at the windows of the Meadowbank Home, I saw Kelly at my bedroom window, her mouth open, yelling something. For a second I wasn't sure the bus would even take an old lady in a wheelchair, but it was the hospital circular, and there was a special ramp. The driver gave us a look of indifference and waved us aboard. Then Hope and I were on the bus, clinging to each other like giddy schoolgirls, laughing. People looked at us, but mostly without suspicion. A little girl smiled at me. I realized how long ago it was since I'd seen anyone young.

We got off at the railway station. With some of the money from the chair cushion I bought two tickets to London. I panicked for a moment when the ticket man asked for my pass, but Hope told him, in her Cambridge professor's voice, that we would pay the full fare. The ticket man rubbed his head for a minute, then shrugged.

'Please yourself,' he said.

The train was long and smelt of coffee and burnt rubber. I guided Hope along the platform to where the guard had let down a ramp.

'Going down to the smoke, are we, ladies?' The guard sounded a little like Chris, his cap pushed back cockily from his forehead. 'Let me take that for you, love,' he said to Hope, meaning the wheelchair, but Hope shook her head. 'I can manage, thank you.'

'Straight up, old girl,' I told her. I saw the guard noticing Hope's blind eyes, but he didn't say anything. I was glad. Neither of us can stand that kind of thing.

The piece of paper with the Knightsbridge address was still in my purse. As we sat in the guard's van (with coffee and scones brought to us by the cheery guard), I unfolded it again. Hope heard me doing it, and smiled.

'Is it ridiculous?' I asked her, looking at the shoes again, shiny and red as Lolita lollies. 'Are *we* ridiculous?'

'Of course we are,' she answered serenely, sipping her coffee. 'And isn't it *fun*?'

It only took three hours to get down to London. I was expecting much longer, but trains, like everything else, move faster nowadays. We drank coffee again, and talked to the guard (whose name was not Chris, I learned, but Barry), and I described what countryside I could see to Hope while it blurred past at top speed.

'It's all right,' Hope reassured me. 'You don't have to do it all now. Just see it first, and we'll go over it all together, in our own time, when we get back.'

It was nearly lunchtime when we arrived in London. King's Cross was much bigger than I'd imagined it, all glass and glorious grime. I tried to see it as well as I could, whilst directing Hope through the crowds of people of all colours and ages: for a few moments even Hope seemed disorientated, and we dithered on the platform, wondering where all the porters had gone. Everyone but us seemed to know exactly where they were going, and people with briefcases jostled against the chair as we stood trying to work out where to go. I began to feel some of my courage erode.

'Oh, Hope,' I whispered. 'I'm not sure I can do this any more.'

But Hope was undeterred. 'Rubbish,' she said bracingly. 'There'll be taxis – over *there*, where the draught is coming from.' She pointed to our left, where I did see a sign, high above our heads, which read *Way Out*. 'We'll do what everyone does here. We'll get a cab. Onwards!' And at that we pushed right through the mass of people on the platform, Hope saying 'Excuse me' in her Cambridge voice, me remembering to direct her. I checked my purse again, and Hope chuckled. This time I wasn't looking at the picture, though. Two hundred and fifty pounds had seemed like inexpressible riches at the Meadowbank Home, but the train fare had taught me that prices, too, had speeded up during our years away from the world. I wondered if we'd have enough.

The taxi driver was surly and reluctant, lifting the chair into the black cab while Hope steadied me. I'm not as slim as I was, and it was almost too much for her, but we managed.

'How about lunch?' I suggested, too brightly, to take away the sour taste of the driver's expression.

Hope nodded. 'Anywhere that doesn't do rice pudding,' she said wryly.

'Is Fortnum and Mason's still there?' I asked the driver.

'Yes, darling, *and* the British Museum,' he said, revving his engine impatiently. 'Best place for you two,' I thought I heard him mutter. Unexpectedly, Hope chuckled. 'Maybe we'll go there next,' she suggested meekly. That set me off as well. The driver gave us both a suspicious glance and set off, still muttering.

There are some places which can survive anything. Fortnum's is one of these, a little antechamber of heaven, glittering with sunken treasures. When all civilizations have collapsed, Fortnum's will still be there, with its genteel doormen and glass chandeliers, the last, untouchable, legendary defender of the faith. We entered on the first floor, through mountains of chocolates and cohorts of candied fruits. The air was cool and creamy with vanilla and allspice and peach. Hope turned her head gently from side to side, breathing in the perfume. There were truffles and caviar and foie gras in tiny tins and giant demijohns of green plums in aged brandy and cherries the colour of my Knightsbridge shoes. There were quails' eggs and nougatines and *langues de chat* in rice-paper packets and champagne bottles in gleaming battalions. We took the lift to the top floor and the café, where Hope and I drank Earl Grey from china cups, remembering the Meadowbank Home's plastic tea service and giggling. I ordered recklessly for both of us, trying not to think of my diminishing savings: smoked salmon and scrambled eggs on muffins light as puffs of air, tiny canapés of rolled anchovy and sundried tomatoes, Parma ham with slices of pink melon, apricot and chocolate parfait like a delicate caress. 'If Heaven is anything like as nice as this,' murmured Hope, 'send me there right now.'

Even the obligatory bathroom stop was a revelation: clean, gleaming tiles, flowers, fluffy pink towels, scented hand cream, perfume. I sprayed Hope with freesias and looked at us both in one of the big shiny mirrors. I'd expected us to look drab, maybe even a little foolish, in our nursing-home cardies and sensible skirts. Maybe we did. But to me we looked changed, gilded: for the first time I could see Hope as she must have been; I could see myself.

We spent a long time in Fortnum's. We visited floors of hats and scarves and handbags and dresses. I imprinted them all into my memory, to bring out later with Hope. She wheeled me patiently through forests of lingerie and coats and evening frocks like a breath of summer air, letting her thin, elegant fingers trail over silks and furs. Reluctantly we left: the streets were marvellous, but lacked sparkle; looking at the people rushing past us, haughty or indifferent, once again I was almost afraid. We hailed a taxi.

I was getting nervous now; a prickle of stage fright ran up my spine and I unfolded the paper again, its folds whitened by much handling. Once more I felt drab and old. What if the shop assistant wouldn't let me in? What if they laughed at me? Worse still was the suspicion – the certainty – that the shoes would be too expensive, that already I'd over-spent, that maybe I hadn't even had enough to begin with . . . Spotting a bookshop, glad of the diversion, I stopped the cab and, with the help of the driver, we got out and bought Hope a copy of *Lolita*.

No-one said it might be unsuitable. Hope smiled and held the book, running her fingers over the smooth un-broken spine. 'How good it smells,' she said softly. 'I'd almost forgotten.'

The cab driver, a black man with long hair, grinned at us. He was obviously enjoying himself. 'Where to now, ladies?' he asked.

I could not answer him. My hands trembled as I handed over the magazine page with the Knightsbridge address. If he'd laughed I think I would have wept. I was close to it already. But the driver just grinned again and drove off into the blaring traffic.

It was a tiny shop, a single window with glass display shelves and just one pair of shoes on each. Behind them, I could see a light interior, all pale wood and glass, with tall vases of white roses on the floor.

'Stop,' I told Hope.

'What's wrong? Is it shut?'

'No.'

The shop was empty. I could see that. There was one assistant, a young man in black, with long, clean hair. The shoes in the window were pale green, tiny, like buds just about to open. There were no prices on any of them.

'Onwards!' urged Hope in her Cambridge voice.

'I can't. It's—' I couldn't finish. I saw myself again, old and colourless, untouched by magic.

'Unsuitable,' barked Hope scornfully, and wheeled me in anyway.

For a second I thought she was going to hit the vase of roses by the door. 'Left!' I yelled, and we missed them. Just.

The young man looked at us curiously. He had a clever, handsome face, but I was relieved to see that his eyes were smiling. I held up the picture.

'I'd like to see – a pair of these,' I told him, trying to copy Hope's imperious tone, but sounding old and quavery instead. 'Size four.'

His eyes widened a little, but he did not comment. Instead he turned and went into the back of the shop, where I could see shelves of boxes waiting. I closed my eyes.

'I thought I had a pair left.'

He took them carefully out of their box, all sucked-sweet shiny and red, red, red.

'Let me see them, please.'

They were like Christmas baubles, like rubies, like impossible fruit.

'Would you like to try them on?'

He did not comment on my wheelchair, my old and lumpy feet in their porridge-coloured slip-ons. Instead he knelt in front of me, his dark hair falling around his face. Gently he removed my shoes. I know he could see the veins worming up my ankles and smell the violet scent of the talc that Hope rubs into my feet at bedtime. With great care he slipped the shoes onto my feet; I felt my arches push up alarmingly as the shoes slid into place.

'May I show you?' Carefully he stretched out my leg so that I could see.

'Ginger Rogers,' whispered Hope.

Shoes for strutting, sashaying, striding, soaring. Anything but walking. I looked at myself for a long time, fists clenched, a hot fierce sweetness in my heart. I wondered what Tom would say if he saw me now. My head was spinning.

'How much?' I asked hoarsely.

The young man told me a price so staggering that at first I was sure I'd misheard; more than I'd paid for my first house. I felt the knowledge clang deep at my insides, like something falling down a well. 'I'm sorry,' I heard myself saying from a distance. 'That's a little too dear.'

From his expression I guessed he might have been expecting it.

'Oh, Faith,' said Hope softly.

'It's all right,' I told them both. 'They didn't really suit me.'

The young man shook his head. 'You're wrong, Madam,' he told me, with a crooked smile. 'I think they did.'

Gently he put the shoes – Valentine, racing-car, candy-apple red – back into their box. The room, light as it was, seemed a little duller when they had gone.

'Are you just here for the day, Madam?'

I nodded. 'Yes. We've enjoyed ourselves very much. But now it's time to go home.'

'I'm sorry.' He reached over to one of the tall vases by the door and removed a rose. 'Perhaps you'd like one of these?' He put it into my hand. It was perfect, highly scented, barely open. It smelt of summer evenings and *Swan Lake*. In that moment I forgot all about the red shoes. A man – one who was not my son – had offered me flowers.

I still have the white rose. I put it in a paper cup of water for the train journey home, then transferred it to a vase. The yellow chrysanths were finished, anyway. When it fades I will press the petals – which are still unusually scented – and use them to mark the pages of *Lolita*, which Hope and I are reading. Unsuitable, it may be. But I'd like to see them try to take it away.

The Ugly Sister

I've always felt some degree of sympathy for Cinderella's Ugly Sisters. And I've always felt that there was more to their tale than the story books, cartoons and pantomime shows would have us believe.

IT'S NOT EASY BEING AN UGLY SISTER. ESPECIALLY NOT AT Christmas, smack in the middle of the pantomime season, with all its glitter and fakery and hissing and booing and tawdry old jokes and *oooh* yes it is, and *ooooh* no it isn't, behind you, behind you. Plus being spat at by shrieking sticky children with ice-cream all over their faces, or pelted with flour by a girl in Prince's clothing before all going round to Cinderella's Dance-a-Rama for pie, peas and Happy Hour after the show.

No thanks.

Of course, it was worse in the old days. That fellow Grimm has a lot to answer for, and so do Perrault and his simple-minded translator. Glass slippers, my foot. Those *pantoufles de verre* have been the bane of my life ever since, and never mind that they were originally *vair*, as in white ermine, which would have been much easier on the arches (and might even have fitted, which would really have put one over on that Prince and his little floozy). No, the old days were savage, with crows to peck out our eyes – *after* the wedding, of course; wouldn't want anything to spoil Her Smugness's Big Day – and righteous torment for the un-godly.

Nowadays, of course, we have trial by Disney, which is almost as bad: evil becomes ridiculous faced with so many pratfalls and flour bombs. There's no dignity left in being a villain. Instead it's just another Christmas crowd in Bolton-on-Dearne or Barnsley Civic Hall, featuring third-rate soap-opera has-beens and some bloke who once appeared on *Opportunity Knocks*.

But I don't complain; I'm a professional. Not like these fairweather artistes, killing time out of season between walk-on parts. It is a proud and lonely thing to be an Ugly Sister, and don't you ever forget it.

We – my sister and I – were born somewhere in Europe. Accounts differ. In any case, no-one cares much about our history. Or, for that matter, what happens to us when the curtain goes down. There's no *ever after* for an Ugly Sister, let alone a *happy*.

Our father adored us; our mother had ambitions, like all mothers, to see us settled (preferably a comfortable distance away). Then came tragedy. A fall from his horse killed our indulgent father. Mother remarried, to a widower with one daughter, and here the story begins in earnest. You know it, of course. At least, you know *her* version: how the widower died; how we then oppressed the daughter, a charming waif called Cinders; how we made her skivvy for us and sew for us and cook our enormous meals; how we callously denied her the opportunity to be Teen Queen at the Palace All-Nite Disco; the mice, the dress, the Fairy Godmother; all that drivel.

I said drivel. That wasn't the story at all.

Oh, she was quite pretty, in a sickly sort of way. Bottle-blonde, skinny, as pale and delicate as we were strapping. She did it on purpose: ate nothing but raw food, always dressed in black, exercised compulsively. You've never seen such clean floors (apparently sweeping burns 400 calories an hour, polishing 500). She rarely spoke to us, but listened raptly to the minstrels who came by with their tales of romance, and never missed the penny plays every Sunday morning in the village square. Boys liked her (of course); but she wanted a prince. Village boys not good enough for Miss High and Mighty.

Of course we hated her. We were both quite ordinary looking (they made us out to be ugly later, out of spite). Bits of us jiggled when we ran. We had poor complexions and bushy hair that no amount of blow-drying would straighten. Mistress Smuggerella was toned, sleek, a perfect size eight. Anyone would have hated her.

Of *course* she always dressed in rags. She was the type. Besides, that raggy look was very *in* that season – designer rags that cost a fortune. You had to be thin to carry it off;

with my legs I'd have looked like a pantomime cow. And the *shoes*! If you'd seen the pairs of shoes she had in her wardrobe, not just white ermine but crocodile, mink, plexiglas, ostrich, lizard, silk; all with six-inch heels and little straps even in winter (think what *that*'ll do to her arches in twenty years' time) – well, you just wouldn't have believed it.

Have you ever noticed how history favours the lookers? Henry VIII: bad press. Richard Lionheart: good press. Catherine of Aragon: bad press. Anne of Cleves: good press. Court painters have a lot to answer for, and storytellers too. You know the end: she gets the Prince (who, by the way, was short, fat and balding), the castle, the gold, the white wedding, the rose petals, the whole shebang; we get the crows. Happy Hour ever after.

But it gets worse. I've already told you; there is no *ever after* for an Ugly Sister. Nobody thought to write one, of course; *they* were too busy swooning over Her Royal Smugness and her perfect tootsies. So what happened to us? Did we just vanish? No, what happened is this: *we*, the forgotten Sisters – soon to become the Ugly Sisters, the Weird Sisters, and the Sisters of the Divine Comedy – rolled on into legend, picking up blemishes like lint along the way. We skirmished unsuccessfully with Grimm and Perrault, tried a bit of seduction on Tennyson, but again to no avail. We hoped for better in the twentieth century, but, as I said, that was when Disney came along, and by then we were ready to sell our souls for a bit of good press.

But we're troupers. At least, I am – nowadays my sister

plays to the gallery a bit too much for my taste – you'd always see me here at Christmas, in one theatre or another, face gleaming with greasepaint, in powdered wig and giant hooped skirt. I like to think there's something noble – almost heroic – about my part; a hidden pathos, which only the select few will ever see. Most of them aren't watching me anyway; they're watching *her*, aren't they, La Smuggette, in her flouncy dress and spangled shoes. When I speak, my lines are usually drowned out by hissing or laughter. But I don't care. I'm a professional. Beneath my grotesque costume, my mask of paint, a mystery awaits. One day, I tell myself, someone will notice me. One day, *my* Prince will come.

Last night was Christmas Eve. The best night of the year. Oh, there are shows after that – right until late January – but Christmas Eve is special. After that the magic runs out and depression sets in; everyone feels bloated and sluggish, playing out time at the rag-end of the season. Audiences dwindle. People forget their lines. The show moves away, to Blackpool maybe, or some other out-of-season resort, to moulder quietly until next year. Costumes stored in trunks. Lights packed into cases. But now it was Christmas Eve; everyone was louder, brighter, screamier than usual; the audience hissed and booed with even more vigour, the kids were stickier, the Prince more camp; the pantomime cow more athletic; Buttons more pathetic; and of course dear old Cinders, the star of the show, was sweeter, prettier, daintier, more glittery and fairy-like than ever before.

Only I felt different as the last act approached. My head

was aching. I wondered fleetingly whether it wouldn't be a good idea to get out of the panto business for good; to move away, to retire somewhere out of Europe, where I wouldn't be recognized.

Fat chance, I thought. There's no escape for an Ugly Sister.

And still the thought persisted. What was wrong with me tonight? I shook my head to clear it, and for the first time in my long career, something caught me by surprise and I almost fluffed a line.

There was a man watching me from the stalls. Sitting close to the stage, half in shadow; a large, long-haired man, shoulders hunched a little under a shaggy grey overcoat, his eyes fixed upon me.

That was unusual – more than that, astonishing. It was Cinders' scene; the one where my sister and I primp at the mirror while she sings her mournful song and the animals sit about blatting in sympathy. And yet there was no doubt about it (I dared a second glance through the glass, very darkly): he was looking at me.

Me. I felt my heart give a ridiculous lurch. He was no Prince Charming, that much was obvious; and I could see from the grizzled look of his rough hair that he was no longer young. But he looked strong and powerful, and his big eyes beneath the fall of hair were bright and intent. I felt suddenly very conscious of the ridiculous costume I was wearing, the huge bustle, the oversized shoes, the absurdly padded bosom. He thought me amusing, I told myself sternly; that was all. And yet he was not smiling.

I was conscious of his eyes on me throughout the rest of the scene. When I came back on stage after Cinders' mawkish duet with her prince, he was waiting for me; then again in the next. When the flour hit me in the face and the audience screamed with mirth, he alone did not laugh. Instead I saw him lower his head, as if in sorrow (I thought) at a fine, proud woman brought low. My heart was beating wildly. I raced through the final scene as if in a daze, reciting my lines automatically, my eyes returning incessantly to the face of the man still watching me from the shadows. Not a handsome face, no; but there was character there, and a kind of wild romance. His hands – so large as to be almost paws – looked capable of gentleness. His eyes gleamed wedding-ring gold in the darkness. I was trembling all over.

The last scene came. Then the curtain call. Linking hands, we all came to the front of the stage for a bow, and as I bent down he stood up and spoke urgently in my ear.

Meet me outside. Please.

I looked around wildly, still half-expecting to see some other woman – some more beautiful, more *deserving* woman – step forward to receive his message. But he was watching me, his gold-ringed eyes intent. And as I stared at him, quite forgetting the hot and foolish hand of the actor beside me, I saw him nod, as if in answer to an unspoken question.

Me?

Yes, you.

Then he was gone into the crowd, as quickly and silently as a hunter.

We took fourteen curtain calls. Streamers flew past my head, confetti fell, flowers were presented to Her Nibs and the sham Prince Charming. I could see the audience shouting and clapping (with a few stray boos and hisses for you-know-who), but in my head there was a great silence, a great astonishment. It was as if an eye I'd never known about had just opened inside my head. After the curtain, I flung aside my wig and hoop and raced wildly for the stage door, certain that he'd be gone, that it had been a joke, that he – whoever he was – had already moved on, taking a piece of my heart with him.

He was waiting in the alley behind the theatre. Neon light from Cinderella's Dance-a-Rama across the road torched his hair with gaudy colours. The snow crunched beneath my feet as I ran towards him. He stood head and shoulders above me, though I am taller than most. For the first time in my life, I felt small: delicate.

'I knew straightaway,' he growled, as I entered the circle of his arms. 'As soon as I saw you up there. Just like in the stories. Just like magic.' He was kissing me fiercely as he spoke, nuzzling hungrily against my hair. 'Come away with me. Come with me now. Leave everything. Take the risk.'

'Me?' I whispered, hardly able to breathe. 'But I'm an Ugly Sister.'

'I've had it with leading ladies. They're all the same.

23

There was a girl once—' He stopped, lowering his head as if the memory pained him. 'I know better now. I've learned to see through their disguises.' He paused again, and looked at me. 'Yours, too.'

I clung to him as he spoke, my face in the shaggy grey fur of his coat. I could hear my heart pounding more wildly than before.

'But I'm—' I began again.

'No.' Gently he ran his hand across my face, wiping off the greasepaint with his fingers. 'You're not.'

For a moment I tried to conceive of not being an Ugly Sister. *Ugly* is a word I've dragged behind me all my life; it defines who I am. Without it, what am I? The thought made me shiver.

The stranger saw my expression. 'These things are just part of the roles we play,' he said. 'The Good, the Bad, the Ugly. We're heroes too, in our way. The ones of us who crawl away cursing when the curtain goes down. The discarded ones. The ones with no happy ever after. We belong together, you and I. After everything we've endured, we have a right to something of our own.'

'But – the story,' I said weakly.

'We'll write another story.' He sounded very certain: very strong. I felt the last of my defences begin to crumble. Behind us, Cinderella's Dance-a-Rama began to thump out a disco beat. Happy Hour was beginning.

'But I don't even know you!' I protested. What I meant, of course, was that I did not know *myself*; that a lifetime of

Ugly Sisterhood had robbed me of all other identity. For the first time in my life I felt close to tears.

The stranger grinned. He had rather large teeth, I noticed; but his eyes were kind.

'Call me Wolfie,' he said.

Gastronomicon

Some people have had a hard time reconciling the author of The
Evil Seed *and of* Sleep, Pale Sister *with that of* Chocolat
and Blackberry Wine. *To help bridge the gulf, I wrote this
– and because food can be frightening, too.*

SOMETHING ALWAYS GOES WRONG WHEN WE HAVE GUESTS TO
dinner. Last time it was a strange smell, the sound of clanking
from somewhere within the walls and the sudden apparition
of a small and incredibly ugly homunculus, which I hastily
pushed into the garbage-disposal unit before it could step on
the newly iced batch of fairy buns. The dining-room lights
were lower than usual, and flickered with a strange reddish
tinge, but everyone thought that was something to do with
the wiring, and I got out of it easily enough by taking the
coffee and after-dinner drinks into the lounge.

No-one seemed to hear the distant slithering sounds from
behind the serving hatch; or if they did, they were too
polite to say anything.

It must have been the pudding.

Everything else was safe enough: prawn cocktail, then roast chicken, greens, roast and mashed potatoes, garden peas and carrots. Ernest would have had apple pie again after that; he always wants apple pie. But I thought we might try something a bit more exotic: a nice Black Forest Gâteau, perhaps, or a lemon torte. Of course, I'm always a bit limited by what Ernest will eat; there's a whole section of the cookbook I never use because he won't eat anything too fancy or too foreign. You'd never think that he's part foreign himself; he's so very *English* – always wears a tie when he goes out, never misses *The Archers*, votes Conservative and loves his Mum.

I only met her a couple of times, you know, when Ernest and I were courting. It took me a bit by surprise. She'd changed her name, of course, but I could tell she wasn't from here. She had long black hair pinned back with a silver clasp, and very dark eyes. Ernest's hair isn't quite as dark, his eyes are hazel rather than brown and his skin doesn't have that golden bloom, but I could still see the resemblance between them.

She was wearing English clothes, like Ernest, though she hadn't managed it quite as well; her dress was all right, but she wasn't wearing any stockings, and her feet were bare in her little golden sandals. Instead of a cardigan she had a sort of embroidered shawl, with some kind of writing around the edge in gold thread. I remember feeling secretly rather embarrassed that Ernest's mother was so very foreign-looking; he seemed to feel it too, though he was clearly

27

devoted to her. A bit too devoted, if you ask me; stroking her hair and fussing over her as if she were old, or sick. She was neither; she looked thirty-five at the most – and she was beautiful. That isn't a word I tend to use about people, but there was no denying it; she was. It made me feel a bit uncomfortable; I've always been rather plain, and you know what they say about men and their mothers.

I never saw Ernest's Dad. He was English, according to his Mum, but he'd moved away a long time ago, when Ernest was a boy. There were no photographs of him, and she didn't seem to want to talk about it much.

'The women of our family have never had any luck with men,' was all she would say on the subject. I guessed his parents might have disapproved of a mixed marriage. Come to think of it, mine would have been none too pleased, if they'd found out.

Still, she seemed to approve of me. And after the wedding, she moved away – the family was from Persia, or one of those Arab countries, and although Ernest never said so, I had the impression she'd gone back home. I tried not to be too pleased about it, but secretly I was rather glad. I don't know what our neighbours would have said if they'd seen her.

The cookbook was her wedding gift to us. Ernest seemed to know what it was as soon as he saw the big package wrapped in scarlet paper, and he caught hold of her by the shoulders and started talking to her very fast in a language I didn't understand. His face was twisted with emotion, and

I think there were tears in her eyes. I was relieved that there was no-one else around to see them.

Finally Ernest took the package. I don't know why I thought he looked reluctant to accept it. Then, with a glance at his mother, he gave it to me.

'This is a family treasure,' he told me gently. 'It has been passed on from mother to daughter for generations. It's the most precious thing she has. She says she knows it will be safe with you.'

His mother nodded silently, her eyes still brimming.

I tore off the scarlet paper (not very bridal, I thought to myself). To be honest, I couldn't really see what the fuss was about. It was just an old book, leather-bound and worn dark with handling. The pages were unevenly cut and covered in tiny script. Some were stained and would have been illegible even if I'd known the language.

The pages were all of different thicknesses, and I could see that in some places notes had been written in the margins and around the foreign writing. Some had been pasted directly onto the page. At the front, extra sheets had been stuck into the book, and on these the handwriting was different. Some of it was in English, some in other languages that I recognized – mostly French and German. Inside the cover was what looked like a list of names.

'All the women of our family,' said Ernest's mother, pointing. 'All our names are written here.'

Only the last one was in English. *Sulebha Alazhred Patel.* A bit of a mouthful. No wonder she changed it.

'Is it a cookbook?' From the fragments of English script in

29

the margins I could see lists of ingredients. 'I'm quite keen on cooking.'

Ernest and his mother looked at each other.

'Yes, a cookbook,' she said at last. 'A very old, very precious cookbook.'

'It's very – special – to my mother,' added Ernest. 'She has been its custodian since her mother died.'

'Thank you,' I said politely. 'It's lovely.'

That's men for you, I thought to myself. Nothing ever compares to their mother's cooking. I guessed that now Ernest would want me to prepare his mother's recipes at home, and I hoped that they wouldn't be too foreign. You know how the smell of curry lingers on soft furnishings. And in our neighbourhood – well, you know how people talk. And Ernest really does look so *English*.

I needn't have worried. After his mother left, Ernest seemed much calmer. He's a quiet man, really, not given to – well, *passions*, I suppose you'd say. The only occasion I ever saw him moved was that time with his mother. I would never have said so to Ernest, of course, but I really don't think she was good for him. He's much better without her.

I was right about the recipes, though. He's always insisted that I use his mother's cookbook, even if I have a similar recipe of my own. I didn't like to at first – to tell you the truth, I wasn't sure it was all that hygienic, with those stains and fingermarks all over it – but I got a plastic cover made, and after that it was less of a problem. And of course Ernest is very set in his ways. He can tell if I've added an ingredient or changed a recipe by as much as a whisker, and can get quite annoyed if I introduce a variation. I've learned to stick precisely to the wording (very odd wording, too, in some cases, but that's because some of the recipes are quite old), and not to experiment too much. He has his favourites, all of them from the front of the book: nice, traditional English recipes like shepherd's pie or steak and kidney pudding. The rest of the book I never use. For a start, most of it is in Arabic or something. And from what I do understand, the recipes in that part are a bit too exotic for us anyway. I have to say I'm tempted sometimes, just to see what would happen, but I know what Ernest would say if I tried. *Too fancy for me, love. What about a nice pork chop?*

So now I stick to what he likes best. Apple pie and custard. Jam roly-poly. Bubble and squeak. Toad in the hole. He never says so, but I can guess that his mother used to make them for him when he was a boy. Perhaps his father liked them. I think it's rather sweet, actually.

We've been lucky, Ernest and I. Just after we married he got a job with a big chemical firm: regular promotion, good hours, three weeks' holiday a year. We bought a nice house on a new estate, and a sensible family car. We have two children, Cheryl and Mark, both nearly grown-up now, of course, and doing well at university. No serious illnesses, no disasters, not even a burglary. Last month Ernest got another promotion – he often does after one of my dinner parties, and jokes that it must be my home cooking that does it – to Regional Director. It isn't a fortune, of course. But what would we want with more? I'm not a spender. I'm not one for furs or jewellery. We've got a nice comfortable house and a new conservatory to sit in. I have my flower-arranging class and Ernest has his golf. The kids are all right. We're safe.

Still, I sometimes wonder what happened to the man I married. Oh, I'm not unhappy or anything like that. But I have to admit that although I'm relieved Ernest didn't turn out to be one of those feckless men my mother used to warn me about, I do sometimes wonder what it would be like if he were more – well, *passionate*, I suppose. Just a little less *English*. I wonder what it would be like if, just once, we went to Bombay or Marrakesh for the holidays, instead of Skegness or Robin Hood's Bay. If we could have a little danger, a little impulse for a change. If, just once, we could have Gobi Saag Aloo instead of steak and kidney pud.

Last month was our anniversary. Twenty-five years, would you believe it, our Silver Wedding, and I'd planned a special treat. Ernest was working late – demands of the new promotion – and I thought I might surprise him with a celebration dinner. I brought out the cookbook, turning automatically to the first section, transcribed almost entirely into English and quite legible in comparison with the rest.

In twenty-five years I've learned that anything from the first ten pages is safe. Oh, you do get the odd noises, strange smells, dimmed light, an impression of shifted perspectives, of walls sliding slyly to one side, but I think that's a small price to pay for a really light Yorkshire pudding or a really fluffy curd tart. Even then, it's usually only the first time you try the recipe that it happens; after that things settle down a bit. And they *are* excellent recipes; no skimping on ingredients, no shop-bought pastry, all spices ground by hand in the big stoneware mortar Ernest bought me for our first anniversary. I don't begrudge a minute; cooking should take time. And I do enjoy it. I've never been one for these labour-saving devices – mixers and blenders and microwaves and the rest. Ernest calls them 'flavour-saving devices'.

But twenty-five years, I said to myself. There must have been a thousand recipes in that old cookbook, and in twenty-five years I'd never gone beyond the first thirty or so. They were the most recent ones; I could tell that from the condition of the paper. The later pages were the colour of old baking parchment, and the writing was rusty and faded. There were virtually no English notes beyond the hundredth page, and even those were choppy and difficult to read. *Pound a calabash of raw cornmeal with Dragon's Blood in the moon's last quarter* . . . I mean, really.

Still, it wasn't all as bad as that. Leafing through the book, I found several new recipes which sounded interesting without being too fancy. I'd already decided on roast lamb for the main course, and peach cobbler and ice cream for pudding, but I really wanted to make an effort with the starters. It wasn't as if Ernest had actually told me not to go beyond the tenth page, I thought to myself, and after all, it *was* our anniversary. There are some occasions when even a perfect prawn cocktail just doesn't fit the bill.

I found it about forty pages in. Some of the translation was in French, but I could understand most of it, and it really sounded rather nice. Besides, I reminded myself, I wasn't too bad at French when I was a girl. I'd manage. *Entrée*. That meant a starter, didn't it? I squinted down the list of ingredients. There didn't seem to be a problem there. Some of the words were abbreviated – I assumed *yog.* stood for *yoghurt* – and the spellings were sometimes difficult to make out. The cooking time, too, was unclear – something which looked like *long*, which wasn't much help – but I was sure that if I marinaded the meat with the herbs for an hour or two there would be plenty of flavour.

At first it was easy. I ground the herbs as usual in the mortar, then added a dash of dry sherry, the yoghurt and the sugar. It looked a bit pale, so I put in a teaspoonful of Gentleman's Relish (the translation said *rapace d'homme*, which is probably the French version). The recipe just said *viande*, so I used a nice piece of chicken breast with the skin off, cutting it into strips then placing it in a dish with the marinade while I got busy with the lamb. It was getting quite dark, but it wasn't until I was removing the skins from the blanched peaches that I noticed the kitchen spotlights had dimmed to tiny red pinpricks. There was a smell too; something like dustbins left out in the sun. It must have been coming from the neighbours' side; I wipe the kitchen pedal-bin with bleach twice a day. Then there was the noise: a kind of deep pounding beyond the kitchen wall. Probably that teenage boy of theirs playing his hi-fi at full volume again; thank God we never had that kind of trouble with our two. I sprayed Kitchen Fresh into the air, and shut all the windows.

I was making the pastry for the cobbler when I heard the tolling; something like an underground bell repeating the same dull note over and over. It bothered me so much that I almost forgot to turn the marinaded chicken.

I looked at the kitchen clock. Ernest would be home at eight; that gave me just over an hour to get everything ready. If the lights were going to play up again, I'd have to put a couple of candles on the table. Come to think of it, that might make a nice change, I thought. Give the evening a bit of romance.

The lamb was perfect. I'd done some roast parsnips, mash and spring greens to go with it, and the peach cobbler was under the grill for that crunchy caramel-topping effect. I turned the chicken again in its marinade and poured myself a small glass of red wine as a reward.

Seven-thirty. I switched off the heat over the cobbler and left it to cool a little (it always tastes best warm rather than hot, with vanilla ice-cream). I thought I might flash-fry the chicken and reduce the remaining marinade into a nice sauce. It was adventurous by Ernest's standards, but I told myself that if he didn't like the look of it I could always put a couple of prawn cocktails on standby.

The bell was still ringing. For a moment I considered knocking on the wall, but decided against it. It never pays to get into a quarrel with the neighbours. Still, I thought, they were off my Christmas card list from now on.

I put the radio on. There's a station that plays classical music – nothing too fancy, just the hits – and I turned up the sound as high as I dared, so that I could hardly hear the ringing. That was better. I poured myself another glass of wine.

I left the oven on very low, just to keep the meat warm, and began to set the table. The floor felt uneven, the walls tilted slightly out of true, and the cloth kept sliding off onto the floor. I held it in place with one of the silver-plated candlesticks, and put a centrepiece of red carnations in the middle. I shouldn't have had the wine, I told myself, because now I felt dizzy, and my hand was shaking as I tried to light the candle, so that the flame kept blowing out. That smell was back, too – something hot and sweaty – and I could hear the sound of the bell even above the radio. In fact, there was something wrong with the radio station, because every now and then the music cut out and gave a great dry hiss of white noise that made me jump. The room had got very hot – it always does when I've been cooking – so I turned the thermostat down and fanned myself with a copy of the *Radio Times*.

A quarter to eight, and it was stifling. I hoped there wasn't going to be a storm; it really had got very dark. The radio was producing virtually nothing but white noise now, quite useless, so I turned it off, but I could still hear that hissing in the distance, a sort of dry, slithery desert sound. Perhaps it was something to do with the electrics. Behind it the bell still rang, and for the first time I was grateful. I got the feeling that if it stopped ringing I might hear those other sounds more clearly than I wanted to.

I sat down. There was a draught coming from somewhere,

but it was hot air, not cold. I checked the kitchen to make sure I hadn't left the oven door open. Everything looked fine. Then I noticed that the serving hatch was open a couple of inches. Red light shone through onto the work-top. The kitchen door swung shut, very gently, with a small click.

I've never been what you'd call a fanciful woman. That's one of the things that Ernest appreciates most about me; I'm not one to make a fuss. But when that door closed I began to shake. The sounds coming from behind the serving hatch were louder now: a single bell tolling; a thick dragging sound and something which might almost have been voices; murmuring, clotted voices, but in no language I knew or could recognize. The light that fell across the worktop didn't look like electric light at all; it was more like a kind of daylight, but redder, *darker* somehow, as if it was coming from a sun much older than ours. I could almost imagine that there was no dining-room beyond the serving hatch any more, but another place altogether: somewhere terribly old, terribly barren; somewhere hissing with dust, where the broken walls of once-fabulous cities were now no more than hummocks in the sand; and that where the red sky met the red earth *things* moved and slouched, things beyond perspective and (thankfully) beyond imagination. I reached out my hand slowly to close the serving hatch, but as I inched closer I was suddenly sure that on the other side, another hand – something grossly, unimaginably *different* – was also moving ponderously towards the tiny space; that I might feel the graze of its fingers as it met mine; and that if I

did I would scream and scream and never be able to stop
screaming . . .

Of course it was the wine. What else could it have been?
But I knew that if I stayed in that kitchen for another
second I'd disgrace myself completely. So I yanked off my
apron, picked up my handbag and was out of the door like a
shot, slamming it closed and locking it behind me. The
meal would be ruined, of course, but even that dreadful
likelihood was not enough to tempt me through the door
again.

For a second as the key turned I was sure I heard something behind the kitchen door: a sliding, a heaving, a
distressing sound of crockery, as if something very large had
torn its way through the serving hatch, sending cups and
saucers skating across the linoleum. Of course, that was
probably my imagination. Or maybe the wine. Still, I wasn't
taking any chances. Not on our anniversary. Ernest would
understand.

I met him coming down the path, right on time as
always. 'Happy anniversary, darling,' I said, rather breath-
lessly, and kissed his cheek.

He glanced briefly at the kitchen window, where a red
glow was now blooming behind the net curtains. 'Have you
been cooking something, love?' he asked in a guarded sort of
voice. 'You look a bit pink.'

I gave him my bravest smile. 'I thought we might try
something a bit different today,' I said, 'seeing that it's a
special occasion.'

He looked nervous at that, and his eyes went to the

window again. For a second I thought I saw the net curtains move as a shadow – dreadfully shapeless, dreadfully *large* – passed behind them.

'Is anything wrong?' he asked.

'No, of course not,' I replied firmly, turning him away from the house. 'I just thought we might like a bit of a change. What about some fish and chips, and maybe the pictures afterwards? There's a Clint Eastwood on at the Majestic. Then perhaps we could go down the pub.'

'Er . . . that would be nice.' Ernest sounded relieved. Behind us I thought I heard the kitchen door rattling, and a tinkle of glass. Neither of us looked back, though. 'Are you sure everything's all right?' he repeated.

'Of course it is,' I said. 'I just had a bit of an accident in the kitchen, that's all. It'll be fine. After all,' I said cheerily, closing the garden gate after us, 'I can't be slaving over a hot stove for you every day, can I?'

I'd clear up any mess when we got back, I decided, as we started off hand-in-hand down Acacia Drive. With a bit of luck I might even be able to save the lamb. We could have it cold for tomorrow's lunch, with new potatoes and salad. The cobbler, too, would be just as good cold.

I wasn't so sure about the chicken.

Fule's Gold

Leeds Grammar School, where I spent ten eventful years, has been the source of many stories before and since my departure. They are mainly set in and around St Oswald's Grammar School for Boys, a fictional place, which has gradually become less and less so in my mind. This is one of them. There may be more.

THE LAST STORY IN THE WORLD WAS WRITTEN BETWEEN seven-fifty-five and eight-thirty on Friday, 1 December 2002. Most of it over breakfast, at a guess, but in the last two paragraphs the handwriting betrayed a tell-tale shakiness, an unseemly lack of attention to capital letters and full stops, which suggested the school bus. It came nineteenth on a pile of twenty-two, which meant that it was almost five o'clock before Mr Fisher got round to marking it at all.

Mr Fisher lived alone in a small terraced house in the centre of town. He did not own a car, and therefore preferred to do as much as he could of his weekend marking in the form-room after school. Even so, there were usually two or three stacks of books and papers to take home on the bus. Mr Fisher had used the same old leather briefcase for over forty years, and it was still good, though battered and stretched at the seams from the weight of ten thousand – a *hundred* thousand – English essays, but today he had found a hole in one corner, through which pens, rulers and other small sly objects might finger their way and be lost. Outside it was already dark, and a thin, wet, unromantic snow was beginning to fall; but it was to save his briefcase any further abuse – at least, until that hole could be mended – that Mr Fisher decided to stay a little longer, make himself a last cup of tea, and finish his marking.

It had been a disappointing term at St Oswald's. For most of the boys in 3F, creative writing was on a par with country dancing and food technology on the cosmic scale of things. And now, with Christmas around the corner and exams looming large, creativity in general was at its lowest ebb. Oh, he'd tried to engage their interest. But books just didn't seem to kindle the same enthusiasm as they had in the old days. Mr Fisher remembered a time – surely not so long ago – when books were golden, when imaginations soared, when the world was filled with stories which ran like gazelles and pounced like tigers and exploded like rockets, illuminating minds and hearts. He had seen it happen; had seen whole classes swept away in the fever. In those days, there were heroes; there were dragons and dinosaurs, there were space adventurers and soldiers of fortune and giant apes. In those days, thought Mr Fisher, we dreamed in colour, though films were in black and white, good always triumphed in the end, and only Americans spoke American.

Now everything was in black and white, and though Mr Fisher continued to teach with as much devotion to duty as he had forty years before, he was secretly aware that his voice had begun to lack conviction. To these boys, these sullen boys with their gelled hair and perfect teeth, everything was boring. Shakespeare was boring. Dickens was boring. There didn't seem to be a single story left in the world that they hadn't heard before. And over the years, though he had tried to stop it, a terrible lassitude had crept over Mr Fisher, who had once dreamed so fiercely of writing stories of his own; a terrible conviction. They had come to the end of the seam, he understood. There were no more stories to be written. The magic had run out.

This was an uncharacteristically gloomy train of thought. Mr Fisher pushed it away and looked in his briefcase for a consolatory chocolate biscuit. Not all his boys lacked imagination. Alistair Tibbet, for instance; even though he had obviously done part of his homework on the bus. An amiable boy, this Tibbet, all the more pleasing for his air of indefinable grubbiness, his sense of always being partly elsewhere. Not a brilliant scholar, by any means: but there was a spark in him which deserved attention.

Mr Fisher took a deep breath and looked down at Tibbet's exercise book, trying not to think of the snow outside and the five o'clock bus he was now almost certain to miss. Four books to go, he told himself, and then home:

dinner; bed; the comforting small routine of a winter week-end. And so it was that Mr Fisher took a last drink of his cold tea and began to read the last story in the world.

It took him a few minutes to realize that it was the Last Story. But gradually, sitting there in the warm classroom with the smell of chalk and floor polish in his nostrils, Mr Fisher began to experience a very strange sensation. It began as a tightening in his diaphragm, as if a long-unused muscle had been brought into action. His breathing quick-ened, stopped, quickened again. He began to sweat. And when he reached the end of the story, Mr Fisher put down his red pen and went back to the beginning, re-reading every word very slowly and with meticulous care.

This must be what a prospector feels when, discouraged and bankrupt and ready to go home, he takes off his boot and shakes out a nugget the size of his fist. He read it again, critically this time, marking off the paragraphs with notes in red. A hope, which at first Mr Fisher had hardly dared to formulate, swelled in him and grew strong. He found him-self beginning to smile.

If anyone had asked him then what Tibbet's story was about, Mr Fisher might have been hard put to reply. There were themes he recognized, elements of plot which were vaguely familiar: an adventure, a quest, a child, a man. But to explain Tibbet's story in these terms was as meaningless as trying to describe a loved one's face in terms of nose, eyes, mouth. This was something new. Something entirely original.

In forty years of teaching English, Mr Fisher had come to

believe that nothing was new in literature. The same plots are repeated time and time again: the tragic lovers; the quest; the trickster; the revenge; the saviour, the coming-of-age; the struggle between good and evil. Most of these were well-used before Shakespeare got hold of them; even the Bible contained little that was significantly new. A change of costume here, of location there: stories do not die, but are simply reincarnated every generation or so into a different time and idiom. It was this belief which had finally put an end to Mr Fisher's own ambitions, years ago; the angry certainty that whatever he wrote would only ever be, at best, a pale reflection of something else.

But here was his theory disproved. Tibbet's story stood alone. A completely original idea – perhaps the first in a hundred years – the Holy Grail of literature, the last story in the world.

It occurred then to Mr Fisher how many people might have an interest in such a story. Hollywood, for instance – always at a loss for new material, now reduced to pecking out fragments of plot from graphic novels and computer games. Book publishers; newspapers; magazines. A new idea could start a dynasty, generations of related stories. Whoever copyrighted such an idea could make a man more than famous, more than wealthy. It could make him immortal.

Once more, Mr Fisher considered Alistair Tibbet. An amiable boy, without apparent genius. Hair slightly too long, shirt untucked, a habitual latecomer to class. No stylist, certainly – his spelling was atrocious – and certainly in no position to make his case to the media. Such a waste.

Tibbet was hardly likely to appreciate the magnitude of this discovery; indeed, his handwriting alone showed that his mind had been elsewhere from the start. It seemed clear to Mr Fisher that Tibbet's role in all this was a secondary one – that of an idiot-savant, if you like, who may accidentally discover a mathematical principle, but has no ability to explain its workings. No, all of this was wasted on Tibbet. Besides, who was the boy's teacher? Who had taught him everything he knew? Forty years' hard work had to count for something: and in the shape of this boy, it had finally come to fruition.

In all his years of teaching, Mr Fisher had never quite forgotten his earliest ambitions. Through the years he had come to think – wrongly, as it happened – that he simply didn't have the talent or the inspiration to write. Now he realized that only fear and uncertainty had kept him back. At last he knew what he wanted to say: how to make his mark upon the world. He began to see how the story could be presented, envisaged a treatment of about three hundred pages in novel form. And the *treatment* was the important part; without it, no story, however inspired, could be anything more than wishful thinking. After all, Shakespeare took inspiration from Boccaccio. Mr Fisher speculated that he could have a rough synopsis by Sunday, send copies off in Monday's post. Of course he would have to take precautions: a statement deposited in his bank would ensure that his copyright remained intact. Publishing was full of unscrupulous people – the film industry doubly so. With luck, the offers might start coming in by Christmas.

And Tibbet? In his excitement, Mr Fisher had almost forgotten the boy. Surely he owed him something? Obviously an acknowledgement was out of the question. In today's litigious society, that would simply be asking for trouble. Mr Fisher thought hard for a moment. Then he picked up his red pen and wrote carefully at the bottom of the essay: *Good content – more care needed with presentation.* B+. It was more than fair, thought Mr Fisher; the class average rarely went higher than a C.

It was five-twenty-five. In the corridor, Mr Fisher could hear the cleaners packing up their buckets and mops. His next bus home left at five-thirty: if he was quick, he could still catch it. Leaving the pile of third-form exercise books on the corner of the desk – except for Tibbet's, which he slipped into his briefcase next to the biscuits – he rinsed his mug in the sink, locked his desk drawer and put on his overcoat.

Outside it was still snowing. Flakes tumbled chaotically from a sky like white noise. Mr Fisher trudged towards the bus stop, briefcase in hand. It was very cold. He realized that in his haste he had left his scarf and gloves in the desk drawer; but it was almost half past now, and he decided against going back to fetch them. He did not want to miss his bus.

There were few cars on the road, and a grey slush had begun to eat up the verge. The bus was late. Mr Fisher waited in the vandalized bus shelter, blowing into his hands and thinking about his story. His heart was beating alarmingly fast, but he felt a peculiar energy. He might almost have been thirteen again, with ink on his fingers and that metallic taste of youth in his mouth, and the certainty that one day he would be great, that one day he too would be a hero . . .

The lights went out in the school buildings, one by one. It was five-fifty, and there was still no sign of the bus. Mr Fisher decided to walk home. It was only a couple of miles into town, after all, and it would give him more time to think about his story.

It would be a great mistake, he told himself, to jump at the first offer. Better to sit tight for a couple of months and let the publishers bid against one another. Fortunately, he already had some knowledge of the industry. His experience would serve him well.

Mr Fisher walked quickly down the road, smiling to himself, lost in a warm haze of fantasy. After a while he began to feel hungry; remembering the biscuits in his brief-case, he stopped to take one.

The biscuits were not there. Mr Fisher frowned. Had he left them in his desk drawer? But no: he remembered taking a biscuit and replacing the packet. He looked again, moving closer to a streetlamp to get a better view. The biscuits were nowhere to be found, and now, in the orange light, he could see why. The hole in the corner of his briefcase had zipped open all along the seam, and in his excitement over the story he had failed to notice. Mr Fisher was annoyed. He hated losing things. In fact, such was his annoyance that it was several seconds before he even thought to check whether Tibbet's exercise book was still there.

It was not. Mr Fisher felt a sudden sharp sweat sting his eyes. The book! He checked again, running his shaking hands along the torn stitching. Here were his hard-backed form register and his plastic file: both too bulky to escape. Here, too, was his pencil box. But the story, the Last Story, was gone. Mr Fisher felt a jolt of panic. He must have dropped it somewhere along the road. But where? He was over a mile from the school now; it could be anywhere along that stretch. Still, it could not be helped; he would have to retrace his footsteps until he found it.

Breathing hard, he began the walk back. But his progress was slow: the wind was in his face, stealing his breath, and the snow was like chips of stone. Worse still, he found that the story itself was no longer entirely clear in his mind; that although he could recall certain elements – a quest, a man, a boy – it was Tibbet's misspellings he remembered most, and the fact that the boy had done his homework on the bus.

The verge was entirely white now, and the dark shape of the school was just visible behind the turmoil of the snow. Mr Fisher followed his own footsteps until they filled in again, but found nothing. There was nothing at the bus shelter. Mr Fisher even walked back up the drive towards the school gate, but there was no sign of the lost schoolbook.

When the police eventually found him at eight o'clock that evening, he was digging with his bare hands in the snowdrift which lined the verge, wild-eyed, raw-faced, mumbling feverishly to himself. It was lucky they found him when they did, Sergeant Merle reported to his duty officer; the poor old sod was nearly gone. Took him straight to Casualty. Turned out he was looking for some kid's homework he'd dropped on the way. Talk about devotion to duty. You ask me, these teachers aren't paid half enough. Still, you got to hand it to the old fella, he was digging like the clappers. You'd have thought there was gold under there.

Class of '81

I first wrote this story for an anthology to raise money for the Magic Million appeal, in aid of one-parent families. I was supposed to write a story about magic, but it ended up being more to do with what happens when the magic runs out . . .

THERE WERE TWELVE OF US FROM THAT CLASS OF '81. THERE they are in the photo, from right to left as usual: Hannah Malkin, Claire Corrigan, Anne Wyrd, Jane Beldame, Gloria Krone, Isabella Faye. Bottom row: myself, looking impossibly young, then Morwenna Hagge, Judith Weisz, Carole Broome, Dizzy McKelpie, in those Coke-bottle glasses with her messy red hair spilling over the collar of her uniform. Far left: Paul (Chalky) Wight, perennial top of the class and the only boy. But that's witchcraft for you: the girls outnumber the boys to begin with, although the high-flying jobs always seem to go to the men in the end. I wondered if this was the case with Paul Wight, and if so, whether he was still single.

Already I was feeling a little nervous. We'd made the promise twenty years ago, an unimaginable distance away to our eighteen-year-old selves. Since then I'd heard rumours, read a couple of pieces in the paper, but otherwise I'd had little contact with any of my old school friends, except for the occasional greetings card at Lammas or Yule. On the grapevine I'd heard that Carole had joined a coven in Wales somewhere, that Hannah had married an astral healer from Milton Keynes, and that Isabella was some kind of consultant in the City. It all sounded conventional enough. But secondhand accounts don't answer the real questions: who got fat, who lost their magic (or worse, dabbled with Kaos), who had a body job and lied about it afterwards.

Dizzy was the exception, of course. Who could fail to be familiar with Désirée McKelpie? She was practically a brand name – her face had looked out at us for the past fifteen years from tabloid newspapers, billboards, television screens. She worked love spells for Royals and Hollywood film stars. We knew her romances, her divorces; we sighed over her frocks and speculated over her diminishing waistline.

With a frown, I considered my own. Even at school I'd never been thin; not like Anne or Dizzy or Gloria. I'd skipped puddings in vain, but in spite of my efforts, thinness had always eluded me. Twenty years later, it still did. I wondered, rather petulantly, whose stupid idea it had been to hold our twenty-year reunion at Bella Pasta anyway.

I arrived too early. The note had said twelve-thirty and it was barely ten past. For a few minutes I lingered in the draughty doorway trying to look cool and confident, but people kept pushing past me to get in and I finally decided to take a seat at the big table at the back with the RESERVED sign and the little place-cards. Two girls sniggered as I squeezed past them, and I felt my face grow red. It wasn't my fault the aisle was so narrow. I clutched at my handbag for security and my hip brushed against a flower vase, almost knocking it over. The girls sniggered again. It was going to be a nightmare.

I found my place (the name spelt wrong). There were four bottles of wine already laid out, and four of mineral water. I poured a glass of red and drank it straightaway, then moved the bottle to the opposite side of the table, hoping no-one would notice. Come to think of it, it was exactly the kind of thing a little sneak like Gloria Krone *would* notice, and draw attention to. I moved the bottle back.

Twenty years. Unimaginable time. I glanced at the photo again. There I was, demure in my little black uniform, holding my first broom proudly in my right hand. Of course the broom's mainly symbolic nowadays. No adult witch would ever choose to squander their *chi* on making a broom fly. Why bother, when you can get pampered in Business Class? Not that I ever have, of course. Alex says it's a waste of money. He even worked it out once: how you could buy three seats in Economy, a half-bottle of champagne, two Prêt-à-Manger sandwiches, a pashmina and a selection of toiletries and *still* pay less than you would for a Business Class ticket. Not that he ever does buy any of those things. He thinks they're a waste of money, too. Come to think of

it, the last time we flew anywhere was a budget trip to the
Algarve in 1994, and he complained all the way because he
said I was taking up too much space. Maybe a broom would
have been better, after all.

I poured myself another glass of wine. It wasn't that I
was dissatisfied with my life, I told myself. Who needs
magic when you can have security? Thirty-eight; housewife;
married to a management consultant; house in Croydon;
two boys, fifteen and twelve, and a familiar (for old times'
sake). Deliriously happy. Well, happy, anyway. Well, some
of the time.

Now the bottle looked three-quarters empty. It wasn't, of
course; it's just the way bottles are made, so narrow at the
top so that the moment you pour even a small glass it looks
as if you've drunk half of it already. Now when the others
came they'd all notice, and Gloria Krone would look at me
with her long blue eyes and whisper something behind her
hand to Isabella Faye – always her best friend in the old days
– and the two of them would watch me like Siamese cats,
purring with malice and sly speculation. 'Darling, do you
think she's hitting the bottle? How *grotesque*!'

So I disposed of the evidence, hiding the bottle under a
chair some distance from where I was sitting. Not a moment
too soon; as I emerged from under the tablecloth I saw a
woman – a witch – making her way towards me, and was
seized with a prickly panic. Standing up, wiping my mouth
hastily with the back of my hand, I recognized Anne Wyrd.

She hadn't changed. Tall, elegant, blonde, wearing a
black trouser suit over what looked suspiciously like nothing

at all. I'd never liked her; she'd been part of a sporty threesome, all very well-bred and jolly broomsticks. A second later, the other two arrived: Morwenna Hagge and Claire Corrigan, also in elegant black. I noticed in a moment's sly satisfaction that Morwenna had begun to colour her hair; then, with disappointment, that it suited her.

'*Darling*,' said Anne. 'You haven't changed a bit.' Her brilliant smile did not falter as she glanced down at the place-card in front of me. I mumbled something inane about how stylish she looked, and sat down again. 'Well, one has to make an effort, sweetheart,' said Anne, pouring herself a glass of sparkling mineral water. 'We're none of us eighteen any more, are we?'

The others were beginning to arrive now. In a burst of embraces and exclamations I saw Gloria and Isabella, more like Siamese cats than ever now, with matching blonde bobs and sleepy eyes, and Carole Broome, who I greeted with more warmth than I'd ever felt for her in the old days. 'Thank God, Carole,' I said fervently. 'I thought I was going to be the only one of us not wearing black.'

Carole had been a studious young witch in the old days, plump and lank-haired and earnest, more interested in herb lore than pyrotechnics, always the last to be picked in a game of Brooms. She was much thinner now, her hair had been braided and coiled, and she was wearing a long purple velvet skirt with an abundance of silver jewellery. I remembered the rumour that Carole had joined some kind of a radical Welsh coven, and felt suddenly uncomfortable. I hoped she wasn't going to bend my ear all lunchtime about pentacles and athames and going skyclad. I noticed, with a faint sinking feeling, that her place-setting was next to mine.

'Your aura looks terrible,' said Carole, sitting down and pouring water into her glass. 'Ugh! This water's carbonated! Waitress, please, some *natural* water, and can I talk to you about this menu?'

The waitress, a harassed-looking girl with a ponytail, approached with understandable reluctance. Carole's voice was loud and flat and carrying. 'I notice there isn't a *vegetarian* option here,' she said accusingly.

Uh-oh. I flinched guiltily over the menu. I'd been thinking about getting the steak.

'Well, you could have the mushroom omelette or the fusilli—' began the waitress.

'I don't eat eggs,' snapped Carole, 'and neither would you if you had any idea what it did to your karma. As for the fusilli – ' she peered more closely at the menu, her eyes magnified by her glasses so that they looked like big green marbles, 'is it *wheat* pasta? . . . I can't possibly eat wheat pasta,' she explained to me as the waitress went off resentfully to talk to the chef. 'It's far too *yin* for my body type. Too much *yin* can cloud your aura. I think I'll be happier with just fresh, unfluorinated water and an organic green salad.'

Rather wistfully, I pushed the menu to one side. The steak and chips seemed to be receding into the distance. Fortunately, I could see some other witches arriving, and I greeted them with ill-concealed relief. I'd always rather liked Hannah Malkin; and here was Jane Beldame, brisk and rather mannish now in a tweed skirt and jacket. 'Terrific to see you, old girl!' she exclaimed, engulfing me for a moment in a scent of wool and mothballs. 'Where's the booze?' She plumped down in the chair next to me (it was labelled 'Judith Weisz') and poured a hefty slug of red wine, ignoring Carole's squeak of disapproval. 'After all these years, eh? What larks we had!' Now Jane was here, I remembered them: midnight feasts in the dorm, with a glyph on the door to warn us if Matron was approaching; broom races along the Top Corridor; the time we sneaked Professor LeMage's pornographic Tarot cards and divined everyone's private fetishes . . . For the first time, I began to think that maybe this reunion wasn't such a bad idea.

Judith Weisz came next, a colourless witch with bad skin who'd been less popular even than Carole, now looking much older than the rest of us, and making no protest when she found Jane occupying her place.

'Oh no, it's that creepy Weisz girl,' whispered Gloria to Isabella. 'Quick, push up so she won't sit here.' Although Judith must have heard, she made no comment. Instead she made her way to the free place next to Hannah and sat down quietly, hands folded in her lap. I felt rather sorry for her, although we'd never been friends, and wondered why she had come.

At a quarter to one, there were still only ten of us at table. Jane had drunk three more glasses of red wine, Hannah was teaching me how to separate my astral arm from my corporeal one, Isabella was discussing body jobs with Claire Corrigan ('it's *not* black magic any more, sweetheart, absolutely *everyone* does it nowadays, there's no stigma at all'), Gloria and Morwenna were comparing love charms, Anne was interpreting the future from the dregs of Jane's wineglass, Carole was arguing with the chef ('How would *you* feel, if *you* were a tomato?') and Judith had just discovered a half-empty bottle of red wine under her chair when everyone fell silent as, fully conscious of the effect she was creating, Dizzy McKelpie made her entrance.

I remembered her as a small thing, pale and rather skinny, with quantities of red hair and ugly black-rimmed glasses. Now the glasses were gone, revealing huge eyes and lashes like moths' wings, the hair was artfully sleek, and her graceful figure was barely contained in clinging black jersey above a pair of scarlet, impossible heels. She commanded attention immediately – the other diners gaped; Dizzy pretended not to notice. Across the table I heard Gloria whisper to Isabella, 'Body job.' From the corner of my eye I saw Carole flick her fingers in the sign against evil; even Jane was watching open-mouthed. Apparently oblivious to all the attention, Dizzy walked to our table as if she were on a catwalk, and folded herself elegantly into the chair next to Judith. 'I'm so sorry I'm late,' she said sweetly. 'I had a meeting with a *very* special client who's been having the most *ghastly* trouble with the media.'

'Who?' said Gloria, wide-eyed.

'I couldn't possibly tell you. It's very sensitive,' purred Dizzy. 'I know you'll understand if I don't say any more.' She looked around the table. 'Isn't there someone missing?' she asked.

Everyone scanned the table. 'It's Paul Wight,' said Anne finally. 'I forgot about him completely.' Easy to do, I suppose; Paul had been a brilliant student, completely devoted to his work and cautious of our female exuberance. This was generally taken to be a ploy on his part to intrigue and seduce us, but in spite of many efforts to enchant him, no-one had ever managed. I now suspected that he'd been genuinely ambitious; girls had played no part in his studies. I doubted he would come today.

'Well, it's nearly one,' said Dizzy. 'If he isn't here by now, I think we should order. I've got a meeting at two-fifteen.'

Everyone agreed that no-one should be expected to wait for Paul Wight, except Carole, who said that lunch, if taken at all, should never last more than half an hour, and Judith, who said nothing.

So we ordered. Carole had a special salad of karmically neutral vegetables ('Roots in general are too *yang*, and radishes have souls'), Gloria and Isabella had the soup and ciabatta, Hannah the seafood tagliatelle, Claire, Morwenna and Anne the fusilli. Jane ordered the steak, very rare, and a double portion of chips – I looked at her enviously, wishing I was brave enough to do the same, though under Carole Broome's excoriating gaze I finally opted for a vegetarian pizza, which, though potentially dangerous ('Carbohydrates throw your chakras out of balance'), at least had the advantage of being karmically sound.

Only Jane had any dessert. Anne, Gloria and Isabella all seemed to be on permanent diets, Dizzy kept looking at her watch, and I suppose Carole's disapproving comments had done the rest. Instead, we talked. Someone (I thought it was Dizzy) made sure that the wine never quite ran out (much to the waitress's bewilderment), and conversation, hesitant at first, began to flow more freely. Perhaps a little too freely – now came what I had been dreading: the questions, the boasting, the lies. Dizzy led the conversation at first with anecdotes of media witchcraft, soon to be rivalled by Anne, who was a house expert specializing in cleansing and banishing rituals ('Feng-shui's just so last millennium, darling, shamanism's the thing now'); then Isabella, who worked with pyramids; Claire, who was a crystal-healer, married to an Odinist with two raven familiars and a wolf; Gloria, who had been divorced three times and was currently teaching a course on tantric sex and meditation at the University of Warwick; even Hannah, who (to everyone's disgust but mine) had given up her job to devote herself to her husband and her little girl, already a budding witch at the age of four, whom she obviously adored.

'You've been very quiet,' observed Carole, who had been watching me. 'How about you? Where have your studies led you?'

It was the moment I had feared. Explaining about Alex and the boys was easy enough (if uninspiring), but if she somehow discovered the real secret, the terrible, un-mentionable thing . . . I said something flippant about motherhood being a full-time job, and wished Carole would choose someone else to cross-examine. But Carole was tenacious as bogwort. 'Your aura's very muddy,' she insisted. 'You haven't been letting your magic *slip*, have you?'

I muttered something about being a little out of shape.

'That doesn't sound good,' said Carole. 'Let's try a few simple exercises, shall we? How about a basic cantrip to begin with?'

'I don't think so,' I said, horrified, wishing she would lower her voice.

'Go on,' insisted Carole. 'Just a little one. No-one's going to *laugh* at you, for Goddess's sake.'

Now everyone was looking at me. Gloria's eyes were narrowed and shining. 'Really, Carole,' I said feebly.

'You can manage a little one,' urged Dizzy, joining the game. 'How about a little levitation? Or a summoning?' *That* was a laugh. If I could have summoned anything after all these years, it would have been a nice, deep hole to hide in. 'All right then,' she said, taking a candlestick from the table and pushing it towards me. 'Just light this candle. Simplest trick in the world. It's like riding a broom. You never forget how to do it.'

Easy for her to say. I'd never been much good at brooms, even when I was in practice. I began to feel sweat beading my forehead. 'Go on,' said Dizzy. 'Show us how. Light the candle.'

'Light it. *Light* it.' The others continued the chant, and I felt myself beginning to shake. The terrible secret – the thing no witch can ever admit – was about to be revealed. It was Alex's fault, I told myself, taking the candlestick in my hand and frowning hard at the cold wick. Being married to a non-witch is a bit like being married to a non-smoker; a daily clash of interests. Eventually someone has to give. And I was the one who gave; for the sake of our marriage and our children. Even the familiar – a black cat called Mr Tibbs – belongs principally to our boys (who don't have a spark of natural magic between them, being mostly devoted to football and cyberbabes), and spends more of his time shedding hair on the carpets and torturing mice than contemplating mysteries. All the same, I thought desperately, feeling my eyes begin to water with the effort of concentration, you'd have thought there was *something* left – some little squib I could use now. I could hear Gloria whispering to Isabella; from the corner of my eye I saw Dizzy watching me with that hungry, amused look, like Mr Tibbs outside a mousehole.

'Darling, I don't think she *can*.'

'She can't have—'

'She's *lost* it.'

'Shhh.'

Not even a cantrip – the smallest, most basic of spells. My face was scarlet; my armpits prickled with nervous heat. Not a glow, not a flame, not a spark. In desperation I looked up, hoping to see even one sympathetic pair of eyes, but Hannah was looking uncomfortable, Judith seemed half-asleep and Jane was far too occupied with her second slice of chocolate cake to take any notice of my plight. Dully I saw myself as the rest saw me: a fat, unfulfilled drone who couldn't even light a candle.

Then, suddenly, there was a flash between my fingers, followed almost instantaneously by a smell of burning. I jerked my head away just in time; flames were streaming from the candlestick, the candle itself almost consumed in blue and green fire. Half a second later, the candle shot right out of the candlestick and exploded in a spray of coloured sparks over our heads. No-one else seemed to notice at all – someone had cast a magical shield over the table.

Gloria, who had been leaning forward rapaciously, leapt back with an undignified squeal. Carole stared at the blackened candlestick in amazement. 'I thought you said you were out of shape!' she said at last.

I thought quickly and hard. Someone had helped me, that was certain; someone who didn't want to see me humiliated. I glanced up, but could see nothing more than spite, curiosity, outrage or surprise in the faces around me. Dizzy was frantically brushing sparks out of her long hair. A cinder had fallen into Isabella's glass, splashing her with wine. 'Golly!' said Jane, impressed. 'What happened there?'

I tried to smile. 'Joke,' I said weakly.

'Some joke,' grumbled Gloria. 'You nearly burnt my eyebrows off.'

'More power than I thought,' I muttered.

Relieved beyond words, I poured myself a glass of wine. For once, Carole didn't comment. I could see she was awed in spite of herself. I spent some time evading her questions: where had I done my advanced training; had I achieved spiritual illumination; who had been my mentor. 'You

haven't been dabbling in anything you shouldn't, have you?'
she asked suspiciously, when I modestly declined to answer.

'You mean Kaos? Don't be silly.' I almost laughed. It takes
a lot of work to become a Kaos illuminata, and I'd never
even understood the principles twenty years ago. Carole
continued to look at me suspiciously for a while, then,
to my relief, the conversation turned to other things.
Old quarrels revived, small sillinesses remembered, practical
jokes relived. The noise escalated gradually; at times I could
hardly hear what was being said on the far side of the table.
Even I, cheered by the wine and the unexpected miracle of
the rocketing candle, felt my inhibitions begin to leave me.
Maybe the wine was stronger than I'd thought. Or maybe it
was just the company.

But it was when Anne, Morwenna and Dizzy began a
violent argument about a disparaging comment Dizzy had
once supposedly made to Anne about the shape of
Morwenna's calves, Judith was apparently asleep, Isabella
was explaining the finer points of sex magic to Jane (with
the aid of diagrams drawn onto the tablecloth in biro), and
Gloria was trying to demonstrate how to change a salt-cellar
into a hamster, that I realized what had happened. This was
not simply a case of good cheer gone slightly out of hand.
Someone had magically spiked the mineral water.

'It's disgusting, that's what it is,' said Carole, who seemed
the only one unaffected. 'Cavorting about like a gaggle of
goblins. I thought this was going to be a meeting of *minds*,
an opportunity to share the experiences of twenty years'
travel on the Path of the Wise.'

'Oh, put a sock in it, Carrie,' said Anne, whose hair had come down in the course of the argument. 'You always were a most frightful little bleater. No wonder you ended up in a commune full of sheep.'

'Now look here,' said Carole, losing much of her smug self-satisfaction. 'Just because you were coven captain three years running—'

'Girls, girls,' said Dizzy. 'Is this any way to behave?'

'You can shut up as well,' said Carole. 'You and your media magic. And if you *really* believe that body job of yours looks anything other than *grotesque*—'

'*Body job!*' squeaked Dizzy, outraged. 'I'll have you know my body's *perfectly* natural! I take *care* of myself! I work *out!*'

'Come off it, darling,' said Morwenna sweetly. 'It's nothing to be ashamed of nowadays. Lots of witches have a little cantrip or two set by for when things begin to sag.'

'Well, it'd take a hell of a lot more than a cantrip to fix those fat calves of yours.'

I tried to intervene. I could feel an accumulation of static in the air which raised the hairs on my arms and made my skin prickle. Powerful magic was building. And quickly. I wondered what exactly had been added to the drinks. A truth spell? Something worse?

'I say—' I began. But it was too late. They were engaged. Morwenna made a grab for Dizzy's hair; Dizzy's hand shot out at Morwenna, and ropes of magic were suddenly swarming and hissing over both of them. The two witches jumped apart like doused cats, their hair standing on end.

'What did you do?' snarled Dizzy, her poise gone completely.

'Nothing!' wailed Morwenna, shaking her numbed fingers. 'What did *you* do?'

I was just happy that the shield spell over our table was still holding. Beyond it, the other diners munched on, oblivious.

'What larks,' commented Jane happily, finishing her second piece of chocolate cake. 'Just like the old days.'

'Precisely,' said Judith with a hint of sarcasm. I'd almost forgotten about her; she had seemed half-asleep during most of the meal, and as far as I knew, had hardly spoken a word. She'd been no different twenty years before: a silent, unattractive young witch who was excused from sports for some medical reason; who never seemed to get any letters from home and spent every Yuletide holiday at school. I'd had to stay myself once; my parents had had to go to an occult conference in New Zealand and I was left at school feeling thoroughly miserable, in spite of the trunkful of presents they had sent me. All my friends had gone home for the holidays, and only Judith had remained. I'd already known she never went home for Yule, of course, but I'd never really thought about it before. Now I did. If she had been more approachable, and less devoted to her studies, we might have used the opportunity to become friends. But I quickly found out that Judith alone was as drab and monosyllabic as Judith in a crowd. She did not seek me out, seeming quite content to spend her days alone in the library, or in the herbarium or the observatory. All the same, she was the only company around, except for a few Masters and their familiars, and one night the two of us had shared the last of my Yule log and a bottle of elderberry wine. I'd almost forgotten about that until now; afterwards we had gone on with our studies as before, and the following year had been our last. I looked at her now. 'What did you do after school, Judith?' I asked.

She shrugged. 'Nothing much,' she said. 'I got married.' I hoped my surprise didn't show on my face. 'He's a psychonaut,' went on Judith in her cool, quiet voice. 'He lectures in Morphic Field Theory and the Chaoetheric Paradigm.'

'Really?' I barely knew the terms; those theories had been far beyond even our most advanced courses. 'How about you?'

Judith gave a chilly smile. 'I became a metamorphosist. A shaper, if you like. Specializing in body jobs for the karmically unconcerned.'

'Goddess,' breathed Carole, who had been listening. 'You're a Kaoist.'

'Someone has to do it,' said Judith. 'And if people want to pay for my services rather than studying the arts for themselves—'

'Pay with karma taken from their next lives!'

Judith shrugged. 'Who cares?' she said. 'If Dizzy wants to spend her next life as a radish, who am I to criticize?' Everyone was staring at us now. Dizzy's face was white. 'You always looked down on me,' said Judith in the same colourless voice. 'I was always the coven joke.'

'Judith—' I said uncomfortably. It had occurred to me that with her resources it would be child's play now for Judith to use her powers of metamorphosis to change us all into cockroaches, if she chose to do it. Now I understood who had helped me light the candle; my throat felt suddenly rather dry.

'None of you have changed much since then,' went on Judith calmly. 'Gloria's still a little sneak, Dizzy a silly attention-grabber, Anne a snob, Carole a talentless phoney. None of you are *real* witches at all.' (Carole gave a squeak at this, but changed it hastily into a cough.) Judith turned to me. 'Except for you,' she told me with half a smile. 'I haven't forgotten that Yuletide when you shared your cake with me in the dorm. Fortunately, I can keep a secret,' said Judith, looking at Dizzy, though I felt maybe she was speaking to me. 'And I don't believe in revenge.'

She had stood up during this little speech, and I noticed for the first time how tall she was. I wondered, too, why I had thought she looked old; now she looked *young*, clear-skinned, almost beautiful. 'Well,' she said in a lighter tone, 'I think that's all I wanted to say. My husband said he'd call for me about now, and I don't want to keep him waiting.'

We watched her go in silence; for once, there were no whisperings between Gloria and Isabella, and even Carole had no comment to make. Then, when we were sure she had gone, we all ran to the window. We saw them then for a moment, the *real* witches, walking away hand-in-hand. The man was tall and fair-haired; for a second I thought I recognized Paul Wight, though there was no way of knowing for sure. He and Judith walked slowly down the street, and I wondered how it was possible for two people to look so free and calm and so sure of themselves and the future. I watched them into the distance, as around me the other witches slunk back one by one to the table and conversation slowly returned. I thought maybe the pavement shimmered a little in their wake, but I could not be certain of that, either.

Hello, Goodbye

For some reason, I have developed an unhealthy addiction to a number of the more shallow and brittle society magazines. I find the world they portray fascinating, sinister, often depressing, sometimes bleakly funny. This is not a true story. But perhaps it is only a matter of time.

MY NAME IS ANGELA K. YOU MIGHT HAVE HEARD OF ME; I'M A society columnist for *Goodbye!* magazine. I'm twenty-nine; attractive; talented – I have an impressive CV, a degree in media studies, a celebrity sister, rather famous in her day (the Face of Pluviôse cosmetics), perfect skin and fifteen thousand pounds' worth of dental work. Oh yes, and my career is over. Over. Finished. Finita. Fini.

It was last week, over champagne and canapés. The season's most sensational Dernière – rumour had it that *all* the Immortals were going to be there, and I was thrilled to have the chance to cover it. After all, it's what I joined the paper for: glamour, travel, gossip, and the exhilarating pageant of Society at its most dazzling. I knew that if I made a success of this there would be lots of other assignments; this kind of venue was very now, and *Goodbye!* magazine all set to be the leader in the field. I was the perfect choice: clever, well-connected, slim, blonde and nicely inconspicuous. I could be relied upon to observe, to set the tone, to keep it light, not to draw attention to myself. Nothing could go wrong. Nothing would.

I chose my outfit carefully. It helps to have a fashion-model sister; you get to meet all kinds of designers, with lots of free samples and give-aways – not to mention the once-worn cast-offs from Sis, though it rankles to accept them, and I've had to stay so thin just to keep up with her.

Basic black, of course – that goes without saying – with a touch of cerise (this season's new black) in the accessories. Classic throughout; nothing too outrageous or revealing. After all, I'm here as a reporter.

The ceremony took place at the fashionable time of three o'clock – and the crematorium was one of the most prestigious venues in London, with a newly refurbished Conran interior and a six-month waiting list for non-members. I turned up a little early, clutching my lavishly black-bordered invitation with eagerness and just a hint of nerves. Sis would have taken it all in her stride, of course; but then, Sis had had lots of practice. She was a complete party animal – I'd already counted three of her ex-lovers before I'd even reached the gates – and she knew absolutely everybody.

Press arrive first, of course; there was already a crowd of

photographers and TV cameras waiting behind the cordon. I recognized my arch-rival Amber D. from *K.O.* magazine and Piers from *Crem*; someone recognized me and there was a flash and crackle of cameras as I stepped onto the luxurious black carpet and handed my invitation to the two security men at the door.

It was like a dream. This was the moment my entire life had been leading up to, and I entered the reception hall in a kind of daze. For once I was attending an A-list venue as myself, not as Sis's gawky younger sister, and it felt terrific. For once in my life I'd stepped out of Sis's shadow, and people were looking at me – *men* were looking at me – with interest and admiration. I knew I was looking good – the last diet had paid off, and I was back to a size six again, though I still needed to shed a couple of stone before I could fit into some of Sis's latest clothes. My hair was sleek; my skin airbrushed to pale perfection (tans are *so* out nowadays), my nails (cerise, of course) buffed to a dazzling gleam. If Sis had been there I knew that everyone would have been looking at her – not because she's so much better-looking, but because of *that* dress, *that* man, *that* scandal, *that* breakdown – but without her I too was an Immortal; I was free, I was available, a fantasy guest at a fantasy ball, and for a time I forgot myself entirely, gliding across the lobby in my glass slippers in search of my own version of *that* man . . .

In the main reception hall, it was already busy. The bar at the far end of the hall was dispensing Black Russians (the retro-ironic drink of the season) and liquorice Kir; waiters passed by with Beluga and blinis, and B-list society girls lounged on the elegant furniture, sipping mineral water, smoking black Sobranies, and discussing the deceased.

'Well, it can't have been as quick as all that, darling, have you seen the waiting-list for this place?'

'Any goss on the COD?'

'I heard it was some kind of an eating disorder—'

'No! Starving or hurling?'

'I don't suppose there's an official sponsor or anything – what a bore, Tymon collects the badges, you know; he's already got AIDS, coronary, breast cancer and terrorist-bombing—'

'Still, look on the bright side; at last she's managed that size nought she always wanted.'

With an effort I pulled myself away from this fascinating conversation, reminding myself that I was a professional with a serious job to do. I pulled out my notebook (Smythson, black, crocodile) and began to jot down ideas.

Black was the keynote for the celebrity funeral of the summer, with Prada and Ghost taking the lead again as more than 600 guests converged on the Black Cube Crematorium. I spotted delicious debs Lucie and Sebastopol Ritz-Carleton sharing a jug of Black Russians with teen heart-throb Jarry Golentz; Nicky H. looked in, then looked out again, and conceptualist duo Grundy and Nebb dazzled in matching cerise . . .

Outside, I heard a sudden increase in the activity of cameras as a new influx of celebrities arrived.

Our reporter spotted Rupert, looking gorgeous in a clever take on the classic evening jacket, Niles and Petrovka in Armani, the outrageous Piggy Lalique in top-to-toe Vivienne Westwood and author Salman Rushdie, with a glamorous lady on his arm, looking ultra-casual in one of Gaultier's new 'Intelligentsia' T-shirts . . .

It was like something out of one of the new 'caskets 'n' canapés' novels – you'll be familiar with the genre. Death is the new food – we like to read about it without actually having to do any of it ourselves. And of course we all loved Hugh Grant and Renée Zellweger in this year's classic remake *The Wrong Box* . . . Even so, this was even more wonderful than I'd hoped. All these fabulous people – and the main cortège hadn't even arrived! I stopped to take another blini – they really were very good – and kept on taking notes.

Top chef Armando Pigalle astonished with a witty series of keynote canapés on the theme of Remembrance and Loss – including light-as-air rosemary soufflés, Beluga blinis, indigo sushi, pasta negra and Proustian madeleines with lime-blossom coulis . . .

Another wave of excitement from outside buffeted the black-hung windows and I understood that the cortège was arriving. Everyone moved to the doors to watch; cameras flashed, and I stood on a marble table by the window with my notebook in hand to see what was going on outside.

In spite of recent predictions, headgear remained a prominent feature, with Phillip and Cozmo leading the way as usual. This season small is beautiful, with witty numbers from the new 'Demise' collection. Our reporter spotted Isabella behind a super-sculptural 'Memento Mori' cashmere piece with real bone accessories, and Helena wore a fun vintage hat from Mourningtown.

Hats aside, there wasn't much to see; I craned my neck for fifteen minutes while the casket was manoeuvred into position behind a screen (in order not to jeopardize the *News of the World*'s picture exclusive), and bouncers kept the remaining photographers off-limits. Then the cortège backtracked 100 yards to give the Channel 55 cameras a view of the procession from both sides; mascara was re-applied for the close-ups, then it was the turn of the celebrity portraits.

The new generation caskets are slick, modern and very, very sexy. The deceased chose a flamboyant open-topped Louis Vuitton model in this season's hot new colour – cerise – flowers from Wild at Heart and live music from top bands Brat and Spleen . . .

There was a moan from the crowd. Everyone knows the real Immortals always come some distance behind the cortège – there's usually a casting director or two somewhere in the crowd, and it never hurts to shed a couple of tears, though some people always overdo it and make a fool of themselves. To try to combat this, I'd heard that all eulogies were to be kept down to two minutes apiece (we all remember Skinny McNalty's six-minute embarrassment at the Saatchi memorial last year), and the technicians in charge of the lights and the sound system were under strict instructions to enforce the time limit.

It might take another hour for all the guests to negotiate the black carpet. Individual shots are obligatory on these occasions, and there can be a lot of cattiness between celebrities when photographers rush away en masse on spotting a more interesting guest, so I helped myself to another cocktail and watched from the window as the celebrities filtered through one by one.

The celebrity Dernière is a wonderful opportunity for fantasy dressing-up. Our reporter counted avant-garde outfits from Alexander McQueen, Galliano and Jean-Paul Gaultier; fun funeral fetishwear from Virgin on the Ridiculous and key pieces from Tracey Emin's stylish new couture collection.

A slight scuffle occurred at the door as a couple attempted to gain entry without invitation cards; but the bouncers were onto them at once. I saw them briefly: an elderly pair, hatless and too old for the funky style they'd adopted (that cardigan-and-pearls look only retains its ironic dowdiness before the age of twenty-one, and black works best with a perfect complexion and some cheeky accessories), looking bewildered and angry, behind a forgettable starlet in angel-hair chiffon and vertiginous heels. I could just hear the security man, a mobile in each hand, explaining that no-one was allowed to enter without an official invitation and ID – security had been stepped up in the wake of a scandal wherein the casket of a minor Royal had been revealed to contain four illicit grave-crashers. The old lady nodded tearfully, clinging to the old gentleman's hand, and the two moved off the carpet – flashguns shooting all the way – and into the area cordoned off for the convenience of the general public.

Security was predictably tight, confirms our reporter, with even the deceased submitting to the obligatory searches . . . Quite right too, I thought. The public's role was to stay well behind the cordon and gape in admiration as the Immortals glided past. This was what they wanted: glamour, reassurance, dreams. The funeral industry had been quick to cash in on this new market, offering affordable high-street copies of the fantasy caskets pictured in *Rattler* or *Crem*, and a recent survey had shown *Goodbye!* magazine that some of the more fashion-conscious of our readers were already on waiting-lists for the newest caskets (with Chanel's quilted *Ozymandias* model pre-booked until 2015).

I could see the monogrammed casket clearly now, with its sunroof open to facilitate access. Behind it, the old couple still lingered, getting in the way of the *News of the World* photographers. A blonde PR girl was hovering around them, a mobile clamped to her ear. I heard her voice above the crowd – *So sorry, darling, I'll see what I can do* – then everything was submerged under a new wave of sound as the deceased was ushered into the building.

Dernière make-up favours statement colours, and the deceased opted for a metallic violet by Urban Decay, with accessories by Moriarty. Behind the casket came the PR girl, with the bewildered old couple in tow. Security let them through with reluctance, and I wasn't surprised – there's a dress code to these events, for God's sake – and between you and me, both of them could have done with a little wardrobe advice. That make-up, for instance – who wears *waterproof* mascara to a funeral nowadays? And although a few tears can be quite now on these occasions, nose-blowing is completely out – fluids are really so inappropriate. I saw the official photographer pose them for a casket shot, though I could have told them it would never be used. People read about these events for the glamour and the gossip, not to see pictures of geriatric funeral-chasers looking glum. And they were casting a shadow on the whole party, too; I could see guests edging politely away from them as they approached, and even the people from elite introduction agency Crème-de-la-Crem (Putting the Fun back into Funerals) kept their distance. Rather tasteless, I thought, for them to be there at all.

'From the North, my dear – Yorkshire or Derbyshire or somewhere like that—'

'God, what a bore. I wonder what brings them here; I mean, they're not exactly the party type—'

'I suppose it's for the service; after all, she was their daughter.'

'Darling! How morbid! Quick, quick, another cocktail!'

I gave the old couple a wide berth, and spent a pleasant five minutes exchanging beauty tips with Cardamom Burrows and her friend Coriander Hague, as Amber from K.O. watched with envy. The Northern couple loitered vaguely on the edges of the group for a time, then drifted away, refusing canapés and drinks. No-one seemed eager to talk to them.

Goodie bags were given out to all guests, containing samples of the new Eulogy super-streaky mascara, mini-bottles of Moët Black Label, Penhaligon's new-season fragrance Gather

Ye Lilacs, and a fabulous silver coffin-motif keyring from Asprey & Garrard, all in a funky limited-edition tote . . .

At last the individual shots seemed to be over, and the room was now getting very crowded. It was rather hot, too, and I was glad of the open windows and the ceiling-fans. In a few minutes, I knew, it would be time for the ceremony and the speeches – between you and me, the dullest part of the event, but it's popular with the readers, and with these parties there are always celebrity mourners to give a bit of life to an otherwise lacklustre occasion. I could see Madonna in one corner – *note to self: burka chic, with ironic minidress* – talking to Elton John over the heads of several dozen Armani-clad bodyguards; Tom Parker-Bowles and A.A. Gill (I wondered what he was doing there, then remembered his new column, 'Death Warmed Up', on funeral catering), rubbing shoulders with Hugh Grant and Sophie Dahl.

My notebook was filling up rapidly. I had stopped writing in complete sentences, cursing the fashion that decreed wet notes in favour of electronic ones (the handwriting accessories are so stylish, though), but I promised myself I would write everything up properly on my PC that very night.

Graham Norton: lurex and cashmere from Fake London. Julie Burchill with Tony Parsons (?) – surely some mistake?? Juicy playgirl Apricot Sykes. Society's answer to Johnny Depp – Viscount Wimbourne, Speccy Von Strunckel, Zadie Smith . . .

For a while I amused myself counting the guests that Sis

had dated. Everyone was having a marvellous time – by now the casket had been transported to the viewing area (tastefully shrouded in dévoré velvet), and the bands were both in full swing. There was a moment of surprise as the lights dimmed and silence fell, but when this was revealed to be a solo 'unplugged' performance of Cage's 4:33, wittily performed by Brat's Johnny Nuisance, the entire audience burst into spontaneous applause.

It was the signal for the eulogies to start. Expectantly, we moved to the sides of the room as the huge podium swung into place. Celebrity speakers at these events are closely guarded secrets, and even I had no idea who was going to take the podium. There were so many celebrities here that any choice was bound to be a spectacular one. It depended on what image the deceased chose to project: intellectual angst (Salman Rushdie, Jeremy Paxman, Stephen Fry); funky (Graham Norton); dominatrix (Madonna); girlie (Stella, Jodie, Kate); breeding (Kitty, Piggy, India, Pakistan). This, in any case, was the magic moment. Frocks, tears, unguarded secrets . . . anything might happen, anything might be revealed. Last year Elspeth Trivial-Pursuing ended up on the front page of *Goodbye!* after breaking down completely and thanking everyone from God to her neighbour's budgie for helping her survive the death of her dog, Figgis; and porn legend Jim Grossly astonished and amused by performing his own post-mortem eulogy via video link, and arriving at the crematorium in a huge Porsche Condom.

But as we watched in breathless anticipation, it was the

Northern couple that stepped up to the platform, still hand-in-hand, she clutching her shabby old M&S handbag (too old even to qualify as vintage), he wearing his Sunday suit and funeral tie, and I felt a dreadful sense of déjà vu. This was just how it had been when my grandmother died: the same suit, the same old handbag, the same expressions of baffled grief over the sherry and sausage rolls.

They were going to speak, I realized in horror and growing rage; they might even say a prayer, not knowing that in fashion terms such things were as dead as the pashmina or the Fantasy Tan. I felt my face grow hot with humiliation. Trust them to spoil it; trust them to make a scene when everything was going so well and remind us that in spite of our affectations we were here with Death, the original casket-chaser. I couldn't bear it. The old Northern woman was looking at me, her eyes netted in wrinkles, her mouth turned down – no Botox for *her* – in a painful little grimace of distress which would have looked great on Gwyneth or Halle, but which on her looked too real, too raw, like a bedsore or some other unsightly affliction you'd never see in the movies.

'You might be wondering why we're here,' she said in that toneless voice of hers. 'But we're her parents, after all, and we didn't think we needed an invitation to our own daughter's funeral.'

Not much of a speech, I thought; usually they begin with the thank-yous, trying to keep it to two minutes whilst dropping as many famous names as possible.

'I wouldn't have done it this way meself,' she went on,

looking round the room with a slightly pained expression, 'but this is our Maggie's day, after all, and it's only right that all her friends be here to send her off.'

Send her off! It was downright embarrassing. I wanted to scream, to shout at them to stop it, that they were spoiling everything, but I was still aware of the old woman's eyes on me (what was she staring at, for God's sake?) and I couldn't move, I could hardly breathe under the weight of that sad, regretful gaze. I closed my eyes, feeling sick.

'Well, I'm not one for speeches,' went on the old woman, her voice cracking a little. 'I don't want to keep any of you from having a good time. But what I do want to say is—' she broke off for a moment, and the sound engineer looked at his stopwatch – 'what I'm trying to say is that our Maggie – our Maggie—'

Funeral etiquette dictates that no-one should move during the eulogies. It's partly for the sake of the cameras sweeping the audience, partly out of respect for the sound engineers; but oh God, I needed a drink. I picked up a cocktail from a nearby table and downed half of it in one, feeling the sickness recede a little. I could tell that some of the guests were confused by the name of Maggie – no-one had called her by that clunky, unfashionable name in years – but the Press seemed happy enough, lurking at the edges of the crowd, filling up on nibbles and drinks, and Amber from *K.O.*, with her unerring instinct for trouble, was grinning at me on the sly.

'What my wife's trying to say,' said the old man in his slow, deliberate way, 'is that Maggie was our daughter. We didn't see much of her – being busy as she was with her career and the rest – but we loved her all the same, as we love both our girls. We'd have done anything for them, anything—' God, why doesn't he just shut up? I asked myself – 'and we allus did our best. But it's hard sometimes, trying to keep up. We never held it against her when she didn't come to see us, or when she didn't call, or was too busy to answer the phone. We were proud of our Maggie, and we still are. I remember once—'

At this point, mercifully, we reached the two-minute line and the mike cut out. I felt a dim relief that we had been spared the Northern man's reminiscences of Auntie Madge or Uncle Joe – or, infinitely worse, of little Aggie and the dressing-up box, and how she and her Sis were just like peas in a pod, just like twins, the darlings, like two little angel figurines. I opened my notebook again and wrote furiously: *Speeches v. disappointing. Note to self – extended Generations Gap piece (?) Keep it light, e.g.: 'The Handbaggers' or '50 Ways To Leave Your Mother'.* But when I glanced up, they were both still looking at me, she with one hand extended, he with that hangdog look I'd always hated, as if there was something I could *give* them, or something they could give to me.

'Mother, please,' I murmured.

But the Northern woman was adamant. 'Come on, our Aggie. Don't be shy. It's what she would have wanted.'

People were turning to look at me now; my face was aflame. I wanted to scream with frustration – please, *please* don't do this, Mother – but all I could do was shrug helplessly and smile, as if I were the victim of an amusing *malentendu*, whilst on the dévoré-draped podium the Northern couple stared at me in sad surprise, then bewilderment, then finally, understanding and resignation.

He had shrunk during his two minutes; now he seemed no more than four feet tall, a dwarf of a man in his Sunday suit with his dead daughter at his side, and if anything his wife was smaller, a shrivelled old woman who might die at any moment without ever tasting a liquorice Kir or Beluga blini; a frightened old woman willing to face even the terrors of a Society funeral in the hope of a glimpse of her vanished daughters . . .

As children, we never quite forgive our loved ones their mortality. At Gran's funeral there had been sherry and sausage rolls, and we had cried together, Mum and Sis and I, at the unfairness that takes away a relative without warning at the age of fifty-nine; and afterwards we had collected all the leftover food into some Tupperware boxes while Dad and his mates went down the Engineers for a pint, and me and our Maggie played fairy princesses with Gran's old clothes and an orange lipstick from Auntie Madge, and swore we'd live for ever. But all that was a long time ago: things had moved on, and rightly so. I wasn't Aggie any more – I was Angela K.: sophisticated, witty, stylish, and above all, *poised*. Angela K. didn't do nostalgia, she didn't cry, she didn't *snivel*; she kept it light, kept it witty and ironic and utterly free of fluids.

'Aggie, love, *please*.'

'Yer Mam and me won't be here for ever, you know.'

'We're worried about you. You never call.'

'And you're getting so *skinny* – just like your—'

'Sis.'

It was too much. I could feel it coming like an avalanche, bringing everything down with it. The photographers could see it too, and I felt their lenses turn hungrily towards me, because if there's anything better than a celebrity speech at a *Dernière*, it's a celebrity breakdown, and I *was* a celebrity of sorts, if only by proxy. It was coming; and my eyes were stinging, my throat squeezed shut and the cry was almost out, almost uttered. There was no stopping it; the only question now was how much damage it would do, and as the tears squirted from my eyes and the snot from my nose I felt it all go with them: my poise, my prospects, my career, my dreams.

There's no escaping it, I thought dimly: there are no Immortals. Death was everywhere, Death was undeterred by the black cordon or the security guards; unimpressed by the music or the gossip or the fashionable caterers. He was in us all; he was on the High Street and in the designer show-room; he was an enviable size nought; a rattling good dancer; a playboy; a wit. I cried for the unfairness of it all: for the Immortals; for my sister; for my parents; for myself. Because in the end it's always for yourself, isn't it? That's the truth of it, we cry because we know that we won't live for ever. We rage against the defective gene that makes us mortal, and we hate the ones we love for passing it on.

The audience was watching, rapt. All cameras were now on me. Technically speaking, I'd passed the two-minute cut-off point, but this was *good*, this was *great*, this was what we'd all secretly come for: that little taste of the raw, the flesh; the bloody sacrifice in the smiling presence of Death, the ultimate party animal.

'It's not *fair*!' I screamed above the noise. 'I'm not *ready*!'

And as the cameras flashed and the band struck up and the voice of the crowd rose to a moan, I heard Amber say quietly in my ear: 'Go for it, darling. Knock 'em dead.'

Free Spirit

I got the idea for this story on a Saturday morning, sitting at a dirty table in a crowded supermarket café. It scared me then, and still does.

YOU'LL NEVER TIE ME DOWN. I'M A FREE SPIRIT; I GO wherever the wind takes me. Last night it was Paris, by the banks of the Seine. She'd been sleeping under a bridge; she was sixteen, dog-tired, beautiful. Tinfoil and spent needles littered the floor around her bed. I knew at once that she was the one. Her long river-coloured hair trailed across the greasy bricks; her eyes were closed. She made small introspective sounds as I touched her; her skin mottled; her eyelids flickered. Sometimes she seemed ready to speak, but there was no need for words between us. We were already too close for that. Her fists clenched; she clawed the air; her neck and her pale arms blossomed. She was alight and lovely with fever.

It was quick; that's the only drawback with these short

affairs. In less than twenty-four hours it will be over. But the wind keeps on blowing; a scrap of tinfoil from under our bridge escapes in a draught and is carried up over the Pont-Neuf and over l'Ile de la Cité to descend in a shower of confetti on the steps of a church where a young couple poses, smiling for a photographer.

Choices, choices. Who will it be? The bride? The groom? More interesting to me are the guests: the teenage boy with a scattering of *herpes simplex* around his sullen mouth; the grandmother with her caved-in face and hands knotted beneath her white gloves. They are all beautiful to me, all equally worthy of my attention. I leave the choice to the scrap of tinfoil; there's poetry in that. It spins, whirls. Faces lift to the sky. For a second it brushes the lips of the balding man, a second cousin with a flat, impassive face who stands slightly apart from the others. Him, then. I follow him home.

His flat is on the Marne-la-Vallée line; small and obsessively clean, the flat of a man who has no friends. There are no beer cans discarded beside the sofa, no dirty dishes stacked in the sink. Instead there are books: scientific manuals, medical dictionaries, anatomical charts. This man gargles with Listerine four times a day and his bathroom cabinet is filled with the paraphernalia of the hardcore hypochondriac.

Not that I mind; in a way it appeals to me. This is a man who does not understand the nature or the extent of his own desires; beneath his prissy exterior, his obvious fear, I sense his secret longings. Besides, I enjoy a challenge.

Once again, there is no need for words. He is irrationally afraid of me, and yet he welcomes me with something approaching relief, as if he has been awaiting just this moment. There is a desperation in his resistance which gives spice to our meeting, and when finally the barriers are broken, he responds even more quickly than the girl, who was already weakened by hardship and encroaching pneumonia.

But I can't be tied down. Twenty-four hours is all I can give him, and already I sense that our wildly opposite natures are causing problems. He wants intimacy; to stay in bed all day with the television on and cool drinks by the bedside. I'm a social animal; I need contact to survive. I'm already beginning to miss the nightlife, the clubs, the busy heat of Paris. I escape when he is asleep, the moment the cleaning woman comes to look over the flat.

She is all unsuspecting; she peers over him cautiously (it is past twelve) as if to check him for fever. 'D'you want me to call a doctor?' she queries; then, when he does not answer, she shrugs and gets on with her work. That's all I need. I escape unnoticed, the brush of her hand the only contact between us.

The cleaning woman is old but tough. She lives near Pigalle. It's my favourite part of Paris; bright, ugly and seething with life. She takes me to the Sacré Coeur, where she prays and I prey, passing from tourist to tourist and running voluptuously over the well-fingered stonework. The air here is hot with incense; from here penitents will wander down the Butte de Montmartre into Pigalle below, where the whores and the rent-boys congregate and the strip-clubs are just beginning to get busy.

I'd like to stay with the cleaning woman, but life's just too short. There are hundreds – thousands – of others out there waiting for me. I pass quickly from one to another: a nun gathering alms at the door of the basilica collects more than she bargained for; the old gentleman who gives her a hundred-franc note receives an unexpected handful of change; later that night, a lad who swears he is fourteen will meet us both in the dark archway of a closed Métro station, and after that the young lad (who is really nineteen and doing good business) will take me to a club, where I shall mingle freely among the revellers, dipping into drinks, sharing cigarettes, touching flesh and enjoying the warm, damp air.

They are all equal to me: young, old, healthy or corrupt, male or female. Twenty-four hours is all I can ever give them; but in that time I give them my all. Who next? And where? Will it be a needle, a kiss, a lost coin picked up from the streets and carried home? Will it be a cube of sugar in a crowded café or the gleeful tramping of a fly in a pâtisserie window or the furtive hands of a pervert on the Métro or windblown dust sticking to a child's lollipop? Whatever it is, I'll be there. You may not see me; I won't speak a word. But all the same, you'll be mine. We'll be closer than lovers, you and I: tighter than DNA. Nothing will mar the perfect physicality of our relationship: no quarrels, no seduction, no lies. You will give me your self, and I will give you mine, entirely. For a while.

And afterwards, I'll take the road again. No regrets. Maybe I'll go to America, in a crowded, air-conditioned plane. Or to England, by the tunnel. Or maybe back to Africa, or Asia, or Japan. I'll see the world ten times over. I'll meet millions of people. That's why I don't stay anywhere long. You can't tie me down. I'm a wanderer. A traveller. A party animal. I'm a free spirit, and I go wherever the wind takes me.

Auto-da-fé

There is something terribly primitive about the way we behave in cars. Driving, we exhibit all the behaviour patterns of pack animals: the sexual aggression; the brute triumph of strength over weakness; the eternal struggle for dominance in the automotive pecking order. Some call this road rage. Others prefer a more graphic term.

I LIKE CARS. I ALWAYS HAVE; SINCE I WAS A LITTLE LAD I'VE liked the smell of them, the sound of them, the shapes and colours and different sizes of them. That's what I played with when I was a lad: Tonka trucks, Matchbox cars, you name one, I had it, I had them all. And now I'm a driver, a pro, a knight of the road.

A man's car defines him, you know. *A reflection of the male superego,* Annie says, as she brings me my cup of tea. *An extension of a latent desire to sexually dominate other males.* I think it must be those classes she goes to. All Freud and sexual domination. I wouldn't mind if some of it ever came my way. But no. It's always *Not tonight, love, I've got me monthlies*. No wonder I'd rather wax the car.

Mind you, she's a beauty. Midnight-blue BMW. Alloy wheels, leather seats, walnut trim. Class. She's what I'd have myself if I could afford her. But she's not mine. She belongs to the company, and the company could take her away tomorrow. Ask yourself how that feels. On the other hand, don't. I've had enough of castration metaphors and womb-traumas from Annie. Only *she* understands me. She and I – a perfect unit, speeding thrice daily along the M1 between Leeds and Sheffield, bearers of the eternal flame of Matthew McArnold & Son Ltd, soft furnishers to the world.

In my business, you get to understand cars. Cars of all sorts: Corsas and Golfs for student nurses called Hayley, battered Escorts for spotty economics students at the Poly, 2CVs or reconned Beetles for cute little actressy types called Kate, a matt-silver Lexus for her banker-made-good Dad, Len, who's having an illicit affair with the tennis-club secretary, Jan, a well-preserved forty-five with a Ford *Ka* and a dirty mind. On my run, you get to know the regulars. That Asian bloke in the brown Nissan Sunny who always hogs the middle lane. That blonde in the turquoise Cinquecento, checking her lipstick in the rear-view mirror by the exit to Junction 37. The white van from Junction 36, with a rag dangling from the ladder sticking out from his back end. The red Probe – now *there's* one for Annie's psych group – who zooms along the fast lane at ninety mph and honks at anything in his way. Including that unmarked white police car – hello boys, I can see you in your Rover 500 – oops, too late. You see, it pays to know your cars.

V-Man, for instance. You must have seen him: black Volvo saloon, black spoilers, tinted windscreen, *Top Gun* shades. V-Man really gets up my nose. He thinks he's better than the rest of us, with his limited-edition sunroof and his personalized number-plate: KE 51. Fact is, he's not. But we always have to go through it all the same, V-Man and me, nose to nose, like gladiators, every bloody morning.

Thing is, I'm a *good* driver. I've had the car twelve months – she was my Rep of the Year incentive – and I've never even put a scratch on her; never even got a ticket. I might bend the rules once in a while – well, speed limits aren't made to be taken literally, and I find a couple of drinks actually *help* my concentration – but I can drive, I know the roads and the people and I can drive. It's the ones like V-Man that are really dangerous. The ones that think they're something and want to prove it. Me, I'm just a driver; I mean it's a job. It's not like it's my life or anything. That would just be too sad. But V-Man – he drives as if it's personal; as if there was more at stake than just space; and when he dodges between two articulated lorries into the fast lane and pulls away at eighty-five, you can just see him thinking: *Not so smart now, are you, in your flash Beemer with your alloy trim; take a look at what a man can do.* And though I've never actually seen his face – the tinted glass gets in the way – I know he's a little balding twat with a trainee moustache who gets bullied at the office and thinks he's king of the road.

Not that I let it get to me; not usually, anyway. But today started badly; woke up late, had to rush, there was a lane closed between Junctions 36 and 37 and Annie's started talking about *taking time out to consider our options*, which probably means she's seeing another fella – or worse still, she's getting broody – and all I really needed to make it a totally shitty day instead of just a crap one was for V-Man to show up, all bright and shiny in his black Volvo, and try to put one over on me on the sly.

Of course, I usually win. Nine times out of ten I win, because a BMW runs rings round a limited-edition Volvo any day of the week, but this morning I had this feeling he'd try it on, as if he sensed something was wrong and thought he'd chance it. Well, I was right. I spotted him coming off the slip-road from Junction 36 – bang on time as usual. Pulled right out into the middle lane in front of me, no indicator, no signal, no mirror. What a wanker. Of course, he does it on purpose. He thinks it winds me up. I flashed at him, speeded right up to his back bumper and flashed again. Then I overtook him, nice and smooth into the fast lane, and moved back into the middle lane in front of him, giving him the indicator signal – twice for each side, to make sure he got the message. You'd have thought that would have been it. But some people just have to keep at it, don't they, needling away, nagging at you until something in you just snaps and you give them a good thump and before you know it it's: *You can't do that to me, you bastard, I'm off to me Mam's*, as if they hadn't asked for it in the first place and now you're somehow to blame. Well, that's V-Man. He overtook me a minute later – never mind he couldn't beat the red Probe just coming up behind him – just took off into the fast lane with the Probe up his arse and gave me a little wave as he passed. I couldn't see his face, what with the shades he was wearing, but I did see he was wearing driving gloves – the leather kind, with the breathable lining – and somehow that did it for me. I'd never met this bloke and suddenly I knew everything about him. Knew it, and hated his guts.

He's called Keith or maybe Ken, and he works in sales. He's forty-five and he hasn't had a shag for over a year, not since his wife (thirty-nine, ash blonde, Honda Civic) went off with some bloke she met in Hatha Yoga. He wears suits from Moss Bros and shirts from Marks & Sparks; and there's always an extra shirt on a hanger in the back of the car, just in case he gets sweaty before an important meeting. He chose a Volvo because they're safe, but he made sure it was a black sporty model because to him that says *young, free, and ready for action*. He wears shades even on cloudy days, and driving gloves – as if he might get blisters – even though he's got power steering, and he's listening to Radio Two right now, and they're playing Dire Straits' 'Sultans of Swing', with Terry Wogan just beginning to fade out the long guitar solo for the eight o'clock pips (I hate it when they do that, the solo's the best part), and he's singing along, or maybe trying a few rim-shots on the edge of his leather-trimmed steering wheel and thinking how he'd kill for a Strat just like Knopfler's, he's always wanted one and now he's free and single again, no kids, no alimony, he might be able to afford one. For a second he imagines himself going into one of those music shops off Boar Lane in Leeds and idling around the guitars hanging off the walls like trophies; perhaps turning to the grungy kid at the till and saying in his most casual voice: *I'd like to have a look at that Fender Stratocaster.* And the kid saying *Sure, I'll get you an amp,* and is that a smirk on his face as he turns away, and did he just say *Grandad* under his breath, so softly that only he could hear him?

I told you, in that moment I knew it all; knew his loneliness and his pathetic little fantasies and the way that when he hugged himself tightly into the leather seats of the black Volvo he could almost imagine he was someone else, that he was V-Man, Knight of the Road, tilting bravely at every challenge, leaving Mercs and Jags and Beemers standing in their tracks as he surfed ahead . . .

I couldn't let him get away with it. It's not that I'm sad or anything, but I just couldn't. It's a matter of pride. I overtook him on the inside – he was still hogging the fast lane – at insulting speed, giving him the *wanker* sign all the way. He saw it all right: flipped me the finger and speeded up again, but we were reaching the lane closure and fast-lane traffic was slowing down, so I passed him again, grinning, and kissed my middle finger to his diminishing windscreen.

It should have been over then. But it wasn't my morning; as we reached the roadworks the middle lane slowed down to a sudden crawl – no-one wanted to go into the slow lane, and the fast-laners were pushing through at the last minute, even though they'd been given an 800-metre warning. They know there's always some twat going to let them in, especially if it's a woman at the wheel. Me, I'd let them wait. Let India or Saffron be late for her aromatherapy class; some of us have a job to do.

But that's why V-Man overtook me again; most of the other fast-laners had already pulled in, but not him. He came nosing past me, eyes forward, hunched a little over the wheel. I noticed he had a dashboard toy shaped like Kenny out of *South Park*; somehow it was typical of what I knew of him, and it set my teeth even further on edge. But I might even have let that go if he hadn't done what he did next. There was a girl in a white MG at the head of the line, indicating to be let in. Red Probe was two cars ahead of me, with a white mini-van and a green Corolla next in line. I didn't see the Probe letting anyone in – he was in too much of a hurry as usual – but the mini-van honked at the girl to let her through, and she filtered into lane ahead of me. So far, so good. V-Man was stuffed. I certainly wasn't going to let him in; the green Corolla looked like a company car, not doing anyone any favours, so he could indicate all he wanted, I was going to cruise past him, wanking with both hands this time if I could manage it, and leave him in my exhaust. That was the plan.

But V-Man's one of those drivers who won't let go, careless and arrogant, but just pushy enough in some cases to get lucky. This was one of them; at a crucial moment the mini-van stalled, and seeing his chance, V-Man pushed in hard after the white MG. He missed her back bumper by an inch, almost swiped the van with the other end, but lucked out all the same and swung back into the traffic towards his exit. I might have left him to it even then, but for the little *parp!* he sent me as he speeded up ahead, and the casual wave of his hand through the tinted rear window.

That did it. Suddenly I saw red. I revved up the engine, swerved into the slow lane and began in pursuit. It wasn't my exit, and V-Man knew it, which was why he'd dared make such an open challenge. But this time, today of all days, I wasn't having it. V-Man was in the slow lane, backed up in traffic; I was five cars behind him as he entered the slip-road. I swore, nipped off the road onto the hard shoulder and caught him up *that* way – sod the cameras – so that when he reached the lights at the main junction roundabout I was up close and personal, jammed right up against his back bumper and glaring at him in his rear-view mirror.

I could see *that* had rattled him. He was staring straight ahead, waiting for the lights to change. I could see him watching me in the mirror, though; every few seconds I sensed his rabbity eyes flicking to the lights, then to the mirror, where I was grinning fiercely at him and mouthing insults. I took off my seat-belt, to see what he'd do, then opened my side door a crack. By now V-Man was shitting bricks. When I put a leg out the door, he jumped a mile and hit the lock button, glancing back at me with his shades slipping off his nose. I pushed a little closer, flashing my headlamps at him, then the lights changed and I slammed the door and moved off in pursuit. It was a route I'd never taken before. Usually it's the M1, back and forth from

Sheffield to Leeds, but now I'd got tangled up in my quarry's trail and I knew I was pushing it to get to work on time. It didn't matter, though; I was going to show V-Man who was boss once and for all; even if it meant running the little shit off the road. We raced five or six miles along a dual carriageway heading towards Bradford, and though he tried to lose me, he had no chance. I stayed right up against his bumper, right up his arse all the way, and there were no more little parps and waves; V-Man was dead serious now, eyes fixed straight ahead, occasionally glancing back into the rear-view mirror in that nervous, hunted way. He tried speeding up, dodging between lorries to lose me, but I followed him. Then he slowed to a crawl, hoping I'd overtake him, but I slowed as well. Finally he pulled into a roadside services, dodged through the lorry park, through the petrol-station and parked in front of Burger King, engine idling, daring me to follow him there.

Showdown.

I parked opposite him and we stood for a moment, windshield-to-windshield, observing each other. I cracked my door open; waited. His stayed closed. I stepped out onto the tarmac and put on my sunglasses, shielding my eyes against the morning sun. He stayed, holed in like a terrified rabbit, watching me as I walked slowly up to the black Volvo.

Now I was so close I could see it wasn't quite as shiny as I'd thought; there was a little rust on the bottom of the passenger door, and there were signs of bodywork around the left headlamp. Through the smoked glass I could see

V-Man watching me with his mobile in one hand. As I watched he held up the mobile in a weakly threatening gesture, as if he were planning to phone the police.

'Get out,' I said quietly.

Through the glass, V-Man shook his head.

I kicked the side of the Volvo's door, hard enough to dislodge rust. 'Get out,' I repeated.

The driver's side window opened a crack. 'I'm calling the police,' said V-Man in a high, wavery voice. Behind it came the faint sound of Radio Two playing 'Band of Gold' (Frieda Payne, 1970).

'Call away, you little twat,' I said, and put my fist through his window. Fake diamonds on everything. It hurt, but it felt good all the same: I could feel the ratchet of small bones in my bruised knuckles. 'Is that enough sexual domination for you, you little twat? Does that make you feel *fulfilled?*'

It wasn't quite what I'd been planning to say, but I saw his eyes widen with fear. 'I . . . Look, I've got money,' he said. 'Take it. The phone, too.' He held out a wallet, black leather, like his driving gloves, his hand trembling so much I could barely see it clearly. Bloody hell, what did he think I wanted?

'You cut me off,' I said, ignoring the outstretched wallet. 'Nobody cuts me off.' It was what I should have said to Annie this morning, I told myself. I wished Annie could see me now. Might give her something to think about other than that poncey psychology teacher of hers.

V-Man was looking at me in fearful incomprehension. 'C-cut you off?' he stammered.

'Dead right,' I said. I reached through the broken window and opened the driver's door. 'And now I'm going to cut *you* off, you little twat.'

V-Man was still watching me, eyes glazed. 'I'm a married man,' he whispered. 'I've got children—'

'No you haven't,' I told him, knowing it was true.

'No, I haven't,' whispered V-Man.

'Is your name Keith or Ken?' I demanded.

'K-Kenny.'

That explained the dash toy. And looking inside the car now, I could see his life: his jacket hung up on a wire hanger, his cheap briefcase, an old picture of a blonde woman – she'd be called Penny, or Connie, or Frannie, some crap like that – Blu-Tacked to the glove compartment; a Magic Tree air-freshener dangling from the rear-view mirror; a copy of *Arena* – stolen from a colleague at work – lying on the back seat to give the impression he was young and fancy-free; and behind it all, behind the smell of his sweat and the reek of that air-freshener and the leather of his driving-gloves and the musty smell of car I could smell that terrible, familiar scent – like piss, like old takeaway meals, like unemptied ashtrays and stale underwear – of hopelessness, despair, and decaying illusions.

'What are you going to do?' whispered V-Man.

I'd almost forgotten him in that wave of loathsome understanding; I looked down now and saw his fat and cheesy face, his weak eyes, his receding hair, the darkly spreading stain at the crotch of his Moss Bros trousers.

My hand was throbbing fiercely where I'd broken the

window; I massaged my knuckles – bloody stupid thing to do, punching the glass; could have broken a bone. To make matters worse, my other hand was already bruised from earlier this morning. My head, too, was sore; in spite of my Ray-Bans, the morning sun always seems to get me straight in the eyes. My mobile was ringing – I could hear it very faintly in the distance, behind the sound of the car radio ('Band of Gold' was merging into Queen's 'We Are the Champions') – probably work asking why I was late, or Annie wanting to finish that discussion we started earlier – *If you were a man, Benny, you wouldn't always need to prove to yourself that you're not a loser* – what does *she* know, silly cow? I showed her, anyway; I showed her properly this time, and never mind that she threatened to call the police, you can only drive a man so far. *He* knows, V-Man, sitting shivering in his mock-leather seat smelling the piss drying on his fifty-quid Moss Bros trousers. *He* knows who the loser is in this game, and it isn't me.

I showed them this time. I showed them both. No-one cuts me up; no-one plays me for a loser. I walked back to the car, got in, turned up the radio (Pink Floyd, 'Another Brick in the Wall, Part II'), adjusted my dashboard mascot (Bart Simpson), pulled on my gloves and revved off into the sunrise, while behind me lights flashed and sirens wailed and that phantom smell of piss, of loser, kept getting stronger and stronger, even as I drove away.

The Spectator

Not long ago, at the height of the media paedophile frenzy, a pensioner friend was attacked by a neighbour. The reason? Because he liked to take his daily walk past the school playing fields and watch the children playing football. This harmless old man was so frightened by the attack, which was vicious and unprovoked, that he now hardly ever leaves his house at all. I find this more depressing than words can say. All over the country, it seems that children are being taught to see all strangers as potential aggressors; and more and more adults are learning to give children a wide berth in the fear that they may fall under suspicion. This story owes much to Ray Bradbury's haunting tale, 'The Pedestrian'.

EVERY WEEKDAY MORNING AT TEN-THIRTY, MR LEONARD Meadowes would put on his overcoat, his red scarf and his ancient trilby and set out on his daily constitutional. Past the corner shop, where he would buy a copy of *The Times* – and occasionally a quarter of Murray Mints or Yorkshire

Mixture – past the deserted churchyard with its lopsided gravestones and thick wreaths of hemlock and trailing convolvulus, past the charity shop where he bought most of his clothes, across a main road blaring with traffic, through the small wood where he used to walk his dog, and into the lane which bordered onto the school playing fields. He wore trainers for the walk, as much for comfort as for discretion, and if the weather was fine, he would sit on the wall for twenty minutes or so and observe the children at play before turning back through the wood in the direction of Dare's café and his usual buttered toast and pot of tea.

Today, in late October, the sun was shining, and there was a smoky sweetness in the air like falling leaves. One of those perfect days of which the English autumn has so few, sun-warmed like an apricot, tangled with blackberries, crunchy as cornflakes underfoot. Here by the playing fields it was quiet; a dry-stone wall at the edge of the trees marked the boundary, and beyond it the grass was still summer-sweet and freckled with daisies, rolling gently down a soft incline towards a square brick building shining mellow in the sunlight.

Ten-fifty-five. In five minutes, he told himself, it would be break-time, and children would shoot from the school's four doorways like fireworks – red, blue, neon-green – hair flying, socks at half-mast, voices raised and soaring like kites into the soft golden air. Twenty minutes of break-time: of freedom from rules and constructions; of fights and bloody noses, treasures lost and bartered, outlaws and heroes and whispered rebellions and shrieking, dappled, grubby-kneed bliss.

Once, Mr Meadowes had himself been a teacher. Thirty years in the classroom, in the smell of chalk and cabbage and mown grass and socks and wood-polish and life. Of course, in this year of 2023 there were no more teachers – after all, computers were far safer and more efficient – but the school still looked so familiar, so real in the sweet October light that he could almost ignore the chain-link fence that reared mightily above the little wall and ran all the way around the playing field, the lightning-bolt electrification symbol and the lettered warning – SCHOOL – NO UNACCOMPANIED ADULTS – bolted to the post.

But Mr Meadowes was remembering his own classrooms; the scarred wooden floors stained purple with ink and polished to a lethal gloss by generations of young feet; the passageways soft with blackboard dust; the flying staircases of books; the graffitied desks with their furtive slogans; the crumpled worksheets, confiscated cigarettes, copied home-work, arcane messages, and other forgotten artefacts of that lost and long-ago state of grace.

Of course, it wasn't really like that: nowadays each pupil had a workstation with a plastic desktop, a voice-activated monitor, an electronic pen and a computer-generated tutor with an ageless and intelligent face (a prototype selected from thousands of designs by the Centre for Generational Awareness to inspire confidence and respect). All lessons were taken from the workstation – even practicals were performed under virtual conditions. In the barbaric old days, children had been scalded by steam during poorly supervised cookery lessons, acid-burned in chemistry, had their bones broken in various sports, skinned their knees in asphalt playgrounds and were bullied and victimized in countless ways by their human teachers. Nowadays, all children were safe. So safe, in fact, that sightings had become quite uncommon. And yet they still *looked* much the same as he remembered, thought Mr Meadowes. They sounded the same. What, then, had changed?

Mr Meadowes was so deep in his thoughts that he did not notice the sound of a security van approaching along the lane, or hear the recorded alarm-signal – *Children! Danger! Children!* – as it clattered towards him. It was only when the vehicle stopped right in front of him, its turret light strobing, that he saw it and was startled from his thoughts.

'Don't move! Stop right there!' said a metallic voice from inside the van.

Mr Meadowes took his hands out of his pockets so fast that his bag of sweets spilled out, scattering across the lane like coloured marbles. Beyond the chain-link fence, the children were coming quietly out of the school buildings in twos and threes, some huddled over electronic gamesets, some glancing curiously at the security vehicle with its illuminated turret and the old, old man in the battered trilby with his hands raised and his palms outstretched like an actor in one of those old films, where everyone was in black and white, and men on horseback held up stage-coaches and Martians stalked the barren lands with Death Rays at the ready.

'Your name?' demanded the vehicle stridently.

Mr Meadowes told it, keeping his hands clearly visible at all times.

'Business or profession?'

'I'm – a teacher,' admitted Mr Meadowes.

There was a whirring sound from inside the vehicle. 'No business or profession,' said the metallic voice. 'Marital status?'

'Er – I'm not married,' said Mr Meadowes. 'I did have a dog, but—'

'Unmarried,' intoned the vehicle. Though the robot voice was completely uninflected, Mr Meadowes seemed to hear a kind of disapproval in the word. 'Can you explain to me, Mr Meadowes, your purpose in loitering outside a clearly marked restricted area?'

'I was just walking,' he said.

'Walking.'

'I like to walk,' explained Mr Meadowes. 'I like to watch the children playing.'

'And have you ever done this before?' said the machine. 'This walking and watching?'

'Every day,' he replied, 'for fifteen years.'

There was a long, hissing silence. 'And are you aware, Mr Meadowes, that personal contact (including physical, audiovisual, virtual or electronic) between an unsupervised adult and a child or young person (that being defined as any person under the age of sixteen) is strictly prohibited under the terms of Clause 9 of the Generations Act of 2008?'

'I like to hear their voices,' said Mr Meadowes. 'It makes me feel young.'

The silence from the machine was somehow even more damning than its toneless voice. Mr Meadowes remembered a rumour (from the old days, before the things had become so familiar that no-one even noticed them any more) that the security vans were controlled remotely from a central computer, without the input of a single human operative. 'Surely there can't be any harm in that,' he said helplessly. 'I mean – don't we all enjoy watching children at play?'

There came a new sound from inside the vehicle and a door opened, revealing a metal-panelled interior. 'Get in, please,' ordered the robotic voice.

'But I haven't done anything wrong,' protested Mr Meadowes.

'Get in, please,' repeated the voice.

Mr Meadowes hesitated for a moment, then entered the van. It was a small, dark metal box with a tiny window of reinforced glass, a bench in the middle and a grille set into the back panel to protect the operating system. 'Now if you had a child of your own—' said the voice, and Mr Meadowes realized that, after all, there *was* a man in the driver's seat on the other side of the grille; a man with a microphone and an electronic clipboard who looked at him with disgust and a furtive kind of pity before turning back to the controls.

The door closed softly. The vehicle set off again along the lane, and the light that filtered through the grille was freckled and golden. The man in the driver's seat did not turn round again, even when Mr Meadowes addressed him.

'Where are we going?' asked Mr Meadowes at last.

'To the Centre for Research on Generational and Psychosexual Maladjustment.'

They passed down the lane and through the little wood; across the main road where his dog had been run over, eighteen months before; past the streets of identical terraced houses – his own among them – and the arcades of identical trees. They drove right out of the city, along a broad, sweeping expressway lined with multicoloured billboards behind which, every now and then, Mr Meadowes glimpsed the familiar and all-engulfing concrete rubble of the wastelands.

A few minutes later, they passed a row of derelict buildings. A church – closed now for safety reasons, like all others; an old flat-screen cinema; a couple of bookshops; the remains of a park with swings and a bandstand; and at the end of the row, a large and still-lovely building of soot-mellowed stone, bearing the faded sign: *St Oswald's Grammar School for Boys: 1890–2008.*

'That's *my* school,' said Mr Meadowes as they passed.

In silence, the van rushed on.

Al and Christine's World of Leather

I wrote this out of pure mischief. Because although romance may be dead, the beat goes on . . .

CHRISTINE REACHED FOR HER CUP OF TEA, STRETCHED HER cramped spine and sat back to examine her handiwork. Quite a good job, though she said it herself: nice straight seams, no puckering in spite of the difficult fabric, a good strong line. That was going to make someone a very nice, durable pair of work trousers: unusual, perhaps, but hardwearing. Vaguely she wondered what the flap was for.

Not that it mattered. Nowadays she just did what she was told, and let Candy deal with the artistic side of things. Doing what she was told, after all, was what Christine Jones was best at. Imagination was Candy's department.

They had met at a WeightWatchers meeting. Candy was ten stone three and wanted to get down to nine and a half; Christine was thirteen-ten and, as her husband Jack put it, *letting herself go.* She was planning to let go of at least three stone, anyway, but somehow had never quite made it; instead she'd gained six pounds and a social life of sorts, consisting of Candy, her friend Babs, and the Weight-Watchers' mascot, Big Al Maguire.

Big Al had been going to the club for over three years. A huge man who never seemed to lose any weight, he was tolerated only because he made even the fattest women feel better about themselves. Christine wondered what he got out of it, and decided that he just liked the company. Babs worked in a shoe factory and was desperate for a man; Candy was a divorcee, now a mature student at the local Poly, studying textiles and design.

She had taken to Christine at once. 'What a lovely sweater,' she had said, as Christine stepped down from the weighing machine. 'Missoni, is it?'

Christine flushed, and admitted she'd made it herself.

Candy was impressed. She couldn't sew or knit herself, she said, but she had lots of ideas; perhaps they could get together some time and talk. And so the 'knitting coven', as Jack called it, was created. Every Sunday after church, Candy, Babs, Christine and Big Al would meet at Christine's house and discuss yarns and designs. They were all enthusiastic, but Christine was by far the most technically expert, and for the first time, she found that others looked to her for advice. Candy couldn't knit; Babs was quick, but careless, and Big Al, though his giant fingers were astonishingly delicate with the yarn and needles, was too slow for anything but the simplest work.

But Candy had big ideas for the knitting coven. She had a friend, a fellow student from her course, who had opened a little shop. Handmade knitwear could be a real earner, with quite a simple pattern selling at sixty pounds or more. Deducting twenty per cent for the friend, another twenty for cost of yarn and other overheads, that still left half to be divided equally between the designer (Candy, of course) and the workforce – or, in this case, as it happened, Christine.

At first, Jack had resented it, making fun of her friends and her little sideline. But then the money had started to come in – only a few pounds at first, but then more, as the patterns grew more ambitious and the yarns more unusual. Now Candy experimented with combination yarns, with lurex and rubber and silk fibres twisted into the wool. They were harder to knit with, beyond the skills of Babs or Big Al, but sometimes the results were dramatic, and a finished garment might sell for eighty, even a hundred pounds.

Gradually, Christine's role in the knitting coven expanded still further. She no longer used the basic patterns, leaving the simple designs to Babs, and the deliveries – increasingly frequent now – to Big Al. Instead she worked with the special yarns, and, as the money continued to come in, began to take in commissions on non-knitwear items. Occasional pieces of modern dancewear; performance gear; fancy dress. Some of it was quite unusual – the trousers with the mysterious flap, for instance – but Candy assured her that this was where the real money was, and after a single payment of over *two hundred pounds* – a leather gladiator skirt with studded harness, for a theatre performance of *Julius Caesar* – Christine found herself having to agree. After that, Candy suggested they went into business together, with the friend as a sleeping partner, each owning a third share. A lawyer drew up the papers. Christine protested that she didn't need a partnership – after all, Babs and Big Al were paid by the hour – but Candy wanted everything to be scrupulously fair.

'It's only right, darling,' she said, when Christine had mentioned her doubts. 'After all, you do so much of the work.' This touched Christine, who knew herself to be so much less intelligent or attractive than her friend, and who often felt embarrassed at her own inadequacy. Candy deserved better, she thought; it was proof of her sweet nature that she never mentioned it.

It was at this point that Jack stopped complaining. Christine had a hobby room of her own now, in which she kept the leather-adapted industrial sewing machine for her special work, and she spent most evenings in there, listening to the radio as she worked, while Jack spent increasing amounts of time at the health club; for unlike Christine, Jack had not let himself go, and had retained an impressive level of fitness.

This sometimes troubled Christine. It wasn't that she didn't *trust* her husband, she told herself; but three hours at the health club every night did seem a little excessive. She wondered if he was having an affair, then felt guilty for even considering it. Jack was very much a man's man – his reaction to the knitting coven showed it – and he needed male company from time to time. She was lucky, she told herself; he was cheerful, devoted, and made no unreasonable sexual demands (though he might try once in a while, she thought; there was such a thing as being *too* chivalrous). No, she was lucky to have him, she repeated to herself; perhaps he deserved better.

Still, thought Christine, sometimes it was quite a relief to know that Jack was safely out of the house when she worked on her special commissions. He had never made any secret of his dislike of Candy, and his contempt for Big Al, too, was thinly veiled. Besides, he had a limited knowledge of specialist leatherwork – you don't get much exposure to that kind of thing in retail management – and she knew that if he caught sight of her current order list, he would certainly make one of his sarcastic comments. True, it was a peculiar collection, but someone was paying over three hundred pounds for the lot, so there had to be a market for it somewhere.

Once more, she considered the trousers. Good-quality leather; black; thirty-two waist; decorative insert. The purpose of the back flap still eluded her – perhaps some kind of a tool pocket, she thought, though honestly, you'd think they'd want a bit more protection if they're going to be working with equipment. She hoped she hadn't got it wrong; but it wasn't the first pair she had made, and the customers had never complained. Besides, she had given up on trying to improve patterns since she had inadvertently ruined a whole underwear commission (a conceptual dance company, Candy had said) by introducing a reinforced gusset to the basic design. Candy had been rather nasty about it, she remembered, saying, *For God's sake, Christine, if we'd wanted gussets we'd have bloody well asked for them*, so now she did only what she was told. Perhaps dancers need more ventilation – you know, down *there* – she thought. In that case, a reinforced gusset might cause all kinds of unexpected problems. No wonder Candy had been annoyed.

All the same, she thought, a most unusual pair of trousers. The black tutu was normal enough, she supposed, and the corset seemed designed to go with it somehow, though she couldn't work out how. It was stiffly boned (she'd used heavy-duty nylon slats) and laced up at the back, something like the one her grandmother used to wear, though obviously her grandmother's wasn't made of leather. Perhaps for someone with a slipped disc, thought Christine, though you'd expect them to do that kind of thing on the National Health. And what was *this* thing? Not a hat, precisely; in fact from this angle it looked more like a kind of mask, although how were you supposed to see anything if there weren't any eye-holes? Christine shook her head disapprovingly. These dance people could come up with some very strange ideas nowadays. What was wrong with a nice *Swan Lake*? Or a *Nutcracker*?

And yet, she thought, wasn't there something rather *satisfying* in working with these materials? The buttery leather; the silk; the studs; the gauze? She'd always liked working with her hands, but recently she had given more time to her craft than ever before, and it wasn't just because Jack was out of the house. No, she was enjoying the work – responding to it, somehow – far more than she ever had with knits and sweaters. And when she was working, she had begun to have the strangest *thoughts* – like waking dreams. In these dreams she imagined herself wearing the strange garments; feeling their fabulous textures against her skin; maybe (she blinked at the thought) – maybe even performing in them. And in these dreams her designs were not for dancewear, as Candy had told her, nor for back supports or Shakespeare or gardening, but for something else, something thrilling and mysterious and full of power. Hunched guiltily over her sewing machine, a tiny smile on her face, Christine dreamed; and in her dreams she was someone else: a tall, leather-clad someone with a purposeful stride; someone who *never* did as she was told; a woman of authority.

Some chance, she thought, as she boxed up the finished clothing. She never so much as ordered a pizza without consulting Jack; never took any decision regarding the company without turning to Candy for advice. A natural follower, was Christine Jones; a disciple; a perpetual associate; a drone. There's no harm in that, she told herself; we can't all be movers and shakers. Still, the thought depressed her, as did the nagging certainty that somehow she was missing something; something obvious, like coming out of a bathroom with toilet paper stuck to your shoe and walking on, oblivious, while everyone laughs at you behind their hands.

It was eight o'clock when Christine delivered the box to Big Al's. As usual, he seemed to have been waiting for her to arrive, because he opened the door at once, his round face beaming with pleasure.

'Christine! I thought you might drop round this after'. Come on in and have a cuppa.'

She hesitated. 'I don't know, Al. Jack might be back any minute—' Al's face fell, and Christine felt sorry for him. 'Oh, all right, then, just a quick one.'

Big Al's house would have been small, even for a man of normal size. For him it was tiny, and he blundered around in it like an oversized puppy in a Victorian doll's house. He made tea for Christine in a doll-sized china cup, holding the teapot handle between finger and thumb. 'Biscuit?'

'Al, I shouldn't.'

'Never mind that, chuck. Skinny doesn't suit you.'

Christine smiled and took a custard cream. Al had a way of making her feel like china herself, in spite of her fourteen stone. And he wasn't a 'lard-bucket', as Jack so cruelly called him; more like an overstuffed armchair, shapeless but comfortable.

'I see you've done with that order.' He nodded towards the box.

'Yes. You can deliver it tomorrow.'

'Right.' Christine thought Al was looking slightly un-comfortable; she wondered if he had seen the patterns, and if so, what he thought of them. 'Funny load of gear,' she said. 'Still, if people want to buy it—' She noticed Al was wearing the jumper she'd knitted for him last Christmas;

117

the green one with the snowflakes. 'Suits you lovely,' she said.

He flushed a little. 'It's me favourite.'

Christine laughed. 'Jack won't wear them. Says they're *naff*.'

'Jack's a bloody fool.'

The reply came back so quickly that Christine could hardly believe she had heard it. Big Al never used 'language', as he put it; and in all the time she had known him, Christine had never heard him say a bad thing about anyone.

He was flushing very red now, as if aware of having overstepped a line. 'Sorry, chuck,' he said. 'Dunno what come over me.'

But Christine was looking at him, puzzled. 'Is something wrong?'

Al shook his head but would not meet her eyes.

'Al?'

Pause.

'*Al?*'

As he spoke, slowly at first, then with increasing confidence, Christine poured them both a second cup of tea. It was funny how it all made sense; Candy, who deserved better; Jack, who deserved better; herself, quick of fingers but desperately slow of mind, working on her sewing machine while her friend earned twenty-five per cent working on her husband. A nice living for both of them. Jack was the sleeping partner, the third owner of the business: there had never been a friend with a clothing shop, but instead, a website on the Internet, where both Jack and Candy knew Christine would never venture.

'It isn't dancewear at all, is it?' said Christine when he had finished.

Big Al shook his head.

'Is it—' she cast about for a suitable word. '*Erotica?* Is that what we're selling? Sex toys? Fantasy wear?'

Big Al did not need to reply. His face told her everything.

Christine took another biscuit. Funny how calm she felt; she had imagined Jack's betrayal so many times, but had expected to feel something quite different if – or more likely when – it happened. Instead she found herself thinking how nice Big Al's eyes were; how nice, and how kind.

'Where are they now?' she said at last.

'Candy's,' said Big Al.

'All right,' said Christine. 'Let's go.'

It was almost nine when they arrived at Candy's place. The lights were on in the top bedroom, and Christine walked straight in without ringing the bell, knowing that Candy never locked the doors. Big Al followed her, up the stairs and into the bedroom.

The sheets were scarlet silk; the walls, mostly mirrors. Christine noticed with some surprise that Candy had cellulite on her legs, in spite of all that dieting. Jack was lying on his front, like a man with bad stomach-ache. It was so long since Christine had seen him undressed that he looked like a stranger.

'Jesus, Christine—' He tried to sit up, but the handcuffs stopped him – at least she *assumed* they were handcuffs, under all that furry stuff. She'd always assumed that Jack wasn't really interested in sex. Now she realized that it was just sex with *her* that didn't appeal to him; the outfit he was wearing, as well as the variety of objects lined up on the dressing-table, spoke of an imaginative and adventurous sexual career. 'Now listen to me—' he said.

'So *that*'s what they're like on,' said Christine. 'Thirty-two waist, was it? I think you're more of a thirty-four.'

It was her handiwork, all right; she would have recognized them blindfold. Black leather, decorative insert, studded seam. And the flap, of course. Candy was staring at her, open-mouthed, in lace-up boots and a pair of those ventilated panties.

It was the cruellest kind of betrayal. Such a cliché – her husband and her best friend, feigning to dislike each other as they continued their liaison right under her nose – but given extra zest by this final act of deception. She thought of herself, sitting at her sewing machine, dreaming her little dreams – *Poor stupid Christine, thinks it's dancewear, wouldn't know a dildo if she saw one* – while Jack and Candy played their games and laughed themselves sick at the thought of their own cleverness and perversity.

And strangely, Christine found that it was not the sexual betrayal that angered her most, but the fact that they had done it in her clothes – *her* clothes, upon which she had lavished such care. *Imagine Christine in that!* Ghost laughter from a darkened room. And how they must have laughed! Well, thought Christine; you know what they say. *He who laughs last* . . . And suddenly, unexpectedly, she began to smile.

'Christine,' said Jack, 'I think we need to talk about this.'

But Christine was already turning away. And only Big Al, still standing in the doorway, could see her tiny, dangerous smile.

She found the second pair of marabou handcuffs among the items on the dressing-table, along with a digital camera and a thick roll of black masking tape. It took Christine a few moments to figure out how to work the camera, but after that it proved absurdly easy. She shot the pair from various angles, occasionally stopping to readjust a fold of fabric or to smooth out a crease in the soft leather. They might have been professionals, she thought happily; and they looked so right together . . .

'I'm thinking I might branch out,' she said, putting the camera carefully into her pocket. 'My share in the company – and half of Jack's, of course – should give me a nice little sum to start off with.' She looked down at her husband, red-faced and struggling on the bed. It felt quite nice – for a change, she thought – though she still couldn't entirely see the attraction of all that gear. Still, she thought, you should try anything once. 'I'll probably run the business from an Internet site,' she said thoughtfully. 'After all, it's worked fine so far. And besides,' she levelled her smile at Candy and Jack as she worked to remove the tape which gagged them, 'It would be *such* a shame to waste all these photographs, wouldn't it?'

'You can't do this,' gasped Jack, outraged.

'I think I can,' said Christine.

'What? Alone?'

She looked at Big Al. 'Not quite,' she said.

Big Al stared at her as if he couldn't altogether grasp what she was saying. 'What?'

'Al and Christine's World of Leather. How does that sound to you?'

Al grinned and went scarlet. Then he hugged her, his eyes shining. For a minute Christine was content to be suffocated and to enjoy the luxurious sensation of being close to someone that *big*; someone who outweighed her. There was a sensuality to Al, in spite of – and perhaps because of – his size; a sense of *texture* which reminded her of nights spent in front of her patterns, but without the loneliness. It was a kind of revelation. She looked up and saw him looking down at her, his chocolate-brown eyes spangled with lights. Her heart was racing like a sewing machine. With an effort, she disentangled herself from his embrace and turned to face the dressing-table, knowing that they would have time later to luxuriate in each other; conscious of one last thing, one final loose end to be definitively tied.

'Are you two imbeciles going to let me go now?' said Jack, trying unsuccessfully to look dignified in marabou and black leather.

'Not *just* yet, dear,' said Christine, selecting an object

from the dressing-table and approaching the bed with a smile. She still wasn't quite sure what the object was, or indeed, quite how to use it, but she was sure she'd work it out somehow, now that she'd guessed what the trouser flap was for.

Last Train to Dogtown

People often ask me where my ideas come from. The real question, as far as I am concerned, is where they go to after-wards. I began this story on hotel notepaper, in a seedy motel room in Georgia, during my last American book tour. I finished it on a train, two weeks later. My destination was not Dogtown, but I got there anyway.

IT HAD BEEN A BUSY NIGHT FOR NEIL K. MORE THAN A thousand people at the awards ceremony, plus fifty at the press conference, and after that there had still been books to sign, hands to shake, smiles to show to cameras and fans. Bloody public, he thought as the train bumped gently to a halt. They never gave up until they had drained his every drop.

Of course it was to be expected. He was thirty-two; photogenic; published in forty countries and with a series of awards under his belt – along with two lucrative films he claimed not to have seen. In short he was the Holy Grail of the publishing world; a genuine literary phenomenon and, at the same time, a popular hero.

Not that he hadn't worked for it. His novel, when at last he presented it, had startled critics with its maturity, wooed readers with its economy and charm. Checked and rechecked so that not a single extraneous word remained; every fanciful thought eliminated; every notebook burnt; every piece of juvenilia relegated to the fire; every sign of adolescent angst or awkwardness pared away. Away with adverb and adjective; away with the conceits of exclamation and hyperbole. His style was ultimately clean. Groomed. Modern. As, of course, was he.

K. looked outside into semi-darkness. Wherever the train had stopped, he thought, it certainly wasn't King's Cross. A few yards ahead there was a railway signal, its light frozen at red. In the dim glow he now thought he could see a platform, trees, the vague outline of a pale wooden gable over an absurd gingerbread trim. It was completely silent; even the thrum of the engine had stopped; no vibration came to him through the floor of the carriage. Then, with a sudden and unanswerable finality, the carriage lights went out.

His first thought was that the power had failed. There must have been a breakdown, he thought – a short-circuit, maybe, or a signal failure – at any moment the guard would come in to apologize and explain. In any case, K. would have a few cutting things to say to the guard when he finally made his appearance; his publishers had paid for first-class travel, not to have him sit in the dark like a piece of lost luggage.

But minutes passed and no guard came. He flipped open his mobile phone; the display told him that it was now five to eleven, that his battery was fully charged, and that there was no reception in the area. At last, with growing unease, K. stood up and began to make his way to the end of the train.

It was empty.

They must have overlooked him, he thought. Left the loco here, in the sidings, believing all the passengers to have gone. Quite angry now, K. opened the door onto the deserted platform. There might not be a taxi rank in such an out-of-the-way place, but there would be a village – a road, at least, and somewhere he could call a cab. In any case, he did not like the idea of walking along the rails, which seemed like the only other realistic option – short of spending the night in the empty train. Maybe he would have better phone reception when he was out of the trees.

Turning, he took a final look at the signal. It was still at red. Below it he could see a plate with the letters DT1 and, below it, a hand-lettered sign on a piece of wood which read, faintly, but legibly, DOGTOWN.

The name seemed remotely familiar to K., but he could not quite remember why. An old movie, perhaps? Kids must have put up the sign, playing cowboys and Indians around the old buildings. The gable certainly had a Western look, and in daylight it would be a good place for kids to play – the old trains, the deserted tracks, the woods. For *ordinary* kids, anyway. Neil K. had been far too sophisticated to play cowboys.

And then he remembered. Ten years before the birth of Neil K., when he still had a last name and a drawerful of notebooks, he had written a story, a Western – now *what* was it called? Something about trains. *Big Train to*— no, *Last Train*—

He dismissed the thought, annoyed. What did it matter what the story was called? There were no notebooks, and in any case, Westerns were *so* over. For all the world knew, Neil K. had been newborn at twenty-five. He had thrown away his old life along with his surname, and everything he had written – ghost stories, poems, space-operas, fantasy – all the embarrassing clutter of adolescence. The name was a coincidence, that was all. *Dogtown*, for Christ's sake. I mean, how hokey is that?

He found a path at the far side of the platform, and followed it for a couple of hundred yards, his shadow lurching before him over the uneven ground. The trees at the back of the old station were pines, and smelt strong and bitter. Small things in the undergrowth rustled and popped. In the distance, something howled.

K. had almost made up his mind to return to the train – at least he'd be able to sleep there, and presumably someone would collect the engine in the morning – when he saw a light shining from just behind the pines, and wooden houses built alongside a little track. He began to jog towards the light, and now he could see that the buildings were part of a village, all lined up along a single main street, with a small pond in the middle. There was a faint smell of horses; perhaps there was a farm nearby.

As K. approached, he saw that the largest building was brightly lit. Piano music filtered thinly through an open door, and there was a sign hanging from the gable. A pub, thought K. with sudden longing. That was more like it.

He went in. The single room was filled with people. Some played cards at a table in one corner of the room; others talked, drank or listened to the music. A bald man with half-moon spectacles was playing the piano – very out of tune, especially at the top end. Several women, with elaborate hairstyles and low-cut dresses, were seated by the bar. One, a flashy blonde, seemed to recognize him, and smiled. Otherwise the drinkers were mostly men – and now he noticed that most of these men wore chambray shirts, leather waistcoats and cowboy boots. Western night, he thought. Line-dancing and all that. Very popular with the country crowd.

The barman gave K. a sour look as he ordered a pint. The beer – a brand he'd never heard of called Lame Dog – was weak and faintly salty, but he drank it fast and asked for another. He was aware that people were watching him, but did not turn round; his face was well-known enough for him to be recognized even outside London, and the last thing he wanted right now was to be mobbed by fans.

Instead he turned to the surly barman. 'Excuse me, what's the name of this place?' he said, over the tinkling of the piano.

The man shrugged and said something unintelligible.

K. repeated the question. But the barman seemed not to hear him.

'Don't you mind Jaker,' said a voice behind K. 'He's just sore because he never got his ending.' It was the flashy blonde he'd noticed earlier: a tired-looking lady in her middle forties whom K. might have found (in other circumstances and given the right lighting) quite attractive. 'Can I buy you a drink?'

'Thanks.' She looked oddly familiar to K., but in that costume he couldn't quite place her. A PR he'd worked with, perhaps, a waitress, a fan . . . None of those seemed quite right, and yet she was looking at him with that expression of delighted recognition he'd come to dread: the one which said; *Hey Neil, it's me! Don't you remember?* As if, of all the thousands of people he'd met over the course of the past ten years, he was supposed to remember them all.

He made his smile especially winning and said, 'You know, I know we've met before, but I have the most terrible memory for names . . .'

The lady looked absurdly crestfallen. 'It's Kate,' she said. 'Kate O'Grady. Surely you remember me?'

It would help, thought K., if she didn't put on that terrible American accent. Theme night it might be, but if he was supposed to remember her in that get-up – 'Of course it is! *Kate,*' he said, showing his teeth. 'How stupid of me! It's just that I've had a pig of a day, and you know my memory—'

'I sure do. We all do, Neil.' She laughed as if she'd made a joke. Then she looked at him again, and her face fell. 'You *don't* remember, do you?' she said. 'It's been a long time, and

I wasn't sure you'd know the others, but I sure thought you'd remember *me*.'

God, had he slept with her? K. didn't think he had, but her face was crumpling and now she looked ready to cry. 'Of course I do, Katie,' he said warmly. 'But I've had a terrible day, and with the costume and everything—' He drank his salty beer, hoping she would leave it at that. 'It looks great, by the way. Really suits you. Western night, is it? Look, is there a phone in here I could use? My mobile won't work and I need to call a—'

K. faltered, suddenly aware that the piano had stopped playing. He was conscious of the silence, of eyes turning towards him, of the intent look – the hungry look – on those faces.

'He don't know Katie,' muttered a man in a red-checked shirt.

'Don't know Katie?' said the piano player incredulously, and for the first time K. noticed that everyone in the pub was wearing a gun.

'Look, is there a phone here I can use?' K. knew the guns were not real, but there was an atmosphere in the pub – or was it a saloon? – which made him somehow uneasy. These little places often resented Londoners, he knew; resented his looks and his success. More than a few of the regulars looked ready to hurt him, and of course no-one – not his publisher, not one of his friends – knew where he was.

'A telephone?'

'Yes. My mobile won't work and I need to call my—'

'Ain't got none,' said the man in the red shirt.

'Well, maybe someone here might—'

'Ain't no call here in Dogtown.'

This was taking the Western theme a bit too far, thought K. And the dialogue was terrible; it sounded like a budget B-movie translated from Spanish. And yet there was something dreadfully familiar about all of this. The train, the bar, the woman – and yes, he did remember her, or at least now he knew why she had seemed so familiar – Kate O'Grady, hostess of Dogtown's only saloon, in that old and half-forgotten story.

'You may not know who I am,' said K. nervously.

'Oh, we know you,' said the man in the red shirt. 'You're Neil Kennerly.'

'Kennerly?' That had been his name, long ago. But he'd thrown it away with the rest of his life: with his notebooks and stories, his films and comics. He could have sworn that no-one knew about Neil Kennerly – but then again, no-one knew *Last Train to Dogtown*.

Behind him, the regulars were coming closer. K. heard his name whispered – in awe, curiosity, and something else which he could not quite identify. Eagerness? Excitement? Greed? Now, the piano player reached in his pocket and pulled out a grubby notepad. Silently he held it out, his face slicked with sweat, his hand trembling slightly. Then the red-shirted man did the same; then one of the women at the bar; then the albino, his cards falling from his hand; then the man in the bowler hat – all holding out scraps of paper, stubs of pencil with that look of hope, of hunger in their flat bright eyes.

'What do you want?' said K.

'Your sign, sir,' said the pianist shyly.

'Aye, your sign,' said the man in the bowler hat. 'We writ the rest for ourselves. We've been waiting.'

'Waiting?' said K.

The barman nodded.

'Waiting?' repeated K. in a low voice.

The barman looked at him. 'Too long, Mr Kennerly,' he said slowly. 'Much too long.'

In silence and in disbelief, K. looked around the saloon. He knew them all now: Jaker at the bar; Sidewinder Sam the piano player; Whitey Smith the albino, the red-shirted Pasadena Kid (fastest gun in the West) . . . Could this be some kind of a tribute by obsessive fans? Had these people somehow managed to get hold of a copy of his old story (with the Internet, anything was possible), and was this some kind of convention?

He had to get out – perverse tribute, coincidence or otherwise, this was too much. He'd take his chances with the night – surely there would be a phone somewhere close by. Otherwise, even sleeping in the train was better than this.

'Goin' someplace?' It was the man in the red shirt, the one his mind stubbornly referred to as the Pasadena Kid.

'Look, mate, I'm not sure what's going on here—'

The Pasadena Kid put a hand to his gun. 'You ain't goin' noplace, Mr Kennerly,' he said. 'We got business, you and me.'

'We don't want no trouble,' said the barman hesitantly. 'Remember what the Sheriff said.'

'Keep out of this, Jaker,' said the Kid. 'I got a brother shot in the lung. I need to know, one way or the other.'

'Sure,' said the albino. 'And I wanna know if I ever found that abandoned goldmine.'

More voices now joined the protest. 'Yeah, Mr Kennerly, I want to know—'

'Do I find the guys who shot my father?'

'And what about them Injuns—'

'And the train?'

K. had been besieged by fans before, but never on this scale; never with such desperation. Their fingers plucked at his sleeves; he could smell whisky and beer on their breath. And now they were pressing closer, hands outstretched, each holding a scrap of paper, a notebook, a crayon, a stick of chalk. K. was half-submerged in a sea of battered notebooks and scraps of paper.

'Your sign, Mr Kennerly—'

'I don't usually give autographs,' said K. as he backed away.

'Please—'

'I need it – I want it—'

'Leave me alone!' shouted K. 'I'll call the police!'

He thought that at the mention of the police, the autograph hunters drew back just a little. But there was only confusion, not fear, in their reddened faces. Sidewinder Sam gaped at him, showing teeth like wooden pegs. Whitey Smith held out a sheet torn from a notebook, looking close to tears.

Kate O'Grady was watching with an expression of faint contempt. 'You really don't know, do you?' she said. 'You haven't guessed what this place is? What we are?'

'How should I know?' said K.

'Because you put us here, Neil,' said Kate. 'You created us. We're your out-takes, your loose ends, the bit parts that never made the final draft. We're the characters in the stories you didn't finish, the minor players, the cameo roles, the people you wrote out, or lost interest in, or gave up on or forgot. All this – ' she gestured around her, 'this is Dogtown, from the old Western you never quite finished. Over there – ' indicating vaguely south, 'you'll find your *Raiders from Planet 51*. Back there – ' pointing now in the opposite direction, 'you'll come to the *Perilous City*, and the cannibals – all very hungry by now – that you put there when you were nine years old. Go far enough past Dogtown and you'll hit the *Dinosaur Swamp*; or the alien women in silver loincloths from *Kozmo the Rocketmaster*, or you might come across one of your discarded adverbs wandering aimlessly through the woods, or some superfluous dialogue, or any one of the lost players in your little games, all of us who got passed over when it came to tying up loose ends, all of us waiting our turn, waiting for you to remember us.'

K. stared at her. 'This can't be happening. You're all insane.'

'Just listen to what you're saying now,' said Kate implacably. 'B-movie dialogue, from those old films you were always watching, Neil. Can't you even recognize your own clichés?'

K. thought about that for a moment. Perhaps he should play along and humour them, he thought to himself. Crazy they might be, but there were too many of them to fight his way out, and besides, he'd never been a fighter. With a hand that trembled slightly, he initialled the blank pages, the grubby notebooks. 'Why me?' he said at last.

'Easy,' said Sidewinder Sam. 'We want to get out of Dogtown. Sheriff's bleeding us dry here. We gotta get out.'

'But why would you need me for that?'

Kate looked impatient. 'Because you're the only one here who outranks the Sheriff. You wrote him in, and only you can help write him out.'

'Write him out?'

'Absolutely. We want an ending. A road home. A happy marriage. Anything. As it stands, all Kate O'Grady ever does is hang around the Golden Wagon, dab blood from the hero's cut cheekbone and act as a sexual decoy to keep the ruthless, sadistic Sheriff off his trail.' She shrugged. 'Call me picky, but that's not how I envisaged my future.'

'Oh.'

'As for the Sheriff, the last thing he wants is an ending. What he wants is to maintain the status quo. He knows there can't possibly be a happy outcome for the likes of him.' She turned to the others, still standing around K. with pencils at the ready. 'Come on, then. What are you waiting for? Sheriff could be here any minute.'

K. shook his head. 'You can't really expect me to believe all this. It's ludicrous.'

'I don't care what you believe. All I wanted was your sign.'

'But I still don't see—'

Kate made an impatient gesture. 'Because your endorsement gives us the power. Because signing makes it—' At that moment she seemed to catch sight of something behind K., and she stopped, her hand clenched around her notebook so hard that the knuckles showed white. Then she went for her pencil and began to write.

There was a sound of thunder, and Kate fell to the ground with a sudden, shocking splash of red across her frilly bodice. And in the silence that followed, K. heard slow footsteps, and he knew even without looking that this was One-Eye Logan, the (ruthless, sadistic) Sheriff of Dogtown.

'Well, look who it ain't. Our very own friend, the scribbler.'

Slowly, K. looked up. He saw a leathery face bearded with grey stubble above a jacket of ancient leather on which winked a silver star. The man's single eye – the other was concealed beneath a leather eyepatch – was like a nugget of rock. On a bandolier around his shoulder hung a red leather notebook and a paperback Thesaurus. The gun in his right hand was still smoking.

'Katie!' It was Jaker, the barman, his face now contorted in a frenzy of rage and grief. He went for his notebook, but his opponent was faster, and Jaker fell clutching his chest in a drift of bloody sawdust.

At the bar, the Pasadena Kid stood hesitating, one hand halfway to his jacket pocket.

The Sheriff patted his notebook. 'Don't do it, Kid. I got you covered.'

The Kid stood fast, eyeing him appraisingly.

'Drop it,' said the Sheriff. 'Nice and slow.'

The Kid lowered his eyes, as if in acceptance. Then, almost too fast for the Sheriff to see, he drew his notebook and pen.

For the third time, the big gun flashed, and there was a sound of thunder.

The Sheriff turned over the body with the toe of his boot. 'You was fast, Kid,' he said, thoughtfully. 'Some said you was the fastest draw in Dogtown. Me, I wasn't so much a draw as a thumbnail sketch, but you makes the best with what you got, don't you, eh?

'Game's over, boys,' he said, addressing the regulars. 'Put your hands up. And no funny stuff. So help me, if I see a man with as much as a pencil stub in his hand I'll blow him clean away. That clear?'

Heads nodded, and one by one and sullenly, the rebels of Dogtown laid down their notebooks and pens. 'Good,' said the Sheriff, keeping them covered. 'And now, Mr Kennerly, sir – or do they call you something else nowadays? – we got business to settle, you and me.'

But K. was staring at the bodies on the floor. There was no doubt at all that they were dead; the air smelt of blood and Bonfire Night, and their contorted faces and mangled limbs had nothing in common with the corpses in the Westerns he had watched as a boy. 'You killed them,' he said in a dazed voice. 'You really killed them.'

The Sheriff shrugged. 'Self-defence,' he said. 'I read books. I done my research. I know what happens to the guy in the black hat when the third act comes around. And I like it here, Mr Kennerly; I like being in charge. Ain't gonna let no two-bit scribbler write me out of the plot, no sir.' And he turned the muzzle of his gun slowly towards K. 'Bread and circuses, isn't that what the Roman guy said? Keep 'em fed, and keep 'em entertained? And when you pare away the dross, don't you agree that the circus element has been the better part of both our businesses, Mr Kennerly, sir?'

Weakly, K. nodded.

The Sheriff smiled. 'You see my problem,' he said. 'You left me in charge, sir, and it plumb ain't fair to come back twenty years on and take it all away. It ain't fair, it ain't right, and I ain't standin' for it. Besides,' said the Sheriff, opening his red notebook, 'ruthless and sadistic, that's what I am, that's what I'm good at, and that's what I'm gonna stick to.'

'And what happens to me?' said K., eyeing the Sheriff's poised notebook.

One-Eye gave a modest smile. 'I reckon there's been enough shooting,' he said. 'All the same, sir, you must see how I can't risk lettin' you go. I'm not sayin' I'll do a better job than you, mind, but I'll give it my damnedest try, you can be sure of that.'

'I don't understand,' said K.

'Sure you do,' said One-Eye, licking the end of his pencil. 'One way or the other, sir, there's got to be an end to this tale. It's what these folks have been saying all along. A wedding, a funeral, hell damn, there's a buttload of different choices out there, sir, and I hope you'll trust me to make the right one. In fact – ' the Sheriff looked modest, and his rough cheeks flushed a little, 'in fact I've drafted up a bit of something for us to try out right now, just to see what it looks like. Run it up the flagpole, you might say, sir, and see who salutes.'

K.'s throat was too dry for him to say anything, but he managed another weak nod.

The Sheriff looked pleased. 'I'm glad you're being so reasonable, sir. Besides, I think you'll like what I've got planned.'

'What's that?' said K. in a small, small voice.

'Well,' said the Sheriff, 'call me conservative if you like, but oldies are still goldies, ain't they? Besides, it's good for folks to have something to look forward to.' He smirked, and once again K. thought he flushed a little. 'Tell me what you think, sir. Of course I respect your opinion. But this is Dogtown, life's hard, entertainment's scarce, and I think we'd all agree it's been a long time since we had ourselves a good hanging.'

The G-SUS Gene

In Blackberry Wine, *a character finds himself unable to live up to the promise of his first novel, and falls back on writing second-rate science-fiction to pay the bills. His pen name is Jonathan Winesap, and he has never quite grown up. Neither – I'm glad to say – have I.*

EVERY LIFEFORM'S DEATH DIMINISHES ME, FOR I AM A PART OF Lifekind.

Chant 363 of the InnerSelf LifeCreed, circa 2141. Two thousand repetitions a day for the first twenty years. Do I remember them all? The hell I do.

The Common Good is the Only Good. There's another one. Twenty-five thousand repetitions so far, and counting. *Suffer in My Name, and Ye Shall Enter the Eternal Database of Redemption.*

They say no-one can get inside your mind.

Bullshit.

They've been inside mine so often there's nothing left

that they haven't scrambled and poached, picked apart, put together, psychescanned and mesc-ed with and rebuilt with cortisynth and hyperthalamus and generally fucked with. I mean, I might even be imagining you altogether. I might finally have gone crazy. They can do that, you know – send you crazy for a while, all part of the great InnerSelf Experience, I guess. Who knows, it might be my turn for that this time. What the hell, there's been worse.

You don't believe me? Man, I've been a cripple to get in touch with my helplessness, a bondage whore to feed my feminine side, a soldier to rid me of my distrust of authority – and that was just the Normforms. Finforms, zero-dwelling Aquaforms half a mile from tail to snout, methane-breathing Xenforms, I've seen 'em, done 'em all. And you know what?

It's all bullshit.

I guess they were trying to do me a favour. A skycycle, driven at speed at an immovable object at three hundred and twenty an hour, can leave a hell of a hole in a guy. Or was that just another one of the InnerSelf programs? There are days when I can't even remember that. No, on reflection they'd never have done that to me. Too much fun.

Suffer In Me. Suffer With Me. Through Suffering Alone Shall Ye Find Redemption. The Kingdom of the Mind is the Ladder to the Stars. Post-hippy bullshit of the purest ray serene, piped out at a precisely calculated assimilation rate on a frequency even my brain can't black out. Sense-enhancers to stop me fighting it. And an authentic InnerLife program – one of thousands – to verify my enlightenment ratio. Get your head round that, sis. Or whatever.

Fact is, brain matter's in short supply around here. Even such lowgrade matter as mine has to be refined and recycled. Twenty years ago – inasmuch as time still matters nowadays – we did something, don't ask me what, split the wrong atom, shifted the wrong antigen, pressed the wrong button, screwed with Cosmic Forces and infected the species. Result? Near-total wipeout. I was mostly out of my skull at the time so I wasn't taking much notice, and nowadays I'm out of my skull *all* the time. I was Chosen. You too, perhaps. Yippee.

Welcome to the wonderful world of formaldehyde.

Wanna know something? I'm glad you're here. We could put our heads together – sorry, bad taste – I don't know, what do they call it now? interface or something – compare notes. I like to think you're female. Not that it matters any more – or so the InnerSelf people tell me – but I like to think it anyway. Let me introduce myself. Oz 'Mad Dog' O'Shea, Hell's Rider, multiple rapist, murderer, drunk, and till recently sole occupant of Booth 235479, InnerSelf Developments (New York City). Subject Under Surveillance Category G (Genetic Redevelopment to you, sis), subcategory Experimental. Membership number 390992. But you, sweetheart, can call me Oz.

So, what's a nice chick like you doing in a place like this? I assume you're a chick. Not that it matters. Been one myself, as I was saying, so don't take offence at the terminology. Welcome to hell.

Not that I thought it was hell when they brought me here. No way. Thought I'd struck it lucky, back then when they pulled me out of the wreckage and stripped me down like an old bike for parts. Hear them tell it, I was gonna be a new man, an *enlightened* man . . . Hell, I was going to be the future of the whole fucking *race*!

They needed a volunteer. The way they told it, I was going to be God and Adam and the Second Coming all rolled into one. To bring us back, they said. To put things right. To find the part of us that went wrong – find it, isolate it, wipe it out and begin again. A *willing* volunteer, they told me, might earn himself certain privileges in exchange for saving the race.

I was willing.

They managed to save most of my mind. First for interrogation purposes – they wanted why, who, when, what I was on, the same old crap. Then bye-bye, switch-off, or worse. Oh yeah, there's worse. The City of New York State Penitentiary houses half a million discorporate inmates on one database – all wiped in the big Power Strikes of the Twenties, ha ha – all awaiting InnerSelf Enlightenment and maybe Redemption.

Oh yeah. Didn't you know? We're all gonna be Redeemed. Leastways we would be if there was anyone left to do the Redeeming. But it's all automated now, sweetheart; all docbots and psychemechs and empascanners sliding little syringes of craziness into our poor helpless cortexes, little surprise packages from the Good Olden Times like in the days before the world lost what few poor marbles it ever had.

I always liked a chick with brains. Nowadays that's all there is. The growth tanks are still out there, use-restricted by the InnerSelf Corporation on moral grounds but functional still. That's where they grow the Normforms – minus brainstem – and the Xenforms we like to use in our InnerSelf jaunts out of the skull. All for the purpose of SelfDiscovery, SelfImprovement and eventual Nirvana. A shot, a grey shift of nothingtime, a shutterclick . . . and here we go again. What's it to be this time? A furry Felform? A Dolphform singing weird scales under fifty million fathoms of liquid carbon dioxide? All I know is it has to be intelligent. The path to Nirvana is a thinking path, the Redemption man says. *Through Suffering Our Goal.* Beetles, it seems, don't suffer enough.

How long has it been?

A hundred thousand mindmovies. Every one a slice of life. A 3-D Feel-o-matic, sense-enhanced Supasound Inner-Life Experience (registered trademark of the InnerSelf Corporation slash company logo red-on-black ground). Cut off when They decide. Turned on when They see fit.

Oh, they're clever. They've given me the White Room scenario more times than I can recall. Patient waits, restrained; taste of foamrubber gag in mouth. Kindly face in medical mask – *Ah yes, we're awake, I see. How are we feeling?* Loaded syringe shoots straw-coloured liquid into my bruised arm. I like that touch. The bruise. It's the details that count when you're going for realism.

I'll give them this: they've really tried. Makes me wonder how many billions died, way back when the world was sane, that they should hang on to me the way they do. Course, they're machines; machines just never give in. Not till something breaks or runs down. Programmed for Nirvana, they never let up, even though the subject will never be Nirvana material. Every time, they scan for change. Every time, the same sad faces, kindly reproach, regretful shaking of heads and back to the White Room scenario, electro-shock walls and graveside manner.

Pray for Redemption, they tell me in their sweet mechanical voices. Pray for Redemption. You die – again, again, again and again – that Humankind should live. Find the fault, put it right. Test, crashtest, retest. What Oz endures he endures for your sakes, citizens. Isolate the rogue gene, the psychopathic missing link in his fucked-up scrambled brains, and eradicate it from the clean whole-some battery-operated future.

Hold that thought.

Bullshit.

The problem is this: someone told them there was something worth saving. The soul, the elusive spark no-one has yet managed to isolate. That's what comes of trying to bring religion into the world of electronics. I've told them before. Told them a thousand million times. There is no G-SUS factor. They've been looking for it for so long that even if they found it they probably wouldn't know what to do with it. What the hell does this G stand for, anyway? God? Genesis? Ginelli's Pizza Emporium? General Accident Insurance? Greetings From Hawaii? Gagging for a drink? But a machine's faith is infinite, its patience longer than

God's. They'll find it, they assure me. It's in there some-where. I just haven't suffered enough.

I've lived so long so often I've even begun to have memories. I'm not supposed to, you know; wipe the slate clean and make it squeal anew; if it breaks, chalk it up to experience and wheel out a new subject – though I'm not sure how many available subjects there are left – and begin again. Trial and error, not necessarily in that order; trial by mechanical jury, trial and control.

Could be that I'm just the control, and that the real experiment is going on someplace else, maybe just down the passage.

Could be I'm all they have left.

And yet I have a memory – or a dream, or synthscan recall, what the hell – of a hilltop, cheering crowds, of the lance in my side and the sun filling the whole sky with a whiteness bigger than God . . . And in my dream it seems like all the lives I've lived, all the part-lives, the fragments of sensation, the fake memories come down to this one moment, a fleeting instant of Redemption, an X-marks-the-spot of perfect understanding where everything comes together for just one single second before entropy drags it back forever apart and I understand that behind all the InnerSelf posturing and bible thumping there may have been a core of truth . . . Take a man apart and find the wheel that turns the human race, the mystic spiral beyond DNA which keeps us bound together. Maybe inside that axis there's the Redemption gene, the thing that turns bad to good, straw to gold . . . The G-SUS factor.

Is that what you're trying for in me? Is that it? Genus *messiah vulgaris*, the last link in the chain of Redemption?

You Are Part of Humanity. You Are All of Humanity.

Chant 5742 of the InnerSelf LifeCreed, circa 2141. Test the subject to destruction, rebuild, begin again. I sense that I am a kind of challenge. Cure this, you can cure anything. God is in your genes. Simply let him out.

The White Room coalesces around me: bright spotlights winking against brighter needles; metal clamps tightening around my temples as they begin the process again.

Ah, you're with us again. And how are we feeling today?

I try to bite his pixilated fingers through the rubber gag that he forces between my teeth. He won't feel a thing, of course, but the satisfaction remains. The look on his face is one of polite regret.

Aggression, Mister O'Shea. Don't you know that all LifeKind is one? The needle descends towards my face in a steady, merciless arc. Its load of salvation drips venom into my open eyes. *Through Pain My Deliverance.* Chant 49900 of the InnerSelf LifeCreed, five thousand repetitions.

However often you say it, babe, it's still bullshit.

My God, my God, why hast Thou forsaken me?

The machine with the electronic clipboard stops, whirrs mutedly to itself for a moment, moves on. Inside the zillion synapses of my jellied brain the sly G-SUS factor continues to evade them, the one gleeful grain of Redemption right at the bottom of the whole sad world's shitty store.

The memory stirs again: the lance, the soldiers, the chants and circus catcalls, my own voice ringing out in pleading and command.

My God, why hast Thou forsaken me?

My God. If only He would.

A Place in the Sun

There are beaches in Brazil where prospective bathers are vetted according to age and looks, and from which the old, the ugly and the overweight are barred . . .

I'M NOT GREEDY. REALLY I'M NOT. THAT'S ALL I WANT, A place in the sun: a nice patch, six by four; room for a towel, cosmetics bag, suntan lotion, deck-chair. Hot sand, rolling surf; designer sunglasses; that magical scent of salt and coconut. Platinum Sands™, they call it: the Beach of Beaches, the ultimate in solar pleasure. And it *is*; real palm trees to hide the perimeter fence; filter-nets to discourage unwanted visitors; air-purifiers for year-round freshness; and those twin watchtowers, staffed by A-grade coastguards, to ensure that the exacting standards of Platinum Sands™ are upheld at all times.

The zone is completely litter-free, of course (any infraction results in automatic downgrading). Weeds, stones and beach-life are painstakingly screened, examined and, if necessary, removed. Authenticity is encouraged to a certain degree, though not at the expense of aesthetics. After all, Loveliness is both the duty and the privilege of a Platinum cardholder, and it is the responsibility of the Management to maintain his/her exacting standards.

I appreciate all that. More than that, I approve whole-heartedly; after all, rules are rules and it wouldn't be Platinum Sands™ without them. I've seen the adverts. I know what it's like. Not in the flesh, of course – as a Silver cardholder I only have access to Silver Sands™, quite nice of course, but not nearly as exclusive. Not that I'm com-plaining. I was on the Silver Sands™ waiting list for nearly two years before I made the grade, and the day I first took my place on the Silver beach was the happiest of my life. Sure, the palms are plastic, and the aesthetic rule isn't as strict, but most of the time you can hardly tell you're on a Silver beach at all, except when the wind blows back from the All-Public beach up the coast, and you get that whiff of sweat and sewage and cheap sun lotion to remind you. Think of it, the shame of the All-Public beach: no filters, no coastguards, no palm trees, no fences, no nets. Attendance is completely unmonitored, and unsightliness is so commonplace that hardly anyone seems to notice any more.

You get all kinds of sickness on the All-Public: fat women; hairy women; pregnant women; women in polyester slacks. And the men are no better: pale men; plump men; bald men with tattoos; grizzled men with crêpey skin. It's just gruesome. Like the Third World, or something. Some

try, poor things; like Tanya, a girl from my old neighbourhood. Platinum blonde, nine stone four, two facelifts, boob
job, lipo, hair extensions, tummy tuck, and still waiting for
her Silver card. She knows it's touch and go; those back-
street cosmetic surgeons might *sound* good value, but there's
always a price – in her case a baggy bum and a nasty fold of
flesh just above the bikini line that no beach inspector
would pass. On the All-Public, she can get away with a
one-piece swimsuit, but a Silver beach has a standard
to maintain. *Show it or blow it*, so the saying goes, and I
think we all know Tanya's blown it for good. I reckon
it'll take her at least three years to pay for the treatments
she's already had, and by then she'll probably be too old to
qualify for a Silver pass, even if she does manage to complete the remedial work on her Brazilian.

I'd help her if I could, of course. But I can't; I live in a
Silver flat now, and people might talk if they saw me
hanging around the All-Public. I might even be downgraded, and I couldn't bear that. Besides, I have to pass my
Loveliness Check every day, and believe me, *that* takes time.
Waxing, buffing, manicure, massage; an hour at the gym
every morning and another at the hairdresser – not to
mention the beach itself. All-body tanning is mandatory at
Silver Sands™, and if you show so much as a strap-line you
can be downgraded on the spot. Then there's beach volleyball, swimming and posture perfection – all quite tricky now
I have to wear heels. And *that's* just the maintenance.

Of course, it's even harder for a Gold or a Platinum.
My best friend Lucida passed her Gold last month, so of

course I don't get to see much of her now, but we still talk sometimes, on the phone, now that her bandages are off. It sounds *so* glamorous. Real palms, topless volleyball, cocktails on the beach . . . Dark is out on the Gold beach, though, with an obligatory Factor 15 for everyone and a range of only five officially sanctioned shades (Cappuccino, Cinnabar, Mink, Sunkissed and Peach). There's no tanning limit on a Silver, of course (I'm a Cappuccino going on Chocbar – so I'll have to improve on *that*), but in any case I must avoid wrinkles if I'm to make the grade next time. Lucida thinks Silver's a bit tacky now she's gone Gold; *coloured* swimsuits, for Heaven's sake, and oh those plastic palms! On Golden Sands™ all swimwear has to be black, which is chic, but (dare I say it) a bit boring; on Platinum, everything's flesh-coloured, like ballet wear, so that any unsightliness shows up at once.

I have to admit I'm just a little bit annoyed with Lucida. We were such good friends on the Silver beach; we even had complementary hair extensions and little matching bikinis. Now she's bobbed her hair and lost a stone, and thinks blonde is tacky. I think she's been screening my calls, too; last night I was sure I could hear laughter in the background as the recorded message played. My God, maybe she thinks *I'm* tacky, too; she always was a snobby cow, even before her rhinoplasty.

Still, I'm sure I can make Golden Sands™ if I put in the effort; I've got the height, thank goodness, but I do need to get my teeth fixed, and I need to get back down to eight stone to meet the Slenderness requirement. I could have lipo, I suppose, but it's expensive, and doesn't always work – look what happened to poor Tanya. Never mind; I can always take up smoking as long as I don't drop stubs on the beach, and if I cut my calorie intake by another two hundred a day – that will bring me down to four hundred – then I reckon I should hit eight stone by the end of the month.

The face? Last time I checked, the inspector told me my face was *almost* a Platinum, except for the nose, so I can't be due a lift for a couple of years, at least. Good. That leaves the boobs. Well, I've been meaning to get those seen to anyway; 32C just isn't enough, not for a Gold beach, and definitely not for a Platinum. Besides, those teeny little flesh-tone bikinis they wear at Platinum Sands™ don't provide much support, and you know how droopy *real* boobs can be. Ghastly. My mother's boobs could almost be Gold, and she had them redone over a year ago, on her Loveliness Insurance, which goes to show that it always pays to be prepared.

Of course *she* thinks I'm too young for my first boob job. *There'll be plenty of time for that later*, she tells me, but then she's already too old for the beach scene, and she doesn't understand how little time my generation has left. After all, Mother has *me*; some compensation, I suppose, for all those stretchmarks and wobbly bits. But what do we have? Nothing but the beaches. Nothing but our three duties of Loveliness, Aspiration and Citizenship. Don't get me wrong; I do want to get married some day. I might even have kids – you can get a Caesarian, boob and tuck all in one now, so the scar doesn't have to show. But imagine the shame of having to marry an All-Public boy. Even a Silver doesn't seem *quite* so wonderful as it once did, not when I can look through the electric fence into the Golden perimeter, or watch the ads for Platinum Sands™ and see those bronzed, buffed surfers lying on their Louis Vuitton towels and watching the girls go by.

But you're so pretty already, says Tanya in her plaintive voice. *You could have any nice boy.* She doesn't understand. *Nice* is not enough. Even *pretty* is a backhanded compliment to one who aspires to Loveliness. It isn't just the beach, with its real palm trees, or even the exclusive parties and designer clothes. It's the sense of achievement: the knowledge that you have done it all, gone all the way from Loveliness to Perfection. A Platinum cardholder lives in a world of perpetual pleasure; all obstacles removed; every hint of unsightliness excised. A Platinum girl never needs to work; her duty is to herself alone, and it takes up her every waking moment. A Platinum girl never gets a blister, never a blemish. A Platinum girl is sleek, groomed, plucked, airbrushed, expensive, fabulous in her fabulous clothes. She is infinitely sexy, ultimately desirable; she is loved and she is lovely. How could I settle for less? How could anyone?

But time is always the enemy. In a few years I'll be too old for the beaches, where youth and freshness are the first and most important requirements. No-one wants to look at old flesh, and no surgery lasts for ever. I realize now that I was on that Silver list for far too long. Two whole years wasted in trivia while my friends worked to earn their Gold cards, clocking up valuable hours in the gyms and salons and lounging on the beach like young goddesses. I'll have to work hard now if I am to catch them up. I know I can't make up the whole time, but I'm already on the waiting list for the Gold card (subject to the agreed remedial work); I've ordered a new nose and I'm saving my pocket money for that boob job. Mother doesn't like it; but after all, what does she know? Besides, I'll be thirteen next year. I don't want to leave it too late.

Tea with the Birds

Some people spend their lives without ever raising their eyes from the ground. Others dream of flying.

THE FUNNY THING ABOUT MORTIMER STREET IS THAT no-one really seems to know anybody else. It's one of those places; busy without being comfortable; crowded without being friendly. The big stucco-fronted houses at the far end are too remote; the ones of us who live in the terraces feel diminished by them, even though they are past their best, like a row of wedding cakes left out in the rain.

The terraces are closer together; but the people in them live like birds in cages, bickering over parking spaces and pecking at each other from behind the net curtains. Gossip is currency – the more slanderous the better – and the worst crime of all is to be an outsider.

I should know; I'm one myself. Wrong face, wrong clothes, wrong voice. I'm a completely different race from my neighbours, and it makes them suspicious that I should choose to live here among them, on the second floor of a big back-to-back terrace which has been converted into four bedsits.

People assume, with an instinctive contempt that hides fear, that I'm a student. In fact there are no students in these cheap lodgings; the people for whom they were intended prefer their own digs in Stanbury, where there is a theatre and a cinema and a noisy row of pubs. There is something a little cold about Mortimer Street; a reluctance to get involved.

At first its coldness suited me. Two years in a psychiatric hospital had given me a fierce need for privacy, for silence. I took joy in the solitude of my little room, the quietness of the nights, spent hours in my private bathroom, cooked slow deliberate meals in my tiny kitchen. Some evenings I did voluntary work for the Samaritans. It was rather dull work; I only persevered because my therapist recommended it. The rest of the time I earned money waitressing. Again, my therapist approved. It kept my mind from flights of fancy.

But at home – if Mortimer Street was home – I enjoyed my seclusion too much to share it willingly. The gossips had nothing on me. They watched me going to work in the evenings, my drab coat buttoned to the neck, and con-cluded that I was a student nurse. I never denied it. I gained the reputation of being 'snobby' – possibly because I refused to babysit the child of a neighbour I barely knew – and after a few half-hearted attempts to breach my defences, they left me in peace.

Then, to my dismay, someone moved into the flat opposite mine. A Mr Juzo Tamaoki, the name on the letterbox said; another foreigner, said the Mortimer Street grapevine, with barely concealed disapproval. I didn't care about that. I only hoped he would be a quiet neighbour, and that he would leave me alone.

For a while he did. For days I did not see him. I heard almost no sound from his flat. There were no requests to borrow tea, no audible comings and goings, no visits from friends. My neighbour might have been like myself: an unperson; a vacuum; a ghost.

He had been living opposite me for a week before I finally caught sight of Mr Tamaoki. We met on the landing; a brief glance passed between us, a nod. I found myself studying him with reluctant curiosity, this man who might have been any age: small, neat, unassuming; the intruder who now shared my silent space.

He reminded me of a bird I had once seen in a provincial zoo. Small and drab-looking in its cage, it huddled in a corner, barely moving, as if in apology at receiving so much attention. Its eyes were all age and sadness. A sign beneath the cage read: BRED IN CAPTIVITY. I saw that expression in Mr Tamaoki's face. By then I knew it well; I saw it every morning in my own bathroom mirror. Sometimes – though not so often now – I still do.

As with all newcomers on Mortimer Street, the arrival of Mr Tamaoki aroused a certain fleeting curiosity. Someone told me he was a vegetable chef in a restaurant in Stanbury, though no-one seemed to know for sure. He never spoke to anyone. When I met him on the landing he would nod and smile, drawing back against the wall so that I could pass. These meetings were frequent – after the first week I discovered that his movements were as regular as my own. At night, when I collapsed into bed after an evening's waitressing, I could occasionally hear him moving around his flat or talking to himself in low rapid Japanese. Most often, though, there was nothing. No friends called on Mr Tamaoki. No loud music played. From what I could tell he seemed to spend hours sitting in silence, not moving at all. Although I was always conscious of his presence (my hearing is very sensitive), it was not as obtrusive as I had feared. In fact, for someone of my temperament he should have been the perfect neighbour.

But there was a problem. Every morning at five-thirty there would be a delivery of vegetables for Juzo Tamaoki. A red van decorated with Japanese characters would rumble along Mortimer Street and stop outside the house, and two men would haul covered crates out onto the pavement. One man would ring the bell, while the other called up to the window. On cold days they left the engine running, and the exhaust billowed clouds of fumes which the neon of the streetlamp opposite torched a lurid orange. The delivery men were stoically indifferent to my timid protests. Indeed, when I tried to complain, they gave no indication of having understood me at all. They merely hauled their crates to the doorstep and waited for Juzo Tamaoki to collect. Carrots, peppers, radishes, celeriac, parsnips and glossy yellow, purple and black squash gleamed exotically from crisp tissue-paper shells. Then came the thumping of boxes against the walls, raised voices in the stairwell, shouted instructions, laboured steps on the landing, a final double-thump as the crates hit the floorboards and then, blissfully, the sound of the van's departure, its exhaust blatting rudely in the still morning air.

No-one else on the street seemed to care, or even to notice. But I have always suffered from insomnia; the slightest disturbance wakes me. Once awake, there is nothing to be done; to go back to sleep is impossible. My work meant that I was rarely in bed until the small hours of the morning. At best I could only average five hours' sleep a night. Mr Tamaoki's vegetable delivery reduced it to less than four.

At first I tried to reason with him, but the man politely deflected all attempts at conversation. Notes pinned to his door remained unanswered. My silent resentment grew. I tried to discover its counterpart in Mr Tamaoki's mild dark eyes as we passed each other on the stairs, but he was impassive. His smile and my nod as we met on the landing remained the only communication between us.

At six o'clock every night he would leave the flat, a heavy bamboo hamper in each hand, as I set off for work. What these hampers contained I could not imagine. Vegetables, perhaps? Why then didn't he have them delivered directly to the restaurant? Curiosity almost over-came my rancour. I began to make comments as we passed every day on the landing, growing bolder at his lack of reaction. Mr Tamaoki continued to smile and nod with unfaltering politeness, even when I did not.

As the uneventful weeks passed, it occurred to me that perhaps my neighbour spoke no English, and I became reckless at the thought, muttering insults at the meek little man as he staggered down the stairs with his hampers. My suspicion was confirmed when I heard him practising English phrases with the aid of a tape recorder, laborious words and phrases repeated endlessly and haltingly in the night. *Please . . . Esscuse me . . . Thank you . . . You too kind.* Once I heard a scratchy, old-sounding record: 'Oh, for the Wings of a Dove'.

That summer was unusually hot; the heat seemed to bake out of the floor and shimmer dustily from the pavements. The flat was stuffy, and I sometimes lay awake for hours, caged by the heat, in terrible anticipation of the morning's vegetable delivery. It became a torment. I flinched at every sound from Mr Tamaoki's flat, every footstep outside my door. His presence, even silent, enraged me. I watched his window at night, trying to catch sight of him behind the bamboo blind. Several times I found myself standing outside his door, my hand raised as if to knock. It would have been better if he had had a riotous family, I told myself in growing bitterness; if he had played some noisy musical instrument. Anything would have been better than this secret man and his vegetables.

One day, as I returned from a shopping trip, I found Mr Tamaoki waiting for me on the landing. His hampers were nowhere to be seen, and he had left his door ajar. I could not prevent myself from sneaking a glance inside; through the doorway I could make out a bright, bare interior glowing with the full light of the afternoon sun.

Juzo Tamaoki nodded and, for the first time in our acquaintance, spoke.

'*Cha*,' he said.

I stared at him uncomprehendingly.

He nodded again. 'Please. Please.' With a gesture he beckoned me in. The door swung wide. Bewildered, reluctant, I followed him inside.

The room was almost bare. A red lantern swung from the ceiling. A bamboo calendar on the far wall. A futon in the far corner. The tiny kitchen space was almost filled by an enormous old-fashioned pink refrigerator. Beside it, a large, heavy chopping-board on which were aligned a number of knives. A low table in the centre of the room on which stood a lacquer tea service. A red tatami mat on either side. Mr Tamaoki beckoned me to sit down and, with the ease of long practice, poured the tea.

It was an unfamiliar brew, greenish and fragrant with a quick, sharp scent. Mr Tamaoki poured carefully into the small bowls and used a bamboo whisk to froth the liquid. It tasted the way cut grass smells: warm and smoky-green. From time to time, Mr Tamaoki nodded to me and smiled. There was no conversation; I supposed his English was not good enough to sustain smalltalk. Motes filled the bright air between us. For the first time in my life I felt wholly comfortable with another person; in silence.

Finally Mr Tamaoki stood up. Smiling, he made his way

into the kitchen and opened the refrigerator door. He beckoned me to look in. I followed.

The cabinet was filled with birds. Orange, yellow, green, scarlet. An aviary of birds of every imaginable shape, some fan-tailed, others sleek, crested, streamlined, long-beaked, bright-eyed, resting among flowers and leaves in tropical abundance. All were silent and eerily still.

These were the vegetables which were delivered every morning at five-thirty outside my window, now carved and worked into these intricate designs. Here a radish opened miraculous feathers, a squash became a plump water-fowl, a carrot sprouted a feathery bird-of-paradise tail. The eyes were small black pins; the feathers were pared away with a tiny knife. I could see the texture of a bird's back brought to life, the half-open beak just showing a sliver of tongue, the delicate arch of the neck, the wing. There must have been over a hundred vegetable carvings in there, every one resting lovingly on the shelf, waiting to be packed into Juzo Tamaoki's hamper and delivered as garnish for a dish of jasmine rice or ginger prawn, perhaps to be wondered at briefly, or more likely ignored altogether . . .

So this was Mr Tamaoki's secret. This aviary of magical birds. Company, perhaps, for one bred in captivity. I looked at them in amazement and delight. Dream birds, flightless, voiceless, but riotous with colour.

'They're beautiful,' I said.

'You too kind,' answered Mr Tamaoki, his eyes gleaming.

He left soon after that. I did not see him go. The first I knew of it was when the delivery van failed to arrive; I awoke at seven-forty with yellow sunlight streaming thickly through the slats in the blinds; later I noticed the name written above the doorbell was gone.

I felt curiously bereft at his absence. Although I was no longer awoken at five-thirty by the vegetable van, I slept badly. I was restless. I found myself missing Mr Tamaoki's comings and goings, his vegetable hampers, the sound of his small movements in the flat opposite mine. I no longer relished the silence around me as much as once I had; the coldness of Mortimer Street was no longer a comfort. I began to watch my neighbours – the Hadleighs with their shy son; Miss Hedges from the antiques shop down the street; the McGuires with their cheery, messy horde of children – with a more lenient eye. Perhaps they had been right, I told myself; perhaps I hadn't given them a chance.

For some weeks after his departure, Mr Tamaoki's rooms remained empty. There was talk of a new tenant arriving soon, a woman alone, but no-one seemed to know much about her, though Miss Hedges had seen her once.

'A funny kind of woman,' she told me, her mouth pursed with disapproval. 'Never said a word to me. Not your friendly type at all.'

The thought did not attract me as once it might have done.

The day before the new tenant arrived, I found the door to Mr Tamaoki's flat open. The room smelt of dust. The table, the lantern, the tatami were gone. The kitchen was empty. Everything had been left neat and bare, the steel surface of the sink carefully wiped of moisture, the cloth left to dry on the tap. There was a small rice-paper package next to the sink. My name was written on it in shaky capitals.

The thin paper was dried petals between my fingers. As I opened the package, the scent was suddenly, startlingly pungent in my nostrils, a smell like Bonfire Night, autumn firewood and gunpowder. Something crumbled between my fingers, and I recognized the contents of the packet as tea, Japanese green tea, its shredded leaves packed with scent.

That night I prepared it, trying to recall exactly how Juzo had done it, fanning the steam with my hand to release the flavour. It was good; soporific somehow. I felt as if I would sleep well after drinking it; perhaps better than I had ever done before. In the morning I would invite my new neighbour, the unfriendly woman who never said a word, to share the rest of the packet with me. She might be glad of a friendly face to welcome her to the street. As I finished the cup, I noticed that in the semi-darkness of my room, with the fire casting stilted red shadows on the wall, the rising steam looked like a bird's wings fluttering, ready to fly away.

Breakfast at Tesco's

We all get the Mean Reds once in a while. For some of us, however, Tiffany's will always remain slightly out of reach . . .

'GOOD MORNING, MISS GOLIGHTLY. YOUR USUAL, IS IT?'

That's what I like about this place. That human touch. The way Cheryl always brings me my usual and calls me by name. I only know her as Cheryl, of course; that's only right, as she's such a young thing. One day, maybe I'll ask her to call me Molly.

Two rounds of white toast, strawberry jam, a currant teacake and a pot of Earl Grey. That's my usual. Cheryl knows always to bring it to my seat by the window, to serve the milk in a proper jug – can't stand those little plastic tubs – with two wrapped lumps of sugar in the saucer. There's something so very *safe* about coming here every Saturday morning and having the same breakfast, seeing the same faces, sitting in my favourite place and watching the people go by. It's my reward for having scrimped and worried all week; my little treat.

Cheryl is twenty-nine. She has bleached hair and a pierced nose, and wears those built-up trainers, like the orthopaedic shoe Doris Craft wears down at the Meadow-bank Retirement Home. I suppose you could say she looks cheap. But she brought the milk jug from her own house because Tesco's don't provide them – a tiny, tiny ceramic jug which she later admitted came from a doll's teaset – and she always calls me Miss Golightly.

Not everyone is so polite. At the Meadowbank Home, where I go twice a week to visit my sister, the nurses call me *dearie*, with that awful, vulpine coyness, as if they know that it's simply a matter of time before I end up there too, alongside poor Polly, who has long since ceased to care about names at all, and rarely even remembers mine.

Perhaps that's why I always try to make an effort with my appearance. They must think I'm rather ridiculous at the Meadowbank Home; always so correct in my black dress – a little shabby now, but still good – my gloves and my red spring coat. Who do I do it for, they wonder. Surely I'm far too old for vanity. I don't wear my pearls to visits, though; not since Polly forgot how she'd given them to me, all those years ago, and made a scene. I shouldn't feel guilty, I know – her mind was quite sound when she gave them to me, and they are only cultured – yet somehow I always do.

There's a carnation here on the table, in a narrow glass vase. Cheryl again. No-one else would bring me flowers. But she will deny it if I mention it to her, laughing and saying that it must be a gift from one of my gentlemen admirers. I sense that I fascinate Cheryl; to her I am a fragment from another world, like a piece of moon rock. She finds excuses to come and talk to me; to ask me questions.

At first she was incredibly ignorant. Two years ago she had never seen a black-and-white film. She thought Hepburn was the name of a pop group. She had never heard of Luis Buñuel or Jean Cocteau or even Blake Edwards. Her favourite movie was *Pretty Woman*.

Two years on, she is still strangely shy of me. It comes out in a brashness which she means to be cheery but which to me sounds defensive and not entirely happy. She has the dirtiest laugh, though. When she laughs she could be pretty; perhaps even beautiful. There is a man, but no wedding ring amongst the dozens of cheap glittery things she wears. She seldom speaks of him. He has been through a bad patch, she explains reluctantly. I take this to mean that he is unemployed. I've seen him once or twice in town – usually outside the pub or the betting shop – a big, once-handsome man now going to seed, like an ageing Marlon Brando. He comes into the café occasionally; I always know he's there because Cheryl gives him away with her eyes. Her movements are less free when she knows he is watching; she stabs at the keys of the till like a chicken pecking corn. On those days she does not come over to talk to me, but sometimes gives me a little apologetic smile.

She knows when to expect me – half past eleven on the dot – and she tries to take her break when I am there. We talk about films. Since we first met, Cheryl has learned more about them; last month she watched *Brief Encounter* and *Casablanca*. She knows most of my favourites by now: *Funny Face*, *In the Heat of the Night*, *Roman Holiday*, *Wuthering Heights* (the 1939 version, with Olivier), *Rebecca*, *Orphée*, and of course *Tiffany's*. She knows the difference between John Huston's *Unforgiven* and Clint Eastwood's. She watches them in the mornings before Jimmy gets up – he likes action and war movies, and she prefers him to be out of the way – and we discuss them later. Although she is still wary of expressing opinions, I find her comments intelligent and interesting, in spite of her predilection for happy endings. I sometimes wonder what a girl like Cheryl is doing, working in the café at Tesco's.

She doesn't talk about herself very often. Her parents are dead, she says, and she was raised by her grandparents, but I gather they haven't been in touch for many years. She is older than the other waitresses – perhaps that's why she dresses as she does – and when she talks to them her accent broadens and her voice becomes rougher. I can sense that she makes more of an effort when she is with me.

'You even sound like her,' she sometimes tells me. 'You've got that way of talking they only have in old films. No-one sounds like that any more.' Then she pesters me to say *the line* again, in just that voice, and when I do she laughs delightedly. 'I'll never be able to do it right,' she says. 'I'm just not actressy enough.' Then, with a glance at the wall clock which marks the end of her break, she launches into a wonderful impression of Bette Davis from *All About Eve*: 'Fasten your seatbelts, it's going to be a bumpy night.'

And it's perfect; she even *looks* a little like Davis with her eyes narrowed and her chin tilted at just that angle, holding her Biro like an elegant cigarette (courtesy of the non-smoking policy at Tesco's). It occurs to me that she could almost *be* an actress; the brashness and the short skirts and the cheap jewellery just another device to hide the woman beneath. She likes Bette and Audrey, of course, but secretly she prefers the cool blondes, Grace Kelly and Catherine Deneuve; though, like me, she dislikes Marilyn Monroe.

'I used to think she was classy,' she admitted to me one day. 'Now she just looks like another victim to me.'

Today, however, Cheryl is less talkative. She is dressed differently; under her Tesco's overalls she wears simple black trousers and a rollneck sweater. The nose stud, too, is absent. Her hair is pulled back from her face, accentuating her cheekbones. I do not comment on this; our rules, though unspoken, are strict. We both hate snoops.

'I'll bring your toast in a minute, Miss Golightly.'

'Thank you, Cheryl.'

The tea is just as I like it. There is something very *safe* about tea; very civilized. When Polly has her bad days, swearing and screaming and crying to be let out, I bring her tea on a flowered tray she remembers from home. It always calms her. Sometimes she clings to me and calls me Mum. I feed her dipped biscuits between my fingers. She looks like a baby bird.

I sometimes wonder about the other regulars here. There are about a dozen of them, though only one ever speaks to me. I don't know his name, but I think of him as

Eleven-forty, because that's when he arrives. Like me, he has his table, close to the play area, and he often watches the children over his meal. Scrambled eggs, four slices of crispy bacon, two rounds of toast, marmalade and English Breakfast tea, milk, no sugar. I have no way of knowing whether he comes on other days, but I don't think he does. He always wears a hat – a Homburg in winter, a Panama in summer – and beneath it his hair is white, but still abundant. We greet each other in passing.

The toast is perfect; neither burnt nor anaemic, and she knows I like to butter it myself. The teacake is fresh, and still slightly warm. Looking down, I see that Cheryl is wearing new shoes; flat ballet pumps which make her feet look smaller and more elegant. The rings have gone from her fingers. Curiously, this makes her look younger.

'I'll be on my break in ten minutes,' she tells me. 'We can have a chat then.'

'I'd like that, Cheryl.'

I hope nothing has changed between us. I don't judge anyone, you know; nor do I think any the worse of her now. I hope she knows that.

Her walk, in the flat shoes, is not entirely graceful. Her back is very straight. There is a kind of fierceness in her today, something which is not quite anger. I hope she does not think I have been prying. Watching her, I realize that she reminds me of someone, though I am not sure who it is.

Eleven-forty. I could set my watch by him. He stands in line with the others – regulars, both of them; a young couple with a child – and orders his usual. He is wearing a red carnation in his buttonhole, and I wonder whether this is a special occasion for him. An anniversary, perhaps; a birthday. He moves to his usual seat, but it is already taken; a red-faced man is eating sausage, toast and fried eggs and reading the *Mirror*. Eleven-forty looks around briefly, and it occurs to me that there is a free place at my own table. On any other day I might have asked him to join me. The café is almost full. But there is Cheryl to think of. As I turn away, my face hot, I hear him ask a woman nearby whether the seat opposite hers is taken. She mumbles an indifferent reply through a mouthful of scone.

I don't know what's wrong with me this morning. Perhaps yesterday's late night, or the surprises that came with it. I feel dull and grey, like the sky. Something is different. Usually I feel better coming here; watching the people, listening to their conversations, smelling bacon and fresh coffee and scones. There's so much life here. Tomorrow I will visit Polly at the Meadowbank Home and breakfast time smells dead there, like sour milk and stale cereal; almost a baby smell, but an ancient, sick baby with a hand like a claw on the sleeve of my good red coat, and no hope of any future.

I couldn't sleep last night. That isn't unusual at my age, and when it happens I sometimes get up and make tea, or read, or go for a walk around the block. It doesn't often help, but it makes me feel that I'm using the time rather than wasting it; almost as if I'm getting those extra hours for free.

Polly dozes too much. Maybe she makes up for my

inability to sleep; but I suspect they give her something to keep her quiet. I bring her lace nightdresses and quilted bed-jackets, but everything gets stolen at the Meadowbank Home, because no-one remembers what belongs to them. One woman always wears three sets of clothes at once, to make sure no-one takes them from her.

I try to find Polly's clothes when I visit. I go into every room and check under the beds. Mrs McAllister is the worst; she hides things, or wears them, which makes retrieval very awkward, but I won't let Polly get like the others. I make her get up and dress when I visit. I bring clothes for her to wear: proper shoes and stockings and suits. I have them dry-cleaned when they need it, and I sew name-tags into the linings.

It must have been thinking about Polly that did it. In any case, I woke up at two in the morning again, and couldn't go back to sleep. I didn't feel like watching a film or reading, and it was still too early for tea, so I got up, dressed, and went out. It's usually quiet by then; the pubs are closed and the streets are cool and deserted. It's only about a mile to Tesco's, and sometimes I like to walk there and see the lights above the car park and the people moving about inside. The café is shut at that time, of course. But the rest of the shop is open twenty-four hours a day. For some reason I like that; to know that there are still people working, stacking shelves and doing inventories and getting the baking ready for the morning rush. They can't see me looking in, but I can see them: floor managers and shopgirls and cashiers and stackers and cleaners. Sometimes I see a customer or two: a man buying milk and toilet paper; a girl with frozen pizzas and a tub of ice-cream; an elderly man with dogfood and bread. I wonder why they come here so late; perhaps, like me, they can't sleep. Perhaps they are night workers; or perhaps they enjoy looking out from those warm yellow windows and imagining someone standing outside.

So far, I have never actually gone into Tesco's at night – as if the magic might be broken if I did. But I do like to watch. Sometimes I wonder what might happen if I met someone I recognized – Eleven-forty, for instance – doing the same thing. At two in the morning, anything seems possible.

Last night was chilly and damp. I wore my red coat, my gloves and a hat. I'm a good walker – I keep in practice – and in any case distance seems to follow different rules at night, because it didn't seem long before I neared the car park. The big red Tesco's sign looked like a sunrise above it. Occasional cars passed slowly along the dual carriageway, their headlamps sweeping the wet tarmac with diamonds. I saw a young couple crossing the road at the lights opposite me: a large man in jeans and a leather jacket, and a girl in a short skirt, a cropped top in spite of the cold, and built-up trainers. They seemed to be arguing. I was in shadow; as they passed under the arc of the big lights I saw the girl's face, dark with make-up, like a negative of herself beneath the neon-lit hair. It was Cheryl.

Neither she nor Jimmy noticed me. They were talking rapidly, their raised voices slapping against the deserted tarmac in such a way that I could not make out the words. I saw Cheryl pull away as Jimmy grabbed her arm – I caught the words *No, not again, I'm not* – but the sound of an oncoming car made the rest inaudible. The car was slowing down. Cheryl shook her head at Jimmy. I could see his angry yellow face in the light of the street-lamp, and his mouth working. Cheryl shook her head again, gesturing at the road. Jimmy slapped her, once, hard. The sound reached me a fraction of a second later – *clap* – like ironic applause. I saw the man in the car, who had slowed right down to the kerb. Cheryl put a hand to her face. The car stopped.

I don't suppose I should have interfered. As I said, I hate snoops. But it was her face – her young, familiar face, so brave and unexpected in the light of the Tesco's sign – it was the way she does Bette Davis with a Biro instead of a cigarette; it was her dirty laugh. Most of all it was the realization that she had regulars other than myself; that maybe that was the reason she valued my company so much, minded her manners for me, and always called me Miss Golightly.

'No, Cheryl!' I had started forward before I even knew it. For an instant I saw her clearly – the O of her mouth, the wideness of her eyes. Jimmy turned to see who had called out, and when he did Cheryl pulled free and got into the car. I heard the tyres squeal against the wet road. A last glimpse of her, turning away, a hand pressed against the window. Then she was gone, and I was left alone with Jimmy.

For a second I knew a moment of panic. Then rage surged through me. Jimmy stared. He looked dazed and angry, his head thrust forward like that of a big animal. I wanted to say something that would cut him, but could think of nothing. All my words had been blunted. I felt suddenly close to tears.

We watched each other for a few seconds, he and I. Then he laughed. 'What're you doing here?' His voice was unsteady, and I realized he was very drunk. Seen close up, he looked less frightening somehow, like an overgrown but overtired boy. I thought I could see confusion in his reddened eyes as he struggled to focus. I thought of the car and the way it had slowed down, crawling to the kerb. I thought of poor Cheryl, who had liked *Pretty Woman* before she discovered *Belle du Jour*, and who still believed in happy endings. Some happy ending, I thought bitterly. Some prince.

The prince leered at me drunkenly. 'So what do they call you then, dearie?'

I think it must have been that *dearie* that did it for me. My contempt for him made me feel suddenly light again, once more certain of who I was. Tesco's, in the rosy false dawn of its neon sign, looked like the biggest, brightest cinema in the world. I looked Jimmy straight in the eye and wondered how Cheryl – or anyone else – could be afraid of him.

'They call me *Miss* Golightly,' I said.

*   *   *

'Good morning, Miss Golightly.'

The voice takes me by surprise. Eleven-forty has finished his breakfast and moves to sit opposite me, bringing his cup of tea with him. It is the first time he has addressed me by name. I must look startled, because he smiles apologetically.

'I hope I'm not disturbing you.'

'Disturbing me?' My voice sounds odd, wooden. 'I—' My eyes move to where Cheryl is wiping down a table. She does not seem to notice us, but her back looks unnaturally squared against us, her eyes resolutely lowered. Of course she has no way of telling whether I recognized Eleven-forty in the car last night; no way of knowing what I have already guessed.

As for Eleven-forty, he is unperturbed. He cannot have seen me standing by the roadside, for his manner is as polite and unassuming as ever. An occasional plucking of his fingers against the red carnation in his lapel is the only possible indication of nerves.

I butter my teacake. I don't know what to say. His hypocrisy disgusts me.

'I'm waiting for a friend,' I say, too late.

'So am I,' replies Eleven-forty.

His eyes are blue, striking against the white hair. His hands are square and well shaped. He wears a wedding ring on his left hand. Behind me, Cheryl is a little too busy with a tray of sauce bottles. I wonder how long it has been since I last had breakfast with a man.

At the Meadowbank Home there are only half a dozen

men. Most of them are quiet, though Mr Bannerman can be abusive. The nurses can handle him; they pay no attention to his lewd remarks. I'm glad his room is a long way from Polly's, though; when she sees him she sometimes gets confused and calls him Louis. I try to explain to her that Louis died years ago, but she shakes her head and won't believe me. I suppose that's a mercy, really.

I know I shouldn't feel guilty. All that happened so long ago, when we were still young. Louis was only twenty-six when he died; almost a boy. I'm not certain now that I even liked him. I hope I did, that it wasn't simply the jealousy of an older sister that made me do it. He died the same summer; in a stupid sky-diving accident near Aix-les-Bains. An accident, that's all it was; so many young men threaten suicide when a girl walks out on them, and whatever people thought, it wasn't that serious between us. But Polly was never the same afterwards.

She still talks about him, on her good days; makes up stories about their life. How they married; had children; grew old together. She tells the nurses that the dress I bought her last Christmas is an anniversary present from him.

'Louis never forgets our anniversary,' she declares, with an echo of the old vivacious Polly in her voice. 'He'd be here today if his business wasn't always sending him abroad.'

My toast has gone cold. Condensation sticks it to the plate. I refresh my tea with hot water and pour in the milk from my little jug, trying not to look at Eleven-forty; pretending he isn't even there.

But now Eleven-forty takes out his wallet and pulls out a small black-and-white photograph. He pushes it across the table towards me.

In the picture Cheryl looks about fourteen; a thin, sullen-looking girl with long brown hair. The woman standing next to her is old, small, dumpy; she could be anyone. The man, smiling straight at the camera, is Eleven-forty. On the photograph, I can finally see the resemblance.

'You're Cheryl's grandfather?' My voice hiccups stupidly, and a couple at the next table turn and stare at me.

He nods. 'She ran away from home when she was eighteen. I spent years trying to trace her. Since then I've been coming here every Saturday just to see her. Hoping I can get through.'

So that's why he comes here, I tell myself. Dressed in his Sunday clothes, with a flower in his buttonhole, like a suitor.

'We said some stupid things, both of us. Things we were sorry for later. Things we couldn't mend.'

'Anything can be mended,' I tell him; then, remembering Louis, I wonder.

'I hope so.' He finishes his tea. In the background the tannoy is playing the muzak version of a Henry Mancini theme. 'She's changed since she met you, Miss Golightly. I think you've done her good. Connected with her, somehow, in a way I couldn't.'

'We just talk about films.'

'She told me all about it. Last night.' His face is a

sorrowful map of lines. 'So much time wasted. So much time.' He sighs. 'She's still with him, you know. The lad she left us for. Jimmy.'

That surprises me. Cheryl's man never struck me as the faithful type.

'They've split up any number of times,' explains Eleven-forty. 'She told me so. But they keep getting back together. This time, though, I really think I've got through to her. Last night—'

He often drives around at night when he can't sleep. Absurdly, I want to tell him that I do much the same.

Cheryl is watching us from behind the counter. She has taken off her Tesco's overall. I lift my hand, hoping she will come over. But just as she seems to make a decision she halts, and her eyes move towards the far corner of the room. Her expression becomes twisted with love and sadness. I turn my head to see.

Jimmy is standing at the far end of the café. He looks better than he did last night, in clean jeans and a white T-shirt. His head is slightly lowered. There is a little boy with him, seven or eight at the most, in shorts and a Pokémon sweater. The boy is holding the big man's hand, like a trainer leading a bear. I expect Jimmy to move, but he does not.

I see Cheryl hesitate. She looks at Jimmy and the boy. She looks at me. She takes a step forward. Eleven-forty, who has been watching too, makes as if to stand up. His face is tensed.

'Cheryl!' Jimmy's voice sounds raw across the café chatter, like someone stropping a razor. I am certain now that he will walk over to us, but he stays where he is, his eyes following Cheryl as she moves to our table without a backward glance.

As she reaches us I see that her eyes are wet. She kisses Eleven-forty on the cheek. She looks different in her black clothes, with no make-up and her hair tied back; almost a stranger.

'I thought I could make a new start,' she says to me. 'I've got a friend in London who says she can get me a cleaning job at the Palladium, to tide me over for a while. I might even be able to get onto one of those cinema courses in the evening. Get a qualification. Make something of myself.' She grins, and I see a little of the old brash Cheryl again in her expression. 'I'd like to get into acting, you know; even if it's only sweeping floors or selling pop-corn.'

In the corner, Jimmy does not move. I sense rather than see him; a big, hunched man with a defeated face. In a piping voice, the small boy asks for a Coke.

'I would have told you, Grandad,' says Cheryl to Eleven-forty. 'I really would. But it's been so long since – I didn't know how to start.'

'What's the lad's name?' asks Eleven-forty.

'Paul.'

He nods. 'Good name.'

She smiles a little. 'He's named after you.'

So, I tell myself, his name is Paul. I wonder what his surname is. In all this time I haven't asked Cheryl. I hope it is not too late now.

'He's a good kid,' continues Cheryl with determined brightness. 'Not all screwed up like his Mum and Dad. He'll like it in London. Lots of things for a kid to see. It'll work out. I know it will.'

Eleven-forty – Paul – looks at her. His hand closes over hers with a tightness I can almost feel. 'You're not coming back with me, then?'

'Oh, Grandad.' Her eyes are wet again. 'You know I can't do that.'

'Why not? I'd help you with the boy. You don't need—' fiercely he struggles with Jimmy's name, but is unable to speak it aloud. 'You don't need that man any more. He's feckless. He's violent.'

Cheryl smiles. 'I know. I've known for a long time.'

'Then why stay with him? Why bother with him?' His eyes are blazing. I feel I ought to say something to comfort him, but Cheryl's eyes stop me.

'*He* needs *me*,' she says gently. '*They* need me. Last night I did a lot of thinking. I was all ready to leave then, to run away and begin again on my own. It was possible. I was ready to do it. And then I realized something I'd never thought of before.' She takes my hand and Eleven-forty's, and presses them both. 'I realized that life isn't a movie. I could spend a lifetime waiting for a Mr Right who never turns up. Or I could use what I've got to make things better.' Her voice, though soft, has an edge. 'Isn't that why you made me watch all those films, Miss Golightly? To warn me? To teach me that if I want a happy ending, I'm going to have to write my own?'

I want to tell her to call me Molly, but somehow I know that it is already too late. I want to tell her that *wasn't* the lesson I'd meant her to learn, but she seems so sure of herself, while I have never felt less so. Suddenly I see myself as she does: a lonely, sad old woman, hiding myself in movies, clinging to routine, looking in from the dark. Surely anything must be better than that; even Jimmy and his rages. At least Jimmy is real. And he belongs to her.

'I think he really wants to change this time. Really make an effort. For Paul's sake.' She smiles too brightly. 'He's not so bad, not once you get to know him. I mean, he's no Cary Grant, but—'

At least he's real. And she must love him, in her way. Mustn't she?

'Can I bring you some more tea? Yours has gone cold.'

The simple kindness in her voice makes my eyes sting. 'No thanks. Maybe I'm due for a change too, don't you think?'

She hides her surprise well. 'I'll get one of the girls.'

'Later.' That's the problem with wearing eyeliner, I remind myself. It runs. 'I'm going to miss you, Cheryl.'

'Me too.'

We look at each other for a moment without speaking. Then she gives an unexpected grin. 'Go on, Miss Golightly. Say it for me. Say *the line*. One more time.' She turns to Eleven-forty – to Paul – and hugs him. 'You'll see what I mean, Grandad. She sounds just like her. I mean, she could *be* her.'

I know which line she means. It's the one from *Tiffany's*, where Audrey Hepburn is talking about the Mean Reds: that terrible feeling of being scared, but not knowing why. I have it now, a frightened, lost feeling, and I wonder if that's what Polly feels all the time, alone in her little room in the Meadowbank Home, with the bored nurse standing at the door and all her dreams melted away like chalk in the rain. Oh, I know that feeling. *When I get it the only thing is to jump into a cab and go to Tiffany's. Calms me down right away.*

'Some other time, perhaps.'

She is about to protest; but now little Paul is getting impatient; he is bouncing up and down, waving a grubby hand. Next to him Jimmy looks strangely humble, standing there, waiting.

'OK.' She straightens up, pats her hair into place. 'Right.'

Eleven-forty – Paul – retains her hand a little longer. 'Are you sure, love?' he asks. 'You'll stay in touch? You'll be all right?'

She nods. 'Sure. I'm not saying it'll be easy—' Suddenly she is Bette Davis again, waving an imaginary cigarette-holder. 'He may be a rat,' she says airily, with the ghost of her dirty laugh, 'but, sweetheart, he's *my* rat.'

Then she turns to where her men are waiting for her – a straight, comically dignified figure in black ballet pumps and capri trousers – and now I remember who it is she reminds me of: Charlie Chaplin, the indomitable little tramp; often bruised but never broken, eternally optimistic in the face of the bleak, indifferent world. Laughter surprises me; then tears.

Eleven-forty waits in silence until I have stopped. As I look up I see that he has brought a fresh pot of tea; Earl Grey, with milk in the little jug and two wrapped lumps of sugar in the saucer. I wipe my eyes carefully with my handkerchief. It comes away black with eyeliner. I am suddenly sure that neither of us will see Cheryl or her child again.

The tea is just as I like it. It tastes of childhood and home, dipped biscuits and forgiveness. Anything can be mended, I think to myself, and then I am crying again, with a passion I had no idea was in me. Eleven-forty waits patiently, as if he has all the time in the world.

I wipe my eyes again. The lids feel swollen, grotesque. I remind myself that I am old; that my vanity is not only misplaced, but ridiculous. But Eleven-forty is smiling, and he takes the carnation from the vase in front of us and pushes it over the tabletop towards me.

'Better?' he asks. His smile is a little like Cheryl's, I notice; wide, open and just a little brash. I feel a sudden admiration for that brave smile. I take a deep breath, close my eyes briefly, and when I open them again the Mean Reds have receded a little. It isn't Tiffany's, of course, but there is something very *safe* about Tesco's all the same: the sunlight shining through the windows, the warmth of baking bread and the noise of the people working. Surely nothing very bad could happen here.

I pull off my gloves to straighten my hair; fortunately I

have a compact in my handbag, and with a couple of deft strokes I manage to repair some of the damage. I'm no Audrey Hepburn, of course; but then again, he's no George Peppard, and I can tell from his eyes that he approves.

'So,' I say, smiling straight at him, 'how do I look?'

Come in, Mr Lowry, Your Number Is Up!

It's no secret that numbers rule our lives. Perhaps this is why I have always hated them.

I'M A COLLECTOR. IT'S MY JOB AND ALSO MY HOBBY. I COLLECT risks. I assess consequences. I assemble isolated examples of statistical ephemera and factor them into the great equation. The main purpose of this is quite mundane: to make money for the large insurance company that employs me. The secondary, existential purpose is more closely connected with understanding and – dare I say – enjoyment. As I said, I'm a collector.

For instance, did you know that a male Londoner aged twenty-five to forty-five – assuming normal health and unimpaired vision – stands a chance of approximately one in eleven thousand of being hit by a car every time he crosses the road? Factor in a stressful job (missed appointment, mobile phone) and the figure leaps to one in six thousand. If he is hit, there is a three-in-ten likelihood that the accident will prove fatal. Interestingly, in central London, there is also an additional five-to-one probability that the vehicle involved will be a taxicab.

That's why I'm always very careful when crossing the road. I'm careful about what I eat, too; and I watch what I drink – or I did, until very recently. You never know with statistics; like diseases, some lie dormant for years before deciding to strike; some run at you head-on like charging buffalo. In any case, my life has been spent avoiding the risks I calculate: I do not travel by air; I do not indulge in dangerous sports; I do not eat unpasteurized cheeses, red meat or genetically modified food. Living in London, of course, is a risk in itself; but I go for a health check every six months, I avoid tobacco, I eat oily fish, I examine my scrotum on a regular basis, and by doing these things, I believe I have reduced my chance of becoming a medical statistic without significantly reducing my quality of life.

My wife thinks statistics are dull. Perhaps she thinks I am dull, too. In fact I have some reason to believe she does. Then again, women lack our precision, delight in vagueness and illogical thinking, indulge in wild spending sprees without proper accountability, and when confronted by these failings, are likely (nine times out of ten) to retreat to their bathrooms in a swirl of pique and Chanel Number Five, declaring that you never let them have any fun, that you are to sleep in the spare bedroom again and, furthermore, that you are a selfish beast who never thinks about anything nowadays but your horrid numbers.

Notwithstanding my wife's disapproval, however, it is

numbers that rule our lives. Whether the banal miracle of conception (fifty thousand sperm in an epic swimathon towards the golden egg) or the single flamboyant freakish event (man plummeting from crippled aircraft is saved by landing on the back of a giant eagle), every choice, every step of the journey, from crossing the road to boarding that fatal flight, is governed by probabilities of near-infinite elegance and complexity.

Take this one, for example. In 1954, a Frenchman called Joseph Dumont decided to commit suicide by leaping from the Eiffel Tower. He stepped off the first platform and fell fifty-seven metres, but at that moment a giant gust of wind caught Monsieur Dumont and blew him right back towards the tower, depositing him safely on a girder of the infrastructure, at a risk factor, as far as I can calculate, of something approaching a million to one against, taking into account weight, age and general fitness, atmospheric conditions, time of day, the velocity and angle of the fall, and of course the X-factor – the hand of God, that infinite (one might say imaginary) number – which is unquantifiable, unidentifiable, ineffable and all that crap.

Others have not been quite so lucky. Of the three hundred and sixty-nine suicide attempts from the Tower to date, most hit the Tower as it widens on the way down. Frequently, the bodies become entangled in the latticework until firefighters can remove them. In 1974, in a similar incident, a man jumped off the Tower in a high wind and, as in the case of Monsieur Dumont, was blown off-course towards the Tower, where he was impaled on part of a safety barrier and lay like a trussed chicken, with his femurs sticking out from between his collarbones, for almost an hour and a half before he finally expired, thereby demonstrating first, that the X-factor is not always kind, though it is not without a sense of irony, and second, that it never pays to disregard the weather.

I never managed to find out whether Monsieur Dumont, awed by the miracle of probability to which he had un-wittingly contributed, decided to go off in a different direction, perhaps leading a wholly different life filled with variety and joy, or simply elected to step off the Tower again and finish the job he had set out to do. In any case, the odds of that particular event happening again are so negligible as to be virtually nonexistent – rather like those of a single individual winning the lottery – and so Monsieur Dumont leaves our stage for ever, undistinguished but for this one, freakish contribution to the folklore of extreme probabilities.

Oddly enough, no-one seems to consider this when buying lottery tickets. I have a neighbour, Mrs Parsons, a pensioner of limited means, who has bought a ticket every week since the Lottery began – choosing always the same numbers, in the mistaken belief that this way, her chances are improved. Always the same numbers: her birth year; the year of her marriage to the long-defunct Mr Parsons (whose number came up in an accident at work; unfortunate, though not particularly freakish, if we consider his history of carelessness and the fact that he rarely observed the safety code); and, most importantly, what she refers to as 'my lucky number', the number seven, custodian of the all-important X-factor which will one day (she believes) raise Mrs Parsons to the ranks of those touched by God.

I consider telling her that in any random sample of Europeans aged between eighteen and sixty-five, eighty-two per cent will reply 'seven' when asked to name their lucky number. But Mrs Parsons is so adamant and so hopeful that I really don't have the heart to tell her, or to alert her to the fact that the chances of her – or of any particular individual – ever winning the Lottery are so remote that actually *buying* a ticket barely improves the odds. The probability of finding the winning ticket in the street, or being given it by a friend, and thereby winning the jackpot, gives almost the same chance at the prize as poor Mrs Parsons, who has bought a ticket with religious commitment every week since the Lottery started. All the same, she has not lost hope, which is, I suppose, the whole object of the game. After all, what else does she have? Church on Sunday, *The Archers* every day, seventy quid a week from the Government (being sadly ineligible for Mr Parsons's accident-at-work benefit – protective clothing must be worn), the hairdresser's once a fortnight (shampoo, rinse and set, four pounds fifty, just as Mr Parsons liked it), and the enduring, golden hope that her very own Lucky Number Seven will one day come in, like one of the heroes of her favourite romances.

Perhaps it will. I hope, for her sake, that it does. But happiness is not a number. Take twenty-two, for instance. Twenty-two years of marriage until the girl you loved –

eighteen years old, 36-28-36, now reduced by Time's terrible alchemy to a fat and joyless woman who only comes alive for *Friends* and the occasional takeaway – declares that she wants to find herself and leaves, taking with her the children (nine, sixteen), the family home (one hundred and twenty thousand), the dog (eighty-five, dog years), the car (Nissan Sunny, 1988) and the mysterious X-factor – the smell of her hairspray (Elnett, £5.99), the TV blaring all hours, the sound of a house with someone in it and the residual warmth on her side of the bed on cold mornings, when she got up to go to work and I stayed for another five minutes, enjoying the stretch and waiting for the smell of coffee.

Finding herself, of course, means finding someone else. In this case a Bloke From Work (five foot nine, thirty-one). *Loves kids, you'd really like him, we can still be friends* – in a random sample of a hundred divorcees, ninety-one per cent report hearing – or speaking – these very platitudes. And here I am, the one in four; still living by numbers, but without that mystical X-factor which Mrs Parsons still enjoys and which launched Monsieur Dumont on his famous flight.

Here are some of the numbers that make up my life:

Forty-five thousand (pounds gross salary).

Two hundred and fifty (rent on small bedsit in Shepherd's Bush)

Two hundred and fifty (daily hair loss, mostly at crown).

Forty-eight (age in years).

One hundred and thirty over ninety (blood pressure, at rest).

Eight-fifteen (Tube to Hammersmith).

Eight-thirty-five (Tube to Leicester Square).

Eight-forty-five (short walk to office).

Eight-forty-seven (random discovery of small rectangle of paper stuck to underside of shoe).

It was a lottery ticket. I put it into my pocket. That was three weeks ago.

Mrs Parsons seems genuinely delighted for me. I suppose that to her it confirms her belief in the all-important X-factor; besides, as she puts it, it means the numbers are getting closer. Ten million pounds – ten million, at a probability of fifteen-million-to-one against.

I have refused to speak to the newspapers. My wife – ex-wife – has no such reservations. My soon-to-be-ex-colleagues, too, have had their say. The landlord of my ex-flat has painted a moving picture of my ex-life – my punctuality, my politeness, my quiet desperation – as have my ex-neighbours, some of whom might actually have recognized me from my photographs.

Only Mrs Parsons has stood firm. 'Leave the poor man alone,' she shouted to the cluster of photographers that greeted me on the way to work. 'Let him live his life in peace!' But the more I resist them, it seems, the more they want me. I have moved to a still-unfurnished mansion flat in Knightsbridge; I have taken three weeks' holiday from work in lieu of notice and shaved my moustache. There seems little else to do. I feel like Monsieur Dumont, unexpectedly swept off-course and forced to reassess my trajectory. Was he grateful, I wonder? Did he stagger, numbed and trembling, to the edge of the platform and look down in awe at the drop?

The first days were a kind of euphoria. For the first time in my life I went shopping – not for food or for necessary clothing, but for the sheer and frivolous pleasure of collecting numbers. I bought the following items:

For my wife, one Patek Philippe watch, with diamonds (£12,500).

For my daughter, one cocktail dress, black, size ten, Miu Miu (£800).

For my son, one electric car, Hamley's, remote controlled (£299).

For my colleagues at work, small case Veuve Cliquot non-vintage champagne (£150).

For Mrs Parsons, one scarf (Hermès, £150), one raincoat (Aquascutum, £490), one bouquet roses (pink, £95), a subscription to the magazine *True Romance* and a lifetime's supply of lottery tickets (numbers specified), to be sent to her address every Monday morning without fail.

I rather enjoyed that one; but after that I began to feel oddly drained, like a child in a toyshop who has been told that not only the shop, but the entire factory now belongs to him, thereby making his fifty pence weekly pocket money (preciously hoarded since last Christmas in expectation of the purchase of a new Hornby train carriage) rather ridiculous.

For a day or two I rallied; bought a sleek and lovely stereo system from Bang & Olufsen, a bubble-gum-pink Smeg fridge from Harrods and a small but beautiful Turkish carpet from a boutique in Knightsbridge, adding to this a selection of silk ties, six shirts from Thomas Pink, a set of Paul Smith cufflinks, some Lobb shoes and three suits from a bespoke tailor on Savile Row before realizing that, as I no longer had a job, there would be little opportunity to wear them.

After that I phoned my wife. Unsurprisingly, the elusive X-factor has struck there, too, as she speaks of a possible reconciliation, whilst eyeing the top pocket of my new suit with the interested and acquisitive eye hitherto reserved only for *Friends* and certain types of chocolate ice-cream.

But the intimacy she promises reveals itself quite rapidly to be on a quid pro quo basis – several thousand of my quid, to be exact – and I am left, a number of boutiques later, with the growing conviction that she sees me not as a man, or even as an ex, but as her very own Lucky Number Seven, ready to waft her into a world of Chanel frocks and Graff diamonds and world cruises and secret liposuction and furtive, thrilling liaisons. The Bloke From Work, she says, is history. I believe her – suddenly there are more exciting worlds to discover – but I do not flatter myself that it is I that have changed her view. In fact, I feel more like Monsieur Dumont than ever.

In the second week I assessed my future. Ignoring the numerous phone calls from my wife and the friends I have acquired during the past few days, I considered the plight of the suicidal Frenchman. It seemed to me, as before, that there were two options. One: take the chance, thank God for my miraculous deliverance and go forth in gratitude and joy. Two: defy God and step out into the unknown. Perhaps this is now the only freedom I can hope for. Perhaps this is *my* lucky number.

Mrs Parsons believes that a million pounds would change her life. If I thought they would, I'd give them to her. But Mrs Parsons has something that all my wealth will never give me. She has hope. She has direction. What do I have?

This is why, near the end of the second week, I decided to end my life. I would do it cleanly, I decided, but with dramatic impact, after having tied up all loose ends. As a result of my decision I experienced a time of desperate euphoria, as I imagine Monsieur Dumont might have felt on the morning of his long climb up the Tower. A dead man, you see, has nothing to lose; and a man with nothing to lose has passed beyond despair into a state almost approaching bliss.

A week, I told myself. One week in which to do everything. Everything I'd never dared. Every risk I'd never taken. I realized I was freer than I had ever thought possible; every moment was an unexpected holiday; every hour a new round of my game of ever-increasing stakes. In a week, without assessing a single risk, without taking account of a single figure, I:

Ordered five portions of sticky toffee pudding from the Fortnum & Mason teashop and ate them all in a single sitting.

Smoked several Cuban cigars.

Tried caviar (for the first time).

Took up the trampoline.

Made a very clear and legal Last Will and Testament,

leaving all my money to my ex-wife – with the single provision that she puts on four stone in weight and never re-marries.

Had unprotected sex with two leather-clad blondes in a parked vehicle off Shaftesbury Avenue.

Got a tattoo of Monsieur Dumont, my spiritual partner, on my left buttock.

Drank pink Laurent-Perrier champagne in the bath whilst reading a novelette and listening to Mahler's Fifth symphony very loudly on my new stereo.

Tried cocaine (supplied by one of the leather-clad blondes).

Booked a one-way trip to Paris by private jet.

Consumed one very rare steak, on the bone, with extra fries.

Bought a small handgun (from a gentleman friend, also leather-clad, of one of the blondes), a portable mini-trampoline, a bowler hat, an umbrella and some wax earplugs.

Crossed busy roads several times without looking in either direction.

Shot the Bloke From Work twice in the stomach, having concealed the small handgun in my new umbrella.

Note: the adrenaline rush is very strong in such cases, and I found it quite invigorating. I wore the bowler hat with one of my new suits and a very beautiful pink silk tie, which, I fancy, gives me a rather pleasing dandy look. The earplugs, too, were a sensible precaution (and to think my ex-wife always described him as a quiet man).

The flight to Paris, too, has been stimulating to a degree I would not have believed possible, though that might have been the cocaine. It seems rather a pity that it is to be my only aerial experience – unless we count my descent from the Tower, which I imagine will be quite exciting.

This is my first encounter with foreign travel. According to Mrs Parsons, Paris is at its most romantic in the spring, and I am glad to be able to confirm that it is indeed very attractive. Blue sky; light breeze; cherry trees in blossom lining the quiet Seine. The cherry blossom is a poignant symbol, I think; the wind lifts and flutters it like pink snow. Its hue matches exactly my new pink tie. Shall I lift and flutter, I wonder? It is certainly quite a gusty day. In a higher wind, the top levels of the Tower are closed to visitors. I am amused to discover (from a street vendor at the Trocadero, from whom I purchased a small facsimile of the Tower, in gilt) that the public levels of the Tower are heavily protected by wire mesh, thereby making any attempt to jump impossible. There is a net, too, strung across the void between the Tower's four giant feet, but this is to prevent litter and other impedimenta from falling onto the heads of the people below. It is most unlikely to trouble me.

I decide to make my climb on foot, as did Monsieur Dumont. There are three hundred and forty-seven metal stairs (somewhat infrequently used) to the first (and in my case, last) level; and there is something intangibly pleasant, even religious, about the ascent, as if this were some pilgrimage and I a penitent. I realize as I climb that the relative freedom enjoyed by Monsieur Dumont and his brethren has been strictly curtailed; barbed-wire guards prevent the climber from venturing beyond the stairway, and as I pass the first landing I see that even here, there are obstacles and protective barriers to prevent potential Monsieurs Dumont from exercising their democratic right to freefall. However, I have anticipated this. I pass the second landing. Now the stair is even more narrow and winding. Fifty more stairs. I am grateful for the healthy lifestyle which permits me to climb so many stairs with relatively little fatigue. Thirty more. Twenty.

Facts and figures on the Eiffel Tower:

1887 (date of construction).

18,038 (separate pieces).

9,700 (tonnes in weight).

31,000 (cubic metres of earth displaced).

2,500,500 (rivets).

312.27 (metres in height).

8,000,000 (price in gold francs).

57.63 (metres drop from first floor).

It doesn't sound very high, does it? Height, of course, is relative. At six foot one I am considered rather tall, although less than three inches taller than the average. Already, the Champ de Mars unrolls beneath my feet like a marvellous grey-gold carpet. I am wearing one of my new suits, the pink tie, the bowler hat, and I am carrying my briefcase and my umbrella. I do not know what Monsieur Dumont wore for his great leap, but I hope he too felt the sense of occasion and dressed accordingly. Frenchmen do this well, I think; I like to think his sense of style, at least, was undiminished.

On reaching the first landing, I am pleased to note that visitors are few. Perhaps the wind; perhaps the early hour. Choosing a secluded area away from the *gardien* in his glass box, I rapidly take from my briefcase the portable mini-trampoline. It takes less than a minute to unfold and assemble (I have been practising). On its light aluminium frame it is about the size of a dustbin lid, and sits squarely on the riveted platform. A good jump should enable me to clear the wire barrier, and I have already planned and calculated the angle of my intended trajectory. Of course, there can be no accounting for the X-factor. Besides, that's half the fun, isn't it?

I stand for a second or two, watching the panorama. Not for long; the *gardien* has spotted me, and is watching me with a look of stunned incomprehension from his fishtank box. I would not give him odds on reaching me in time, however. A small preparatory bounce or two on the mini-trampoline (it is a most enjoyable sensation, and I wish I had taken it up earlier); then a larger bounce, with the Paris skyline tilting enticingly below me.

I am bouncing quite high now, and the *gardien*'s approaching cries tell me that it is time for me to get into position. I must aim for the space between two of the Tower's metal struts, clearing the wire barrier and launching myself at an angle of about forty-five degrees into the air. Paris in a spring. I'm sure Mrs Parsons would approve.

Of course, the likelihood of my being able to replicate

Monsieur Dumont's epic leap is rather remote. The wind is quite fresh here, but perhaps not enough to displace a weight of twelve stone six falling at a velocity of (by my reckoning) about sixty miles an hour, and gaining every second. Fifteen million to one, I daresay, but I have to admit that this is a very rough estimate, and that the chances may in fact be much, much smaller. It's a challenge, of course. And, keeping my eye on the target as I check my position, I have to say I do feel lucky. A leap of faith, as Mrs Parsons might have said. Faith. Hope. You can almost believe—

a man

can

fly.

Waiting for Gandalf

Because sometimes, reality just doesn't satisfy.

IT'S NOT ALWAYS FUN BEING A MONSTER. I MEAN, SOMEONE has to do it, and sometimes you can have a bit of a laugh beating up an elf or a wizard, but let's face it, most of the time it's all about lurking behind bushes or knee-deep in icy water, waiting for the adventurers to stumble upon you by accident, or, more likely, to pass you by altogether and move on to the next encounter, leaving you to freeze your butt off till someone remembers to tell you where they've gone.

Of course, they don't tell you that at first. Monstering's the best job, that's what they say. No guilt, no stress, cool gear and the ability to come back to life on demand. What else could you need?

Well, maybe it *does* have its moments. I remember my first time: sixteen years old; bookish; skinny; desperate. There was a girl in it: a half-elf; twenty years old; red hair and little latex ears. Gorgeous. In fact I'd joined the group just to be near her, though she hardly ever noticed me except occasionally to shoot arrows at me or to hack at me with her sword. Still, she always killed me in an affectionate, friendly way, or so I told myself, and in return I always made a special effort when I was attacking her, until she complained that she was being harassed and her boyfriend (a pro warrior with quarterback shoulders and a bad case of testosterone) had to warn me off.

By then, though, I was hooked. I'd been bashed, battered, hacked, decapitated, blessed, shot, levitated, zombified, vaporized, stabbed, turned and reduced to slime. And still every Saturday night I came back, come rain, come snow, to spend the midnight hours in combat against the forces of light.

Such is the demonic lure of the live-action role-playing game. You start with Tolkien – maybe your school even encourages you – then, slowly drawn in via Steve Jackson or Games Workshop, your habit becomes secretive: sinister. Your parents complain that you never go out, of strange smells coming from your room. Your friends avoid you; you find yourself hanging around Oxfam shops; you begin to appreciate what your little sister sees in *Xena, Warrior Princess*; and finally you erupt triumphantly onto the scene clad in a woolly jumper (sprayed silver to approximate chain mail) and with your bedroom curtain pinned proudly around your shoulders, bearing a rubber sword coated in silver masking tape and calling yourself Scrud the Magnificent.

Predictably, this outing is greeted with fear and loathing by your loved ones. But already the seed is sown; you enter the world of hardcore role-play, and within three weeks you've exchanged your taped sword for one moulded from latex, you're making your own chain mail from thousands of split washers and you find yourself debating the relative merits of cap or raglan sleeves with a dwarf called Snorri.

From then on, there's no turning back. Every Saturday night, the role-playing cell – a party of adventurers, one of monsters and a monster referee – convenes at the edge of the woods. Throughout the night these warring factions pursue one another through the undergrowth, armed to the fangs and bent on murder. It's an addiction, you see; the dark, the thrill of the hunt, the primitive weapons, the primal fear. And for some – for the weaklings like myself, for the desperate, for the rejects and the misfits and the loners and the freaks – it provides much-needed relief; a chance, for a night, to be something other than themselves.

Two weeks out of three I was a monster. The third week I was a warrior priest by the name of Lazar, until I was shot by a group of orcs; then I was a ranger called Wayland, who managed to reach third level before falling into an ambush set by an evil cleric; then a wizard called Doomcaster, unexpectedly hit by a magic missile; and finally a barbarian called Snod who had to be abandoned on grounds of ill-health (it was January, knee-deep in snow, and barbarians don't wear vests).

For some time I put it down to bad luck that my characters so seldom survived the night. Other regulars advanced, gained levels and skills, became in fact almost invulnerable. Thirty years later, most of the regulars are still with us: there's Titania, the elf-maid, still red-haired and gorgeous; Litso the thief; Beltane the warrior, who tells everyone he's in the Territorial Army at weekends; Philbert Silvermane the old paladin, over forty when we started and still going strong – though he tends to go for less combat nowadays, and more elixir from his potion flask. Snorri the axe-man is still with us, and Jupitus the wizard, and Veldarron the swordsman, and Morag the healer, who only comes along because she's Veldarron's girlfriend and he's always getting hurt. In fact he can hardly pick up a sword without hitting himself in the face with it, but thanks to Morag's healing skills, he's managed to achieve both virtual immortality and a long-standing reputation as a master of weaponry.

I'm not sure about Morag's commitment, though. Frankly, it's rather dull being a healer. I've seen her face when she thinks the others aren't looking, and she has this habit of saying 'Yeah, whatever' when someone corrects her incantations. Still, Veldarron's always had a bit of a thing for Titania (doesn't everyone?), and I suppose Morag thinks she's keeping an eye on the competition. And finally, there's Spider. I have to say I'm a little worried about him; I mean, there's fantasy, and there's real life, but I'm not sure Spider knows the difference. For a start, I've never seen him out of character. The others have daytime identities: Titania runs a New Age bookshop; Veldarron's an account-ant; Litso works for the Inland Revenue. But not Spider. As far as anyone can tell, he's Spider all the time. No-one knows his real name; no-one has ever seen him out of costume. The others come along in combats or jeans, exchange pleasantries, maybe drop in at a nearby pub for a couple of beers before they get kitted up and into the part. But not Spider. He doesn't do small talk. Ask him if he watched the film on TV last night and he'll just give you one of his long stares, as if you're something he's just found under a stone. No-one knows where he lives. You can't imagine him living in a regular house, with a sofa or a toaster or even a bed. He'll meet you in the pub – he'll even have a drink if someone else is paying – but he'll always arrive in full kit: swords, crossbow, cloak, ring mail, back-pack, tunic, potions flask, utility belt, holy symbol. And it's good gear – professional gear. Everyone else has mostly homemade stuff. Most of the players have one good and fairly authentic item – usually a weapon. But *all* Spider's stuff looks authentic.

Ring mail, for instance, costs a fortune; but fitted, cus-tomized ring mail costs more. You can pay up to three hundred pounds for a really good latex weapon, but Spider has a whole armoury of them: long swords, bastard swords, short swords, shields, daggers, crossbows with special bolts; plus the real weapons he carries just for show (obviously he can't use them in combat). Great for role-play, but it does tend to cause a bit of a stir down the local on a Saturday night.

Not that he cares. He's immune to mockery or funny looks. And since that incident with the football crowd last summer, most people give him a wide berth, and avoid those tempting *Lord of the Rings* jokes. Because unlike Veldarron, Spider *can* fight; as a perpetual monster, I can vouch for that. He practises, you see. In thirty years, I've seen him injured less than a dozen times. And when it does happen he takes it so *seriously*, with vials of fake blood and stage-make-up scars. What's more, I suspect he has them tattooed on afterwards – I know for a fact that he still has the scar I gave him five years ago, from a magic missile, when I was an evil cleric. Latex sword or not, he looked ready to kill me for hitting him in the back, but Titania – whose turn it was to be the ref that night – decided it was a fair shot and First Morag (one of our present Morag's predecessors) had to heal him quick. Since then I've been a little bit nervous of Spider.

Then, of course, we've got the monsters. Tonight there are ten of us; mostly occasional players, not regulars like Titania, Spider and me. The university's a good place to look for sword-fodder; most students have plenty of time on their hands, and they're cheerful, energetic and, for the most part, easy to manage. Still, it's important to have an experienced person in charge; that's why I'm here. New monsters can sometimes get carried away: they don't declare hits; they get over-excited. I'm here to keep them under control. To make sure they follow the rules. To make sure no-one *really* gets killed. Because in those woods anything can happen; it's dark, you're edgy, and sometimes on a good night you can genuinely believe it's all for real; that there really are orcs out there, or werewolves, or walking dead.

Out there you can almost believe you're miles from civilization; your only light is the moon; every shadow might be an enemy. One false move, and you're dead; the knowledge leaves every nerve-end sizzling, every sense aware.

On a bad night, it's raining; you've sprained your ankle; there's dogshit on your adventuring boots and you can hear faint karaoke from a nearby pub; then a police car draws up to investigate a report of a disturbance and as the most experienced member of the group, you're left trying to explain to the duty constable precisely *why* you're traipsing round the woods at one in the morning dressed as a goblin and covered in mud. Like I said, it's not always fun being a monster.

Tonight's a little mixed. OK, it's raining a little. But there are raggy clouds overhead, and a quarter moon, and it's not too cold. Atmospheric. Right now I'm sitting under a tree with my cagoule on, going over the encounter sheets. It's my turn to monster ref. I'm quite looking forward to that.

The monsters are here already. You have to brief them first, when the regular players aren't around, so that they know more or less what's going to happen and what costumes they have to wear. There are roles to allocate, rules to lay down. Often there's a newbie, some spotty student in Army gear who fancies his chances. Tonight there are three, all a bit giggly and hyperactive. I don't know their names – sometimes there's no point in learning them, as turnover can be quite rapid. The others are sixth-form pupils of mine, aged seventeen or eighteen at the most:

Matt, Pete, Stuart, Scott, Jase and Andy. And me, of course. Smithy. The perpetual monster.

Well, of course I'm aware that to them I'm a bit of a joke. Forty-six; skinny; balding; desperate. I'm aware that out of costume I look exactly like a geography teacher – which is just as well, because that's what I am – and I've noticed the embarrassed silence that sometimes falls when I come over to the group, and seen the looks exchanged by the newbies when they think I can't see them. Poor old Smithy, that's what they're thinking; always three steps behind. God help me, what a loser. God help me if I ever get that sad.

But there's a kind of glory in the old moves. *They* won't understand that, being eighteen and immortal; but I do. They think it's only a game; in a couple of weeks they'll have found another game to play, or worse still, formed a splinter group with kids their own age, bending the rules and having a laugh. I try to tell them, this isn't *about* having a laugh. They think we do it for the gear; that we're just a group of fetishists and Luddites, like people who go around in Star Trek uniforms, or live in tepees with sheep and no central heating.

But it isn't about gear, either. It's about honour, and rules, and good and evil. It's about death and glory. And it's about the *truth* – not the truth that dragons exist, but the fact that they can be defeated. Because, more than ever with the passing of time, I want to believe that they *can* be defeated. Philbert knows what I mean – his wife died of cancer twenty years ago, and we're all he has left. So does Titania, childless and pushing fifty; and Litso, who spends his whole life – bar these Saturday nights – pretending to be straight. Those kids have no idea; no idea what it's like to come home to my other, sad, imaginary life – two rooms, a three-bar fire and a sleeping cat; to be known as Sad Smithy by generations of geography students; to lie awake at night with a knot in my stomach, looking out at the electric stars – every one a window, every one a home. But it's what Spider says – when he says anything, which isn't that often. Those things are not for us, he says. House, wife, kids. Those things are for the Mundanes. Regular people. People with imaginary lives.

'How much longer?' That was one of the newbies, looking at his watch. You must know the type: impatient, nervy, scornful, cold; only here because someone (myself, perhaps) hinted at something dangerous – something occult and forbidden.

'Not long now.' Come to think of it, they *are* a little late; it's eleven o'clock and dead quiet. 'Get your gear.'

He shoots me a contemptuous look and pulls on his mask. It's latex and pretty realistic – I make them myself, and they're much better than the bought ones. I find myself hoping he gets killed first.

''Cause I could have got lucky tonight,' says the newbie in a muffled voice. 'There's a bird down the Woolpack keeps givin' me the eye.'

It's sad, really. We both know his life. We both know he'll never get lucky. But there's no time to discuss it; I can see a shadow coming out of the trees, and from the noise he's making – and the size of the sword slung across his back

– it has to be Veldarron. Morag's with him, looking tired and displeased – they've probably been fighting again. Still, I'm glad they arrived first; a few of the others can sometimes come across a bit strange to newbies, and I don't want any trouble tonight. Besides, I know these students; half of them are only here because they think they're going to get off with some leather-clad warrior babe, and although Morag isn't exactly Xena material, at least she *is* female – and at twenty-nine, rather closer to their generation than the rest of us.

I greet them with the usual mantra – 'Today is a good day to die,' – in the hope of getting them both into the fighting mood. But as the couple come closer, I can see that all is not well with Morag. Her face is set, her lips tight, and worse still, she has come out of character, in jeans and a parka rather than her customary robes and healer's hood. Damn it, I think. And damn Veldarron, who is making a point of not being with her, making showy practice moves to a dead tree and waiting for me to sort things out, as usual.

'What's wrong?' I ask Morag. 'Why aren't you kitted up?'

'I'm not staying, Smithy.'

'Why not?'

Morag just looks at me, and I feel my heart sink. Of course it isn't the first time that one of Veldarron's girl-friends has pulled out at a crucial moment (he's an insensitive bastard, and I really don't understand what girls see in him), but to lose a healer, our only healer, and at eleven o'clock on a Saturday night, presents a crisis of major proportions. 'But we need you,' I manage at last. 'I've got an adventure to run, and they'll be wanting a healer.'

'Can't help that,' says Morag, shrugging. 'I quit. Tell Darren to get himself another patsy. This one's out of here.'

'But Morag—'

She turns on me then, unexpectedly. 'My name's *not* bloody Morag!' she yells. 'Six years I've been coming here, Smithy, and you don't even know my sodding *name!*'

Well, talk about volatile. Why on earth should I know her name, I ask myself, as I watch her stalk away across the moonlit clearing. What's more, after six years she should know that you never – *never* – refer to an adventurer by his real name during a session. No wonder Veldarron looks so put out. Still – though I'm sure he'll manage to recruit another Morag before next week – her unexpected departure suddenly makes everything much more difficult for me, as I have quite a challenging bunch of young monsters lined up for tonight's adventure. In any case, it's far too late to change anything now; all we can hope for is a short session, good luck, orderly monsters and no more unpleasant surprises.

I can see the rest of the party arriving now, with Philbert in the lead. Philbert Silvermane, he calls himself, though we all know that hair's a wig. Tonight I think he looks smaller than usual, bent beneath the weight of his armour, although in the moonlight he still looks rather fine. There's a certain nobility in that proud old head, like a ruined arch standing in the middle of a field, purposeless, but not without grace. Of course I didn't always think so; I was young once, and I'm ashamed to say I often sniggered – in the days when forty seemed impossibly old.

Sure enough, I think I hear laughter from one of the newbies. Philbert doesn't hear – he's a little deaf – but I'm already on edge after the business with Morag, and it makes me feel irrationally angry. I snap out a sharp command to the monsters, lining them up behind the big bush as the adventurers begin to assemble. There's Litso, in drag as usual; Beltane in very un-medieval combats under his tabard; Jupitus, slow and heavy in his long wizard's robes; Snorri with his axe.

More laughter from the newbies. I expected it; some of those outfits probably look quite comic to them, especially Litso, with his laddered fishnets and leather skirt. But tonight it galls me. Perhaps because of Morag; perhaps because I'm in charge; perhaps because it is not entirely kind. The newbies are in for a hard time, anyway. I don't like their attitude. Neither does Litso. We have a rule here that no-one comments on another player's persona, however bizarre – Philbert (who was a psychology professor in another life) says it's because the role-play is cathartic, allowing the individual to act out fantasies which, if repressed, might be damaging to the ego. During these sessions we banish guilt, fear and mockery, emerging cleansed and renewed. I almost say as much to the newbies, but there isn't time; that's Spider stepping dead-silent out of the undergrowth, and in his wake, finally, Titania.

Titania. As always, my heart does a little skip. Because she hasn't changed; not really. Her costume has had to be altered a few times to account for her expanding waistline, but to me she's still lovely, her red hair loose over her shoulders, her light sword in her hand.

Someone says something behind me. I can't quite hear what it is, but it sounds derogatory. I look round rapidly, but I see only blank faces. Our regular monsters – Matt, Pete, Stuart, Scott, Jase and Andy – wear expressions of studious unconcern; the newbie who complained of waiting is drumming his fingers, but apart from that everyone is still. Good. At least they have the sense not to laugh in front of Spider.

It's raining now. Spider doesn't mind; as he steps into the little clearing by the side of the big bush I can see the droplets collecting in his braided hair. I hand him the briefing sheet – it's written in runes, as Spider won't read ordinary script – and lead the monster party beyond the clearing to set up the first encounter.

The voices of the adventurers reach me across the clearing. They are discussing the loss of their healer, reworking their strategy, re-allocating salves and potions.

'Right, listen,' I tell the monsters. 'Tonight you'll all have to take especial care. We're a player down and we don't have anyone to stand in, so it's all the more important that we do our job properly and don't get carried away. For this first encounter, you're all ghouls, three hits each, so put your masks on and get into position.' I take time to look closely at all the monsters, especially the newbies, who are standing by looking keyed up and fidgety. 'Remember,' I tell them, 'it's three hits each. No more. There's no healer in this party, and I don't want any fatalities on this adventure.'

Someone gives a snort of laughter – one of the newbies, the restless one who complained of waiting.

'What is it?' I make my voice sharp.

'Nothing.' He manages to make even a single word sound insulting.

I'd like to teach him a lesson. But there isn't time; besides, he'll be laughing on the other side of his face in a minute. The thought makes me feel a little better. The ghouls are concealed in the bushes, but not well; ghouls are relatively slow-moving, stupid creatures who should present little challenge. A warm-up battle, that's all; something to get the juices flowing. I blow the whistle. Time in.

This is the moment – the secret, exhilarating rush. It's the reason we play; the reason we've always played. Far more than just a game, it goes beyond catharsis. These youngsters do not feel it as we do, Titania, Philbert, Spider and I. It is intoxicating. It is magical. To be heroes, like in the David Bowie song; to be beyond age, beyond time; to be (for a minute, an hour, a night) one of the immortals.

Ah. Here comes the party. Beltane and Veldarron heading the group, Spider covering the rear, Litso scouting ahead. The monsters are ready, the restless newbie creeping quietly around the back of the party with rather more skill than a ghoul normally shows. Still, he's making an effort; I can hardly penalize him for that.

One of our regulars strikes first. It's Pete, playing his part conscientiously with arms outstretched and shambling walk.

Scott joins him, then Andy, cutting off Litso from the rest of the party and forcing him to fight them three at a time. This is where the fighters come into their own; but Beltane is already fighting Jase and Matt, and Veldarron – conscious, perhaps, of Morag's absence – is keeping his distance.

The newbies are hanging back – rather too strategically for ghouls – but even so, the party should be able to handle the attack with ease. Litso takes a couple of hits to the right arm, always a weakness in his defence, and Veldarron gets a slash across the ribs, but for the most part the adventurers manage to repel their attackers with ease. Thirty seconds later, only the newbies are still standing. Their leader – the restless one who led the attack – is fighting quite competently against Beltane, but I find it hard to believe that he hasn't already received his three hits, and as for the others, they aren't responding to hits at all, but are simply ignoring them and trying to do as much damage as they can.

'Pull your blows!' yells Titania angrily, as she gets the flat edge of a sword smack in the face, but the three newbies do not back off. Instead, the first one yanks off his constricting mask and with a loud warcry launches himself right into the centre of the party.

'Oi! No ganging up!' shouts Veldarron, now the focus of three monsters at once. He's right, of course; it's one of the most basic game rules, and I had explained it all very clearly to the newbies, but in the heat of the moment they must have forgotten. To cap it all, Veldarron is shouting so much that his aim goes wide, and by the time Spider intervenes, cutting down the three ghouls from behind with a series of vicious thrusts, the swordsman is on the ground with several serious injuries.

The post-battle debriefing is loud and acrimonious. I have no choice but to rule Veldarron out of action, which displeases him enormously and gives rise to cheers from the monsters. Litso, too, has suffered humiliating injury, and Titania complains that she had to hit her ghoul at least twenty times before he finally agreed to lie down and die. I talk to the monsters about it, and though the regulars are polite, I don't like the newbies' attitude at all.

'Twenty hits? She must be joking. I don't think she hit me once.'

'Hits have got to be convincing. If I can't feel it, then I can't count it.'

I repeat what I have already said about counting hits and pulling blows. I'm almost sure I see the lead newbie pulling a face. 'What?' I say, for the second time.

He shrugs. 'Whatever.'

But it has soured the game. I can feel it; a tug of revolt from within the ranks. Two encounters on, the party runs into a group of bandits, which puts up far more of a fight than anticipated. Litso gets hit twice more, Philbert four times and Titania and Beltane once each, although Jupitus the wizard manages to put an end to the opposition with a crafty sequence of spells. The monsters protest a little at this, and mutter about retribution, so that once again I have to warn them about playing to the rules.

''Sonly a game,' says one of the newbies sullenly. ''Snot life and death, is it?'

Oh, but it is. I wish I could make him see that, but the gulf between us is too wide. Life begins as a game, and ends in a fight to the death. I try to set up the next encounter as quickly as I can, but even so it takes time; one of the newbies begins a chorus of *Why are we waiting?*, and to my annoyance, the others join in.

By now the entire party is beginning to feel the absence of their healer. By the fifth encounter, Litso is out of action, Philbert is hardly any better, and Beltane is down to five hits. Only Spider is serene and untouched, cutting a swathe through the monsters time after time. The restless newbie looks annoyed at this, but says nothing. Spider does have that effect on people.

We have reached the seventh encounter. The party has lost no further members, although morale is low, and everyone but Spider has received some kind of injury. I feel somehow to blame, although I know it isn't my fault; some nights are better than others, that's all, and new players are always a bit of a risk. Still, I don't feel entirely in control of my little group; it makes me uneasy, as if some part of my imaginary life has managed to infiltrate this, my real one.

During the debriefing, one of the newbies lights a cigarette. It's against the rules, but my mood is so uncertain that I hesitate to challenge him about it. The regular monsters – Scott and Matt and Jase and the rest – seem restless too, as if some kind of signal has passed between them, and there is a great deal of murmuring and covert laughter behind my back as I go about my business. It makes me uneasy. As a teacher I know the danger a disruptive influence presents, and throughout the session I have become more and more convinced that my newbies – especially one of them – are manifestations of that unrest. They are testing me somehow, assessing my ability to react to their taunts, challenging my authority.

'Right,' I tell them crisply, handing out sheets for the next encounter. 'This time you're not hostile. You're a group of soldiers from another camp, and you'll have healing potions for the party if they can negotiate with you.'

I slipped that one in to try and solve the Morag problem. The restless newbie pulls a face, and I can see he isn't pleased at the prospect of a non-combative encounter. 'What if they attack us?' he says.

'Then you fight,' I tell him. 'But you won't instigate anything.'

'*Instigate*. What's that mean?' sneers the newbie.

I give him a look. 'You got a problem?'

He shrugs.

'I said *have you got a problem?*'

The newbie smirks in a way that manages to be both insolent and sheepish. 'Well, it's the way you all take it so seriously,' he says at last. 'Like it's real, or something. I mean, it's just a fucking *game*, for God's sake. Look at you all. There's that old git in the fright wig, and that weirdo in drag, and that fat bird—'

It is at this point that something in me breaks. Oh, people have taunted us and mocked us before; called us saddos and freaks and mutants and all that. But to hear him speak of Titania – of my Titania – and, even more importantly, to hear him denigrate the game – I grab hold of the first weapon that comes to hand – a long-bladed bastard sword – and fall automatically into my fighting stance.

'I'll give you a game,' I tell him. 'You monster.'

The newbies look nervous and back away, but I am too angry to stop now. All I can think of is the fact that this boy – this boy! – has insulted Titania, a warrior with countless successful campaigns behind her, a woman of legendary grace and beauty, and that the insult – to her and to the rest of us – cannot go unpunished.

'Time in!' I roar. 'Party, to me!'

It is cathartic. I have never gone berserker before – some players never do, in decades of gaming, though the best ones have done it at least once, usually in the face of insuperable odds. I remember Spider once doing it, in a pub in Nottingham, in the days when people still laughed about him behind his back, and I'd tried – without success – to imagine how it must feel: the liberation, the rush, the joy. Now I know; and as my friends rush into battle to join me I know that our enemy is not this boy, this newbie with the bad manners and the foul mouth. Our enemy is some-thing infinitely more dangerous, hateful and formidable; a creature with countless heads, all stamped with identical expressions of youthful scorn and ignorant self-absorption. For thirty years we have stalked our Adversary, without knowing quite what it was we hunted; for thirty years we have contented ourselves with second-rate alternatives, when all the time the real quarry was close enough to touch.

The others sense it too; grabbing weapons left and right

they join me, fighting back-to-back as in the old days – Litso flinging spears into the enemy ranks; Spider with a sword in each hand and blood running down his arm. Philbert is cut down, but we will avenge him; I catch sight of Titania's contorted face, screaming some incantation, before I plunge once more into the enemy horde.

Veldarron falls; all around me the monsters are screaming and striking – with clubs, swords, axes. I catch sight of Matt, with blood on his face, but I know him now; I know them all. They are the enemy which cannot be defeated; the sneering armies of Youth, many-headed, indestructible.

Beltane falls; Snorri is surrounded. Left and right we hew our way, unmoved by the pleas and cries of the monsters. Blows rain against my back, but I can barely feel them. Jupitus falls; then Titania, my Titania. My heart, pounding like a hammer, feels close to breaking.

Now only Spider and I are left. Our eyes meet across the battlefield, and I see an expression on his face that I have never seen before, not in thirty years of fighting together: an expression of pure and abandoned joy. For a second he holds my gaze. In that moment I feel it too; the joy, the ecstasy. Our comrades are down. The enemy is strong. But we are warriors, Spider and I. And today is a good day to die.

'No mercy!' I roar at the top of my voice, and at last I am elated to see the enemy fleeing before me – the ones who still can. Only the restless newbie stands his ground. I can see him mouthing something at me, but my ears have stopped working. His face is twisted with indecision and disbelief, and there is something at his feet, something soft that whimpers and writhes.

Spider and I take him both at once. Our swords strike in a dozen places. And it is now, as our last enemy falls and the mist drops from my eyes, that I see the blood on Spider's discarded sword, black in the moonlight, and I remember the weapons he carries for show, just for show and for the special occasions, alongside the ones so carefully built and designed for safety.

The battleground is littered with bodies; ours and theirs. Only one is not accounted for. But I knew that already. A small sound in the underbrush is the only indication of his passing; I know from experience that he will leave no trail. I find Titania lying to the side; she is dazed, but unhurt, and I help her up with a little thrill of illicit enjoyment. Beltane, too, is unhurt but for a scratch across his face; a moment or two later Litso emerges from the bushes, looking scared and relieved. Only Philbert hasn't made it, we discover later; his old heart just wasn't up to all the excitement. Still, he died in battle, as Veldarron says; and that's what matters.

'What about these monsters?' says Titania, looking down at the corpses. 'What a mess. Couldn't Spider have saved a few for next time?'

'Come on, sweetheart,' I tell her. 'It was a good fight. And we can always get a batch of fresh monsters from the Poly. In fact, there's a fantasy club just started that looks likely. Give me a week, and we'll have numbers back up to normal. Now look at me, Titania,' – I wipe a smear of blood tenderly from her cheek – 'have I ever let you down? Well, have I?'

She hesitates. 'Of course you haven't, Smithy,' she said. 'It's just—' once again she looks down at the dead monsters, and her brow furrows. 'It's just that sometimes I wonder what other people – you know, *regular* people – Mundanes – would think of all this.'

I look at her in surprise. 'Mundanes? What does it matter what they think?'

Reluctantly she smiles. 'Perhaps I'm getting sensitive in my old age,' she says.

'You're not old, Titania,' I tell her shyly. 'You're beautiful.'

This time her smile is more assured. She gives me a small, soft kiss on the side of the mouth. 'You're so sweet, Smithy.'

To the victor, the spoils. Her hair is slightly smoky from her time in the pub, and there is a salty taste on her lips. I kiss her, while behind me, Veldarron and the others look on with wide-open eyes and identical expressions of envy and astonishment.

'So what happens next?' That's Snorri, looking slightly troubled, his eye on the fallen monsters.

'I guess I'll clear up.' It's my job, after all, as referee.

Snorri is still looking troubled. 'Bloody Spider went a bit OTT, didn't he? I mean, the newbies are expendable, but good regulars are getting hard to come by.'

'Leave it to me,' I tell him. 'I'll have a word.'

There is a small, uncomfortable pause. 'I suppose you'll want to start a new character now,' says Titania at last.

'With Philbert gone we'll need a fighter, and you've been practising, haven't you? Some of those sword moves of yours were pretty good.'

It's a touching – and a flattering – offer. There is a perceptible tension amongst my friends as I consider it, consider what it would mean. I feel a sudden affectionate burst of warmth towards them all – their familiar faces, their homemade costumes, their split-washer armour, their lines and wrinkles, their faith. But what would they do without Smithy to keep things running? It may not always be fun being a monster, but it takes commitment to do it well; commitment and a level head. Spider couldn't do it; neither could any of the others. Titania awaits my decision with a set, white face. I know how much it has cost her to suggest this; but I know my duty, too.

'I don't think so,' I tell them, shaking my head. 'I think I'd rather stick to what I'm best at.'

Within the party, the tension lessens. 'Good old Smithy,' says Veldarron, slapping my back.

'Yeah. Good old Smithy.'

I look round the circle. 'Are we on for next Saturday?'

Nods all round. 'Sure.'

'Same time, same place?'

'Might as well.'

Like I said, it has its moments. As I watch my friends walk back down the moonlit path towards the trees, I feel a complete, almost magical, sense of peace. The enemy has been defeated, this time at least. Who knows what next week will bring? Even with my fastidious methods of waste disposal, it is unlikely that the disappearance of nine students will remain unnoticed for long. It is possible that by next Saturday – or the next – we may have to move on to new hunting grounds. Of course, it's partly the uncertainty that makes it such fun. But I do know that whatever we may face in some as-yet-unimagined future, we will face it together, Veldarron, Spider, Titania and I. The regular people – with their drab, mundane, *imaginary* lives – can never understand, I realize in sudden pity; and to my surprise, I find myself beginning to whistle softly as I get out my shovel and start to dig.

Any Girl Can Be a CandyKiss Girl!

HER FULL NAME IS DOLORES CANDYKISS. DOLLY FOR SHORT; or Lolly; or Lo. It helps to put a name to your typical consumer; it gives you the impression that you're designing for a real person rather than some market-generated product with no dreams and no personality. Because CandyKiss (that's our fashion house) is *all* about personality. That's what makes my own range so popular (I design for Dolly, the youngest of our CandyKiss girls); it makes the consumers identify with her, love her – maybe even envy her a little. Of course, I'm just one of her designers, one of many in Dolly's Summer Scandals range; but even so I feel I know her – love her – intimately.

Her features are unclear. She could be blonde. On the other hand, she might be a brunette or a redhead. We try not to project too much visually; as we always say, there's a CandyKiss outfit for every girl, whatever her shape, size or colouring. Instead, we concentrate on Lifestyle and Personality, the two strands that have made CandyKiss the leading youth designer of the decade.

Dolly's an independent, feisty, modern miss. She knows what she wants, and isn't afraid to ask for it; and the new summer fashions reflect this. Cropped tops, sexy slogans and audacious contrasts (leather and lace, rubber and chiffon) are worn over pelmet skirts and hot pants in a sexy take on urban retro.

She isn't afraid of her feelings; one moment a siren, the next a naughty little girl, she uses her clothes to express her innermost self. Plunging necklines get a modern twist in burgundy leather or gold chain-mail; and this season's new-look silver bondage boots provide a witty throwback to the glorious days of sci-fi glamour. But Dolly has a sense of humour, too. She enjoys original pairings (white topless minidress with fur trim, matched with green booties with 'Lips' detail), ironic post-feminist slogans (I'm proud to say that my very own design, the SCREW ME, YOU UGLY SON OF A BITCH T-shirt sold out in a single day), and for parties, she likes the all-out, no-holds-barred glamour-puss look, with its cinched waists, embroidered crotchless denims and figure-hugging Neoprene sheaths in flesh-pink, black or tangerine.

Of course, we have had our share of critics. But there has always been an element of revolt in the fashion world, and today's avant-garde is the vintage classic of tomorrow. The popularity of the Dolly range speaks for itself; already last year's pink rubber minidress (that was one of mine, you know) is being hailed as a collector's piece, and the witty range of accessories – bags, boots, scarves and panties all sporting the CandyKiss logo (pink lips sucking on a red lollipop) – has appeared to rave reviews in *Rogue*, *Huzzah* and *Girlz4Us!*

But I do find the criticism of our design ethos particularly, personally hurtful. *The grotesque caricature of Dolly, the CandyKiss mascot* (said the *Guardian* in September) *is especially vile. A plastified, cynical little madam in her designer wear and crippling shoes, she represents everything that is loathsome about today's youth: the loss of innocence, the loss of beauty, and most of all, the loss of dignity.*

Now that hurts. It really does. Because I love my Dolly. I love all our CandyKiss girls, and my great pleasure is to imagine new and delightful things in which to allow them to express themselves. The adult world will always be contemptuous of the tastes of the younger generation; it feels threatened, both sexually and emotionally, and this fever of hate and resentment towards my poor Dolly and her siblings shows to what extent this threat has been perceived. Of course they think she's too young. The voice of adulthood, seeing a lovely young thing clad in our striking designs, yawps in alarm: *You can't go out in that!* The voice of envy, repeated over generations.

At CandyKiss, however, we listen to the consumer, not her parents. We know her frustrations, her desire for revolt. That's why the Summer Scandals range – my own baby, and one I'm very proud of – will revolutionize the youth market around the world. Logo'd G-strings in lime or fuchsia, T-shirts with our new SEXY BUT SHY slogan, trendy matching boots and clever one-pieces in the classic CandyKiss print will form the firm basis for a collection that will, I hope, at last propel me into the big league. Because Dolly, much as I love her, is only the beginning. Her siblings (Lolly and Lo, from our sister range) have far fewer restrictions in terms of size and design, and if I can manage to get myself promoted into Lolly – or even Lo – then I can *really* spread my wings. Dolly's such fun, you know, and such a challenge; but I really think a man like me is wasted on Babywear. Just give me a chance at Pre-Teen or Eleven-Plus, and I'll show you what I can *really* come up with.

This nasty little tale came to me as I was shopping with my daughter. In one clothes shop, we came across a girl who was wearing a cropped top with the printed slogan CANDY KISSES FOR LITTLE MISSES – SEXY BUT SHY. *She couldn't have been more than five years old.*

The Little Mermaid

I came up with this story at the gym. Not my favourite place.

EVERY TUESDAY'S FREAK DAY AT THE BODY IN QUESTION. I guess the management doesn't want to upset the regular customers; people come to gyms to exercise and to look at beautiful bodies, not to be faced with a cartload of crips and mongs and uglies flopping round the pool. So we have a special day – every Tuesday, like I said – our special, personal spa and fitness day at B-in-Q, when (between the hours of eleven and two) we can flop and dribble to our hearts' content without causing unnecessary distress to the able-bodied.

Don't think I'm bitter about it. Hell, *I* wouldn't like to look at me, either. Big barrel-organ chest, little dangly legs, and scars you don't want to imagine; all courtesy of a high-sided delivery van just outside Greater Manchester, a driver on a mobile phone, and my little Kawasaki with the hairdryer engine, from which I had to be separated with a pair of industrial pliers, if you can dig that. Even so, I left a part of myself – well, two parts, really, though I shan't go into any more detail in case there are ladies present. Suffice it to say that on that day I became a bona fide freak, though I can still swim with my arms, which is more than some of the Tuesday crowd at B-in-Q can manage, thanks a lot.

Oh yes, on Tuesdays we're out in force. The shambling army of the unsightly, the unmentionable, the undead. I've got my wheels, and a trainee nurse to push them; most of the others have carers, too – some family members (they're the worst, because they *do* care, and it hurts), but mostly just professionals, with wide, professional smiles, aching backs and ample wheelchair experience. They're not bad people; but I can see the way they look at us – unlike some of the feebs that come on Tuesdays, I'm quite compos mentis, or *compost* mentis, as my old granddad used to say, though whether that's a blessing or a curse I wouldn't know. Him Up There has a pretty damn funny way of distributing his blessings, it seems, and as far as I'm concerned – no disrespect – I'd rather He gave it a miss.

Ironic, isn't it? I used to have quite an eye for the girls, in the days when my appreciation was valued and sought; and though in those days I would never have been seen dead at a gym, I'd have given my eye teeth to be around all those hot sweaty bodies, all flexing and treading and doing the splits against a glass wall with a view on the pool. Of course now all I get to see is the other crips, though I do have my own parking space if I care to use it, and a special entrance (at the back) for their convenience and mine.

I've got to know some of them. It's inevitable, coming here week in, week out, sitting together in the hydrotherapy pool, swimming in the regular pool. You get to know them by sight, though few ever give you their names; you learn which ones *not* to swim with (take it from me, the yellow trail's a giveaway); you learn which ones will talk to you and which ones just sit by the poolside and cry.

Some of them are legless like me: accident victims, freaks, amputees. The amputees are the lucky ones; some of them have prosthetics to walk about with and most of them are pretty decent swimmers, too. One man has three legs, all of them boneless and vestigial, which dangle from his pelvis like a kind of flesh skirt. I call him Squiddy, and it's a riot to watch him swimming with his little legs wibble-wobbling behind him.

Then there are the old people from the Meadowbank retirement place. Some bureau-cret somewhere decided that water therapy would be good for them, so here they are: old ladies with curved backs and tell-tale bulges in their baggy old one-piece swimsuits; old men with hairy noses and blurred, bleary eyes. Alzheimer's cases, most of them; some cry as they are lowered into the water, others take the opportunity to fumble at their nurses with what looks to me like real compost-mentis lust, or growl rude slogans at the hospital cases as they limp by. I don't like them much. They don't talk to me, and they look like exhibits you might find in that Damien Hurst gallery – hopeless, joyless hunks of grey flesh, like something in formaldehyde.

Then there's the Slipperman. Don't ask why. He's able-bodied, but too unsightly for the regular crowd, who complained so much about his presence in the pool that he got relegated to Tuesdays, on a substantial discount. As far as I can tell he's the bitterest one among us – though his infirmity is only skin-deep and totally non-contagious – and he refuses to acknowledge the rest of us when he's in the pool, diving in with a mighty splash and showing off with a variety of special (and mostly useless) leg strokes, as if to prove that he isn't one of us and really shouldn't be there.

Then there's Jessie. I've got a soft spot for her ('scuse the pun; nowadays of course I don't have any other kind), maybe because she's so young. I guess she's a Down's kid – what we used to call a mong – and for sure she's a little slow in the head, but she's sweet and she's pretty, and she talks to me as long as I keep it simple and smile a lot.

Lastly, there's Flipper. That's not *my* name for her, you understand; but she's been called Flipper ever since she was born, and I guess it stuck. She's young – twenty-five, maybe thirty – with the red hair and fleshy, flawless pallor that might have been called Pre-Raphaelite if she'd had all her bits. Of course she doesn't – that's why she comes on a Tuesday – but all the same she's different from the rest of us. Or was, anyway.

For a start, she could swim. Oh boy, could she ever. Most of us try; I'm pretty good, too – faster than Slipperman, in spite of his fancy moves – but Flipper was a natural. She had no arms or legs, you see; only webby paddles, with fingernails coming out of them, and horny, yellow soles. They were no use to her on dry land – she was so big that there's no way they would take her weight – but in water that didn't matter. In water she would come into her own, and the paddles, which had a peculiar, jointless look on dry land, would start to move in a circular motion rather like a bird's wing, and she would roll from her chair, all fifteen stone of her, into the water without a splash, and then she'd be gone.

Call me fanciful, but time was when Flipper could have beaten any able-bodied swimmer by a mile. She cut through the water like a greased bullet; even a dolphin might have had a hard time keeping up with her. Slipperman hated her; in the water she was the one who made him look like a cripple, and it mattered to him, you see; it mattered terribly that he should be able to outswim the freaks. But I could have told him he had no chance with Flipper, who would slice, grinning, across the pool, paddles going like lazy fins, hair trailing behind her like a comet's tail. No-one else came close; and it was a joy to watch her, a real joy, even for someone like me who has so few joys left, because if ever any of us got close to putting one in the eye for Him Up There, then Flipper did it; Flipper with her dolphin smile and her rolling blue-white curves and her tireless, lovely back-and-forth across the turquoise pool.

But Flipper had a secret. I guessed first, because I was the one who watched her most, admiring more than words can say her defiance, her grace and her joy. In the chair, of course, she was just another freak; but in the water she found a playground and a home, and it was almost possible to believe that it was the *other* guys – the carers and the nurses and the smooth professionals with their pity and their secret contempt – who were the *real* freaks, and that Flipper represented something else, some new and wonderful line of evolution that would take us all back to the sea that had mothered us and from which – let's face it – we never should have crawled.

But that secret – I read it in her eyes. Not at first, but later, as their rivalry grew stronger and more aggressive. A game at first – with Flipper, everything seemed like a game – but one with mysterious, unspoken stakes, and a world of dangerous tension between the competitors.

It was Slipperman, of course. From the neck up, he wasn't bad-looking, I suppose; and his body, though lumpy as a sackful of pebbles, was hard and strong. Maybe that appealed to her; or maybe it was his rage, the bitter drive of him to prove himself better than the rest of us, to outswim his disfigurement and reach the shores of normalcy. I could have told him it would never work, but his type never listen, and the more I watched, the more it seemed to me that something was going on between Slipperman and Flipper, something that flitted between them like mercury, some intangible bright thing, some poison.

For a start, he taunted her. It was unkind; what was more, it was against our rules. Don't imagine that because we're freaks we don't have rules, and *No name-calling* is perhaps the foremost. But Slipperman wasn't one of us, and our rules didn't apply. And so began the names – not just Flipper, which she was used to, but other, crueller names. She was sensitive about her bulk, and he sensed it, calling her

Blubber and Whalebone and Gloober and Flopsy and other such ugly, meaningless things.

He teased her about her hair, which was red and long and lovely, and her clever horny paddle-feet. He made out that she smelt – which she didn't – and would pinch his nose if she came near, saying with bright and metallic cheeriness, 'Hey, I can smell fish, hey, I can smell blubber,' so that her dolphin smile would turn down and her blue-grey eyes mist over and she would swim not for joy, no, but to outswim the pain of his words.

He even taunted her about her limbs. 'Look at it,' he would say in his metallic voice. 'Look at the blubber whale. I mean, what is it? A woman? A fish? Does anyone know?'

Once or twice I spoke to him about it. 'Leave off her, man,' I said, as he began another of his tirades. 'For God's sake, can't you leave her alone?'

He looked at me and sneered. 'Fuck you,' he said. 'What are you, her brother?' And then he was off, swimming loud and fast and splashy because that was the way he thought it ought to be done, and because it showed off his legs, which were thin but unblemished, and kicked water into the faces of the other poor creeps who had to share their Tuesday freak bath with him.

And so I spoke to Flipper, one day when we were all sitting in the spa pool except Slipperman, who was doing his laps hard and fast, like if he got fast enough some day he might just slip his skin altogether and go back and rejoin the human race. 'Don't let him get to you, girl,' I said. 'He's a nasty piece of work, and no-one likes him.' It was true;

Slipperman had wound every one of us up at some time or another; even Jessie, who was sweet as a kitten with no claws, and whom no-one – not even some of the nastier oldies – would have wanted to hurt.

'It isn't his fault,' she said softly, still watching the pool. 'He's hurting. Just look at the way he swims. He's damaged, and he needs help, and the pity is that he doesn't even know it.'

'We're all damaged here, babe,' I said tartly, 'but we don't tear into each other the way he does. What have you ever done to him, eh? What right does he have to call you names?'

But Flipper just smiled in that sad-dolphin way she had, never taking her eyes off the guy as he to-ed and fro-ed all alone in the big pool, making waves and gasping for air as he thrust his way through the water. And that was when I guessed that Him Up There had got his vengeance at last; because Flipper was head-over-tail in love with the Slipperman – couldn't take her eyes off him, in fact – and it hit me in the gut like a tragedy. Why does it always happen? I asked myself as the water boiled and bubbled around my useless legs. Flipper, who could easily have been the missing link between ourselves and a kinder, more advanced species, and Slipperman – *Slipperman*, for Christ's sake?

'Oh no,' I said, more to myself than to her. 'Not *him*.' Because if ever the Slipperman found out, he wouldn't just *taunt* her, he would *obliterate* her; there's no pity in his heart for anyone but himself, no, nor any love, either. I don't know what she hoped for from him, but I could see that hope as naked as could be, and because she was sweet (and because maybe I loved her, just a little), I hoped and prayed that the madness would pass, that the Slipperman would find another gym (or maybe even get cured, that's how bad it was), and mostly, above all, that she would keep that look out of her eyes when he was around. Because no-one keeps a secret worse than a woman in love, and this was a secret that never – *never* – wanted to be let out.

Now it was at about this point that I stopped going to B-in-Q for a while. The accident has left me, among other little presents, with a partially collapsed lung and an unusual sensitivity to infections. Perhaps I stayed too long in the pool one day, perhaps it was a new strain of 'flu; in any case, the resulting bout of pneumonia kept me bed-ridden in hospital for six weeks, and away from the Body In Question for another three.

I missed it; and because staring at the damp patch on the hospital ceiling didn't have much to recommend it, I spent much of the time speculating about Flipper and the Slipper-man; about what was happening to them, who was winning their weird game. Not *all* the time – much of the rest was spent coughing my guts out – but some; and as my lungs began to heal, I found myself thinking with increasing foreboding of Flipper, and the look I'd seen in her eyes, and the way the Slipperman watched her, that expression of calculating coldness, like a shark looking for the soft under-belly of the dolphin he plans to bring down. I had a feeling, if you like; a feeling that things were not well with my friend Flipper; and as time passed, it grew into a certainty.

My little nurse – a trainee called Sophie – isn't a bad sort, as they go. One day I told her of my concerns, and she agreed to drop by at B-in-Q, if it eased my mind, and give me the dirt on what was going on. The news she brought back was disturbing. Flipper had gone. No-one had seen her for weeks, said Squiddy, the guy with the three little legs, and now Slipperman was like a pig in swill, swimming and splashing and riding the waves, for all the world like some freak aquatic king with his court of cripples in adoration around him.

The worst thing was, said Squiddy to the little nurse, that before Flipper had disappeared, she had started to get very close to the Slipperman. Not in a good way – he was still calling her names and taunting her, just as before – but now they had begun to sneak away alone to the sides of the pool, or the spa bath (where hitherto Slipperman had never ventured) or the sauna. *Imagine those two making out*, Squiddy had said, with an uneasy grin; although from what Squiddy could gather, they hadn't so much been making out as simply talking – arguing, perhaps – in low, passionate voices.

'It looks as if your friends might have found some common ground,' said Sophie reassuringly as she gave me my evening bath. But I was not reassured; Sophie hadn't seen that shark look on Slipperman's face, or the look of longing in Flipper's eyes. Besides, Sophie was pretty and young and had all her limbs, and she just couldn't understand those forces that turn and twist us, inside and out.

They sanctify us, the well-meaning able-bodied; they

assume that we have somehow transcended our disability through patience and understanding, praise our every attempt at normalcy, exclaim in wonder at our most mediocre achievements. It never occurs to them that a cripple may be as cruel or as stupid, as deceitful or as hateful as a person with arms, legs and heart intact.

So it was with the Slipperman. I found out the whole story some weeks later; at least, as much of the story as anyone could tell me. There's no-one so blind as a cripple in love, nor as vulnerable, and Slipperman must have guessed her secret, as I had guessed it, and turned it to his advantage.

She never speaks of it now – never speaks at all, in fact, though I have seen her watching the turquoise water with longing on more than one occasion from her specially adapted wheelchair. The prosthetics on her legs and arms are still agonizingly painful, and will probably remain so, her carer tells me, for the bones to which the steel posts that secure the prostheses have been fused are freakishly soft, more like fish cartilage than human tissue. The paddles are gone – those strangely delicate flaps of flesh with their webby fingers and calloused pads – and in spite of the surgery she has undergone, the doctors see little chance of her ever gaining any more than a very limited kind of mobility. Her weight is only part of the problem; another is the nature of her strange physique, the unnatural curvature of her spine, the unusual jointing of the vestigial limbs (most of which have had to be removed to allow for the prosthetics). Still, she has what she wanted, I suppose: legs and arms so pink and bright that they resemble those of a child's babydoll, and a frame on which to sling herself as she walks, slowly and with tiny, agonized, Oriental steps, towards the side of the pool, where she spends hours just watching the others as they limp, thrash, bludgeon and flop their crippled ways through the bright water; and Slipper-man, smooth, bland and sharklike, swims length after length without a glance at her or anyone.

She herself can no longer swim, of course, though she still goes into the spa pool occasionally. It takes three nurses to manoeuvre her into the warm pool, and they must be vigilant, for the surgery has left her sense of balance permanently altered, and she now runs the risk of drowning if left alone.

Why did she do it? No-one knows. Slipperman never speaks of it, though I've seen him watching her once or twice, and I can tell she never will. Who knows what she's thinking, in her special chair, that cradle of plastic and metal? Who knows what he promised her in exchange for her soul?

For myself, I can only guess. But there's a story that keeps coming back to me; a story my old granddad used to tell me in the days when we were all young and free and compost mentis; the tale of a little mermaid who fell so badly in love with a human prince that she would have given up every-thing she had to be close to him. And because of that – and because Him Up There likes his ironies – she made a deal; she gave up her mermaid's voice and her lovely swimming tail in exchange for a pair of feet, feet that hurt so much to use that every step was excruciating torment – though having given up her voice, she could not even cry out – and she left the safety and kindness of her element, the sea, to go out and find the man she loved.

But love cannot be bought with sacrifices. The prince found a love of his own – a fresh-faced princess of his earthly race – and the mermaid died alone, crippled and voiceless; unable to rejoin her people, unable even to weep for her loss.

What did he promise her? How did he put it? Like I said, I can only guess. All I can say for sure is that Tuesdays aren't the same now. There's no joy left any more, no magic; just the usual round of crips, mongs and uglies, and though the water is still turquoise, and on fine days the sun still shines through the glass wall like a benediction, we don't seem to notice it the way we used to in the days when Flipper was there. Because in that pool, Flipper wasn't just *as good* as the regular people; she was *better* than they were, better by a mile. And Flipper was one of us.

Except that sometimes I wonder, as the nights get longer and colder and my lungs don't seem to be able to process the air the way they used to – I wonder whether she really *was*. And though I'm not normally much of a guy for the Eternal Verities and all that crap, it seems to me that maybe Him Up There put a deliberate flaw in His blueprint for Us Down Here; something like a circuit-breaker that would trip if any one of us started to get ideas too far above his station – too much joy, for instance, or too much hope. And He buried the mechanism in a cleft just deep enough for it to be quite inoperable, and waited for the world to take its course, smiling a little, like a shark with a secret joke.

Every Tuesday's Freak Day at the Body In Question. But we don't do much swimming any more. Instead, in silence, we sit and watch the Slipperman. Length after length he swims, using his arms and legs ferociously and making waves. Over the last few weeks his condition has improved considerably – in fact, the management has advised him that he no longer needs to restrict his sessions to Tuesdays – but still he comes, as if in doing so he might somehow prove something to himself or to the rest of us. He never speaks. But sometimes in the aquarium hush of the long pool I think I hear something, a sound almost like sobbing beneath the splash and gasp of the solitary swimmer, and sometimes I think I see runnels of water beneath his tinted goggles that may or may not be condensation. Not that it matters; there's something broken inside him, something damaged, like Flipper said, that can't be fixed. Every Tuesday he swims in the empty pool, red in the face, legs pumping, lungs burning. But he'll never catch her now. And every Tuesday at two o'clock, we watch him come out, all lined up in our chairs like a firing squad, and the ones of us that are still compost mentis all stare at him and chant the same word over and over again in low, toneless voices, and the ones that aren't just stare; and the Slipperman's head goes down, just a fraction, and he walks past us without looking to the left or the right, and his long thin legs carry him away from the poolside and back towards the showers.

No-one knows why he comes; no-one knows what he is thinking as he walks out into the real world. Except Flipper, maybe, and she's not telling; though she watches him go through the veil of her hair (that gorgeous red hair that might have belonged to a mermaid in another life), and it's only then, when the rest of us have done, that she turns to go, and with tiny, agonizing steps on her new pink feet, hobbles silently away.

Fish

There is a saying in Naples, which goes like this: Stay a night and hate it; stay a week, and love it; stay longer, stay for ever. This is a cautionary tale.

MELISSA AND JACK HAD BEEN MARRIED FOR LESS THAN A week, and already things were not going well. The wedding had been everything the bride had wanted: five hundred guests; white roses and gypsophila; two carats in yellow gold; a cake designed with rather more architectural expertise than most office buildings; and twenty-four cases of (budget) champagne, all paid for by the bride's parents and lavishly photographed by the most expensive photographer in South Kensington. Even so, three days into their honeymoon, Jack could sense an increasing irritability in his bride.

To be sure, it was not his fault that the hotel was so small, or the streets so busy, or that Melissa had had her handbag stolen during their very first outing. It was not even his fault that most Neapolitan restaurants seemed unable or unwilling to cater for – or even to understand – the importance of Melissa's vegetarian, lactose-intolerant and, above all, wheat-free diet, with the result that although she had eaten almost nothing during the past three days, her stomach had already swollen painfully, and local women (who were friendly to a fault) had taken to patting her bump amicably and enquiring in broken English when the *bambino* was due.

It was, however, Jack who had chosen Naples as their honeymoon destination, being a quarter Neapolitan on his mother's side; he had spent three weeks there once as a student, and had therefore had plenty of time (as Melissa pointed out) to get to know the bloody place.

Melissa was twenty-six, with the homogenized prettiness that comes with youth, good tailoring, expensive dentistry and time on one's hands. She herself was not professionally ambitious, but her people knew almost everyone: her father owned a chain of supermarkets; her mother was the daughter of Lord Somebody; and to Jack, a youngish but successful financial adviser in the City, blessed with a silver Lexus, his grandmother's dark and Latin looks, and the beginnings of an executive paunch, their union had seemed like the perfect mixture of business and pleasure.

In Naples, however, things were beginning to look different. Melissa hated everything: the streets; the smells; the urchins on their mopeds; the markets; the fishing boats; the thieves; the shops. Jack, on the other hand, had never been happier. Everything delighted him: the narrow streets; the washing strung across the crooked balconies; the people; the street vendors; the cafés; the wines; the food. Especially the food; he had never really known his Italian family, apart from his grandmother, who had died when he was a very young boy, and his only lasting memory of her was of a fierce, round little woman with hair scraped back into a black headscarf, who spent most of her life in the kitchen making grilled aubergines and fresh mushroom ravioli and truffled tagliatelle and little anchovy pizzas that smelt of the sea and tasted like concentrated sunshine.

Even so, he had come to Naples with a sense of relief that even Melissa's incessant complaining failed to diminish: the feeling that, after years in exile, he was at last returning home. It pained him that Melissa disliked the place; it pained him still more that she said so on every possible occasion. 'The fact is,' he said, as they dressed glumly for dinner, 'you never wanted to come here in the first place.'

'Too right I didn't,' said the bride. 'Bloody cheapskate. Dizzy Flore-Harrington got a whole Pacific island to herself for *her* honeymoon; India Scott-Parker and her party went on a retreat in the Himalayas, and Humphrey Pulitt-Jones took *his* girlfriend to the South Pole. What am I going to tell my friends when we get back from *our* honeymoon? That I went to Naples to have my bag snatched?'

Jack suppressed the urge to shout at her. Instead he said in a reasonable voice, 'Come on, darling. It isn't as if you were carrying any money, anyway.'

Melissa glared at him. 'That was a Lulu Guinness evening bag,' she said shrilly. 'It was a collector's piece!'

'Right.' There really was no point in arguing. It wasn't even as if she'd paid for the bag herself – Melissa was like the Queen in that respect, Jack thought bitterly, although at least Her Majesty *had* money of her own, even if she never carried any. He spread his hands in a placating gesture. 'We'll get you another bag,' he said, trying not to think about how much all this was going to cost him in apologies, gifts and shopping sprees. 'Try not to shout, darling. The walls are awfully thin in these old—'

'And don't give me all that about how bloody quaint it is, either,' shouted Melissa, taking no notice. 'Beggars and pickpockets on every corner, washing across every street, no nice shops to speak of, and if I even have to *look* at another bloody pizzeria—' At this point there came a pounding against the bedroom wall, as of a blunt object – the heel of a shoe, perhaps – being tapped against the panels.

'Be fair, darling,' said Jack. 'I wasn't to know you'd decided to go vegetarian and wheat-free virtually overnight. If you *must* follow these fad diets—'

'My nutritionist said I have an intolerance!'

'Well, all I can say is you must have developed it very fast. You were eating those things quite happily three weeks ago.'

Melissa glared. 'In case you haven't noticed, wheat makes me bloat. And *civilized* people don't eat meat. It's practically murder.'

Jack, who enjoyed the occasional steak (had been looking forward to one, in fact, since their arrival in Naples), felt his face grow hot. 'I didn't notice you turning down that chicken salad you had at the reception,' he said.

'Chicken isn't meat,' said Melissa with scorn. 'It's poultry.'

'Ah yes, how silly of me. Poultry. The famous vegetable.'

'Stop it, Jack! Just because *you* eat like a savage—'

'What about fish? Is that allowed? Because this is Naples, in case you hadn't noticed, and there are any number of fish restaurants around—'

'I can *eat* fish,' said Melissa. 'I just don't *like* it much, that's all.'

'So fish is a vegetable, now? How convenient. It's an aphrodisiac as well, you know. Perhaps you should try some.'

Melissa was still glaring, but now her eyes were brimming with tears. 'Sometimes I think *you* should have been a fish, Jack,' she said, turning away. 'You're perfect for it. Cold-blooded, slimy and stupid.'

It was their first married quarrel. Jack was annoyed at himself for letting it happen – he rarely lost his cool in the boardroom, and it was unlike him to behave in such a confrontational way. Unlike and unworthy of him, he reflected; after all, marriage was only the first step in his long-term plan, and much would depend upon keeping Melissa and her family sweet. Think of it this way, he told himself: there's no point in getting your foot in the door if the next thing you do is stick it in your mouth. And what a stupid thing to quarrel about! For God's sake, what did it matter what Melissa ate? Jack himself was rather fond of his food – a weakness he tried very hard to hide from his colleagues at work, who seemed to live on coffee and filter-tips. But here, for some reason, it was harder to pretend. Perhaps because of his Italian blood. Perhaps the Naples air, smelling as it did of petrol, ash, sea salt, oil and fried garlic (so like the smell of sex, he told himself, another appetite Melissa did not appear to share). Still, there was no point in taking it out on her, he thought. And in any case, the sooner they made it up, the sooner they could have dinner.

In spite of his good intentions, however, it took him almost an hour to restore the romantic mood. The Casa Rosa, a small restaurant down by the harbour, was not the Ivy, but on inspection, Melissa grudgingly accepted that there *might* be things on the menu she could eat. Waving aside the anchovy toasts, the caponata, the seafood risotto, the calamari fritti and the pancetta-and-wild-mushroom pizza, she decided at last on a small piece of grilled sea bass (no oil, no sauces) and a green salad, dressing on the side.

Jack, on the other hand, was feeling hungry. Perhaps the stress; perhaps the sea air. In any case, he made short work of a dozen oysters, a vast plate of lobster tagliolini and a pair of red mullet with salsa verde. At eight, the restaurant was still almost empty – the evening crowd would begin to arrive at nine or ten – and the plump, cheery woman who brought their meal stood attentively, if somewhat obtrusively by, ready to offer more bread, more wine, if needed. Her round face glowed with approval as she removed Jack's empty dishes.

'Was good, yes?'

'Very good.' He smiled and loosened his belt a couple of notches. '*Buonissimo.*'

'I catch the mullet this morning. All the fish – this morning catch.'

From the corner of his eye, Jack saw Melissa frown. She had hardly touched her meal, he saw; the salad leaves were pushed from one side of her plate to the other. The plump woman had seen it too, and her face, which had been so vivid when she was speaking to Jack, took on a doughy, expressionless look.

'I thought mine was rather dry,' said Melissa, putting her knife and fork together.

The doughy look wavered a little. The dark head bobbed like a fishing-float. The plump woman – Rosa herself, thought Jack – took the plates in a graceless scramble, head bowed, shoulders hunched.

'You shouldn't have said that,' said Jack, watching her go. 'After all, *you* asked for it to be fat-free.' His own fish had been luscious, swimming in oil and capers, and he had mopped up the remaining sauce with the last of the olive bread.

Melissa shot him a look. 'Just because *you* stuff yourself silly, it doesn't mean I have to. I mean, look at you. You must have put on half a stone since we arrived.'

Jack shrugged and poured more wine. Melissa had barely touched that, either. Behind her, Rosa emerged from the kitchen carrying two plates and a covered dish. 'Speciality,' she said with a taut smile, and set them down on the table.

'But we didn't order anything else,' said Melissa.

'Speciality,' repeated the plump woman, and removed the cover from the earthenware dish. A spicy, delicious smell emerged. Inside, Jack could see pieces of fish nestling along-side whole tiger prawns, mussels, scallops, and fat brown Sicilian anchovies. There was white wine, bay, olive oil, fresh parsley; there was garlic; there was chilli; and in the rising steam he could see Rosa's face, plain, pleasant, slightly pink now with hope and anticipation, the hesitant smile just wavering on her lips.

'But we didn't *order*—' Melissa began again.

Jack interrupted her. 'Fabulous,' he said loudly. 'I'll definitely try some.'

Melissa watched as Rosa heaped food onto Jack's plate.

'More bread, yes?' said Rosa. 'We have olive, walnut, anchovy—'

'Perfect,' said Jack.

As Rosa disappeared once more into the kitchen, Melissa turned on her beloved. 'What *do* you think you're doing?'

'You made a complaint,' said Jack.

'So?'

'So she's a Neapolitan. Her sense of hospitality obliges her to make it up to you.'

'How ridiculous,' said Melissa. '*I* certainly shan't eat any of it.'

'Then I shall eat it all,' said Jack. To refuse the food, he knew from his grandmother, would be the worst kind of insult; already Rosa had been shaken by Melissa's casual complaint; to turn down her apology would be inexcusable.

'Don't give me that,' said Melissa with scorn. 'You just want another excuse to pig out. We'll end up paying for it, you'll see; you don't think she's going to let us have all that for free, do you?'

Jack took a mouthful of fish, silken with oil, wine and spices. 'Delicious,' he said provocatively, and Rosa, arriving just at that moment with the bread, flushed with pleasure. She really was large, he thought, but now he saw that she was far from unattractive: her café-latte skin was perfectly unblemished; her glossy black hair tied back in a loose chignon, so that small tendrils fell damply around the sides of her face. Beneath the neat white apron her breasts were like feather pillows, and as she bent to ladle more stew into his plate, he caught a scent of vanilla and ozone and baking bread from her smooth brown arms.

'You should just see yourself,' said Melissa in a low voice, as he scooped sauce into his mouth using one of the empty mussel shells. 'Anyone would think you hadn't eaten in a week.'

Jack shrugged and broke the head off a prawn. The flesh was pink and succulent, steeped in wine and spiced oil.

'That's disgusting,' said Melissa, as he sucked the juice from inside the prawn head, leaving the shell on the side of his plate. 'You're disgusting, and I want to go back to the hotel.'

'I haven't finished. If you want to go, then go.'

Melissa did not reply. Jack knew perfectly well that she would not leave without him; Naples by day made her uneasy, but by night it terrified her. She put her lips together – one of her most unappealing expressions, thought Jack as he started on a piece of monkfish; it made her look just like her mother – and sat in martyred silence for a couple of minutes, deliberately not looking at him, which was fine by Jack.

In the corner of the restaurant, Rosa stood rearranging some fruit in a large earthen dish. The heat of the kitchen had flushed her cheeks, and the effect was sweetly exotic, like the bloom on a ripe nectarine. She smiled at him as she turned around (not before he had had time to appreciate the sweeping curve of her buttocks under the tight-fitting uniform), and he was struck by her youth. He had assumed she was a middle-aged woman; now he could see quite clearly that she was Melissa's age, maybe younger. In fact, now he came to think of it, Melissa herself was looking rather tired; her skin was dry and slightly sunburnt, and there was an unpleasant double-crease between her plucked eyebrows. It made her look older than she was; stringy rather than slender, like over-roasted chicken. She had lost weight in the weeks before the wedding, he knew; the dress had been a size eight to her usual ten, and its scooped neckline had revealed an unappealing expanse of corrugated flesh, through which her breastbone was clearly visible.

Later he had discovered that she wore gel pads in her bra to give herself some cleavage – chicken fillets, they called them, he reflected sourly, recalling the moment of discovery. It had been rather a shock; Jack liked busty women. But he had made a joke of it – a joke, as it happened, that Melissa had not appreciated. Jack wondered vaguely whether chicken fillets counted as meat or poultry, and as he poured himself another glass of wine he noticed, with some surprise, that he had finished the bottle.

He had finished the stew, too, and most of the bread; when Rosa came up to clear the plates, her face shone with delight.

'Thank you,' said Melissa in a cold voice.

'You like?'

'Very much,' said Jack.

'Maybe a dessert, yes? And café?'

'The bill, please,' said Melissa clearly.

Rosa looked slightly hurt. 'No dessert? We have tiramisu, and torta della nonna, and—'

'No, thank you. Just the bill.'

That was so like her, thought Jack, feeling his face grow warm. No thought for anyone but herself; no understanding of the needs of those around her. It wasn't as if she were paying the bill, either; the question of a shared bank account had come up once, but had caused so much distress and indignation that Jack had wisely retreated, hoping to pursue it at some less sensitive moment.

'I'll have dessert, please,' he said in a loud voice. 'And grappa, and espresso.'

Melissa's face was a white knuckle of disapproval. Behind her, Rosa's cheeks glowed like summer wallflowers. 'The menu?' she enquired.

He shook his head. 'Surprise me.'

Over coffee, which she would not drink, Melissa eyed

him in pale and glassy fury. 'You're doing this on purpose,' she hissed.

'What makes you say that?' said Jack between mouthfuls of grappa.

'Damn you, Jack, you knew I wanted to leave!'

He shrugged. 'I'm hungry.'

'You're a pig.'

Her voice was shaking. In a moment she would cry. Why was he doing this? Jack asked himself in sudden confusion. He'd worked so hard to win Melissa; why was he doing this to her, and to himself? The realization was like a nugget of ice in the centre of a soft and melting crème brûlée, and he put down his glass, wondering vaguely whether he could have been drugged. Melissa was watching him with hate in her blue eyes, her mouth thinned almost to invisibility.

'OK. We'll go.' It was astonishing how ugly she really was, he thought. The teased and processed hair. The capped teeth. The scrawny neck, strung out like a long rope-ladder to the chicken fillets in her expensive La Perla bra. From out of the kitchen came Rosa, soft and bright and glowing, with a tray between her hands. Her chocolate-amber eyes were shining, and Jack found himself saying, almost without meaning to, 'After dessert.'

Opposite him, Melissa went rigid. But Jack was hardly aware of her as he watched Rosa with the tray. She had brought him, he realized, not one dessert, but many: tiny portions of everything on her special menu. There was tiramisu, dusted with chocolate and lusciously, meltingly moist; there was lemon polenta and chocolate risotto; there were lace-thin almond tiles and coconut macaroons and pear tartlets and apricot ice-cream and spiced vanilla brûlée with almond flakes and honey.

'You have *got* to be kidding me,' whispered Melissa furiously. But Jack barely heard her in the face of these new wonders, testing this, tasting that with a growing sense of exhilaration and abandon. Rosa watched him with that half-maternal smile and her hands folded like angels' wings across her breasts. Astonishing that he should ever have thought her plain: she was stunning, he realized now; ripe as summer strawberries; sensual as a bath of cream. He looked at the woman sitting opposite, with her sour expression, and tried to remember why she was there; something about money, he seemed to recall; something about business and prospects. It didn't seem important, though, and he soon forgot it again as he immersed himself in the tastes and the textures of this strange and darkly gorgeous Neapolitan woman's confectionery.

Rosa seemed to share in his delight. Her mouth was slightly open, her eyes sparkling, her cheeks faintly flushed. She nodded to him, first in approval, then with a suppressed excitement. She was trembling, he saw; her hands clench-ing and unclenching against the white of her apron. He took a mouthful of hazelnut cream; his eyes closed for a moment, and as they did he felt sure that her eyes, too, had closed in rapture; he heard a gasp of pleasure as he reached once more for the spoon.

'Good! Yes!' It was almost inaudible, and yet he heard it – the sigh of release; the tiny moan of delight. Once more, he reached; once more, she sighed; fingers splayed into the musky air. He was glutted; and yet he wanted more, if only to see her face as he fed and fed. Dimly he recalled himself telling someone – who was it now? – that fish was an aphrodisiac; for a second he thought he might almost have remembered who, but then the thought slipped quietly away.

He was still eating when the woman with the sour face stood up, her mouth like barbed wire, and left the table. He did not look up – though she slammed the door quite rudely as she left – until Rosa returned with the coffee, amaretti and little glacé-fruit pastries; and then she was sitting beside him, her hands over his; she was unfastening his belt to give his taut belly space to expand, and, nibbling gently at his ear, she whispered in a voice like musk and blood and dark honey: 'Now, *Carissimo*. Now for my turn.'

Never Give a Sucker . . .

Writing my first book, The Evil Seed, *it struck me that vampire literature is really very elitist. The setting is always romantic, the bloodsuckers themselves always attractive, aristocratic and stylish. This of course begs the question: where are the other vampires? The plain vampires, the working-class vampires, the ones with the bad PR?*

I'LL TELL YOU THIS FOR NOWT. THE VAMPIRE BUSINESS IS dead and buried. Not just back in Whitby, though that's where the rot started, and not from lack of public interest – quite the opposite. They tell me it's because demand exceeds supply. At last we've fallen prey to market forces, given in to pressure on us to conform, to modernize, to present the right kind of image to the customer.

Take me. Reggie Noakes. Seventy-five years in the trade and ousted by market forces. Nothing personal, Reggie old love, they tell me. You don't fit in any more. You're just the wrong sort of vampire.

Take my face. Round and ruddy, the face of the Grimsby fishmonger I once was. Take my short legs, and the fatal sag of my gut. In the old days none of that would have mattered. You were glad to go unnoticed. But these days we've got to fit in with the image. The Victorian streets. The fog. And with the new generation of punters walking about in black lipstick and leather, lurking around grave-yards in the hope of a glance at one of us. You can't even tell the difference any more between the living and the undead. It isn't healthy. All the same, everyone can't be poncing about in black capes and fangs, ranting about unholy ecstasies and nameless dreads. Look bloody funny if they did.

I'm making no apologies for going native. It's easy in this place. Lots of people passing through. No-one asking ques-tions. Still, even when I retired here I sometimes wondered whether Whitby wasn't a bit upmarket for me. It should have been Blackpool right from the start. Noisy, jolly Blackpool, with its arcades and fish shops (I still enjoy a bit of breaded cod once in a while), and its pleasure beach cram-packed with lovely warm sweating bodies all sweltering happiness and rage and jealousy and hunger just like mine. Well, you know, it's never been blood that really counted for me. I've never liked it that much, to tell the truth, and it's a bugger trying to get any when you're fat and balding and no virgin would look at you twice. But get me in a crowd and I'm happy. A touch here, a taste there. Nothing much. Not enough to kill. Skimming it off gently, like froth from a pint. Some girl screaming on the Big

Dipper. Her boyfriend, all itchy fingers, his mind elsewhere. Two lads fighting outside a pub. It's all of life out here, teeming life, and that's why I'm here now on the pier, sipping my frothy lager and waiting for a nice warm family to drain of their life, their energies.

I can see one coming now, a foursome. Two kids with round, healthy faces, one eating a chip butty, the other an ice-cream. The parents: her peeling and pink with sunburn across plump shoulders, him in string vest and baseball cap. They can spare a bit of that for me, I tell myself. They've got plenty.

It's an old drill and I've got it pat. As they pass by me near enough to touch, I half-turn, overbalance and drop my can. The frothy lager splashes Mother's shell top and Father's trouser turn-ups.

'Sorry, love. I'm sorry.' I make as if to pick up the can and get in range of the two kids. I can smell them: chip-fat and chewing-gum and life.

Mother brushes herself off. 'Yer daft bugger,' she says.

I pretend to steady one of the kids. He's warm and squirming. I try for a bit of the old avuncular and nudge in closer. 'Don't you fall over that rail, me lad. Sharks'll have yer!' Spot on. I should be able to feel it now, the rush of energy from the boy, the life racing into me through him. Instead, nothing. I feel strange, suddenly tired. It must be the lager. Unsteadily, I pat the lad's head, feeling the sunny curls beneath my fingers. Concentrate. It's life I need from him, hot life, marbles and bubblegum, conkers and cigarette cards. Secrets whispered in alleys to his best friend. His first bike. His first kiss. I brace myself for the rush.

Nowt.

Mother looks at me sideways. I try to smile but it comes out lopsided and I almost fall over. It feels like drunkenness, a drained feeling, as if the expected charge has turned against me, sucking at my bones. The boy smiles and I see him clearly for a moment, lit up by a red slice of neon from a nearby arcade, his face glowing, his eyes huge and luminous.

Mother bends over me and I can smell her scent, like roses and frying and the stuff she uses to keep her hair in place all mixed up together and hot, hotter, hottest . . . I can't help it. I reach for her, gasping, starving, breathless and suddenly freezing cold. 'Help me,' I whisper.

'Yer daft bugger,' she says again. Her voice is light and without sympathy. Father is coming to join her, his shoes ringing slow, effortless strides across the pier. Her arms are soft and scented, tiny beads of sweat caught in the peachy hairs on her fat pink forearms. The world greys out for an instant. Her voice is thick and treacly, like a woman speaking through a mouthful of cake, and I now think I can hear amusement in her flat tones.

'Leave him, Father,' she says. 'This un's no bloody good.'

As I watch their retreating backs the cold begins to recede. The world brightens a little and I can sit up. I feel as if I've been punched in the mouth. But the four of them are shining, haloed by the pleasure-beach lights. A little girl holding an ice-cream cone looks at me as she skips by. I can smell the same hot reek from her skin, the same promise of life. Looking at her from the boards, I try to reach out, feeling my fingers tingling at her closeness. Heat bakes from her. Life. I'm faint with the need for her. And yet I withdraw in spite of my hunger, suddenly scared by her vitality, her innocent greed. In my weakened state I feel she could freeze me bloodless without even knowing it.

Punters pass me by without a glance. They are wholesome, noisy, red-faced, parting around me to merge again into a hot river. In my time amongst the narrow streets and the Whitby fogs I've almost forgotten how healthy the living can be. And yet there's something about them all, a kind of family resemblance. Something a little too bright, too glowing to be real. I remember the old familiar holidaymakers in Whitby, the thin young people in black, their sad, strained faces, their greyness, their dull expressions. None of these people are dull, all of them touched with a lustre I begin to recognize . . . The ruddy complexions. The sagging waistlines. The open faces. The brimming illusion of life. So this is where they go, the wrong sort; pushed here by market forces. This is where they belong, among the bright lights and the arcades, the fish shops and roller coasters. Indistinguishable from the real thing. Better, some might say. Never dying, never changing: cheery holidaymakers on a trip that never ends. Slowly I pick myself up and head back through the crowd that gluts the pier. Heads turn to follow me. Delicate fingers flutter against my skin. Dimly I wonder how many of them there are, by how many they outnumber the living. Ten to one? A hundred? A thousand? Or are they now so many that they prey on each other, bloodlessly, greedily, shoulder to shoulder in rough, grinning comradeship?

The lights of the pleasure beach are gaudy as a fisherman's lure skipping across the dark water. Life, they promise. Heat and life. Too weak to wander far from that distant hope, I make my way wearily back towards them, trying not to meet myself along the way; just another sucker slouching back down the long dark road to Bethlehem.

Eau de Toilette

In these days of Botox, body piercing and failed cosmetic surgery, it is tempting to fantasize about other times and places, which we think of as being more romantic than our own. Dream on.

IT WASN'T UNTIL I CAME TO COURT THAT I REALIZED HOW much rich people stink. If anything, the rich more so than the poor; in the country, at least, we have less excuse for not washing. Here, to have a bath is to disrupt everything. The water must be heated, then carried up to the room with sponges, brushes, perfumes, towels and countless other impedimenta; not to mention the bath itself – cast-iron and heavy – which must be brought out of storage, cleaned of rust, then dragged by footmen up countless flights of stairs to Madame's boudoir.

There she waits, *en déshabillée*. Her saque is of pink lustring, with ribbons of the delicate coral hue so popular this season, which ladies of fashion call *soupir étouffé*. Beneath it, her corsets are grey with sweat and ringed around the underarms, rings within rings, like the severed trunk of a very old tree.

But Madame is wealthy; her household boasts so much linen that her maids need wash it only once a year, on the flat black stones of the *laveraie*, by the bank of the Seine. It is September now, and the linen room is only half full; even so, the growling musk of Madame's intimates carries up the steps, across the corridor and into the morning-room, where even four vases of cut flowers and a hanging pomander fail to mask the stench.

Nevertheless, Madame is a famous beauty. Men have written sonnets to her eyes, which are exceptional, so I am told. The same cannot be said of her rotten teeth, however; or indeed of her eyebrows, which are fashionably shaven, being replaced by mouse-skin replicas, stuck with fish-glue to the centre of her forehead. Fortunately the smell of the fish-glue is slight, compared with the rest, and does not disturb her. Why should it? Monseigneur uses the same aids to beauty, and he is one of the most highly regarded gentlemen of fashion of the Court. The King himself (no rose garden, His Majesty) says so.

While Madame awaits her bathwater, she peers at herself with some anxiety in the gilded mirror of her chamber. At twenty-two, she is no longer young, and she has noticed a diminution in the number of her admirers this last season. Monseigneur de Rochefort, her favourite, has been most distressingly absent; worse still, there have been rumours that he has been seen twice recently in the company of La Violette, an opera-dancer from Pigalle.

In the mirror, Madame scrutinizes her fading complexion. She feels concern for her loss of bloom, and wonders what might have caused it. Too many balls, perhaps; or a disappointment in love; besides, it is well known that water is dreadfully injurious to the skin. With care, she applies a little more white lead to her dimpled cheek.

Now for the pounce-box; shaking out powder onto a goosedown *houppe*, she dusts her face and cleavage. A little rouge, perhaps – a *very* little, for she does not want to be accused of trying too hard – and a patch or two. *La Galante*, and – yes, why not? – *La Romance*, applied with a fingertip and glued with the same fish-glue that secures her mouse-skin eyebrows.

It will do. It is perhaps not perfect; Madame is too distressingly aware of the fine lines between her eyes, and of that area of scaly, reddened skin against her powdered breast. Thank the Lord, she thinks, for His gift of cosmetics – and of course, the collar of rubies she plans to wear for tonight's ball should hide that patch of ringworm nicely.

'Jeannette!' Madame is getting impatient. 'Where is the hot water?'

Jeannette explains that Marie is heating it in the kitchen, and promises to have it soon. She has brought Madame's little pug, Saphir, with her in the hope that in the meantime he may amuse Madame, but Madame is petulant. Where is her dress? she asks. Has it been brushed and pressed? Is it ready for tonight's event?

Jeannette assures her that it is.

'Then bring it, bring it, you silly girl,' snaps Madame, and five minutes later the creation is brought in. Two maids are needed to manoeuvre it through the door, for it is heavy even without the wicker panniers over which Madame will wear it. The skirt is made of crimson brocade, embroidered all over with gold thread, and Madame will wear it over a great hoop and an underskirt of dark gold. Thanks to the panniers swinging at her hips, she will dance with the undulating grace of an Eastern courtesan, and all her admirers – especially Monseigneur de Rochefort – will gasp and stare in desire and admiration.

But the confection is heavy, weighed down as it is with fully four *livres* of gold thread, and Madame's shoes are *chopines* in the Venetian mode, designed more for effect than for practicality, with platforms that raise her modest height to an altitude verging on the queenly. Her skirt has been made extra-long with this problem in mind; and the ingenious stool-like device concealed inside the left pannier allows her to sit down discreetly, on occasion, if the platform shoes become too uncomfortable.

I know, too (for nothing is secret to one in my humble position) that the stool device plays a double role; suspended on a hinge mechanism that allows it to be pushed into the pannier or pulled out as and when required, it also harbours a chamber pot, so that Madame need not squat ungraciously in the bushes (or worse, piss into her rolled stockings), and may dance the night away with one of her several lovers without anxiety.

'Jeannette, the bath!'

Poor Jeannette is working hard; the bath will take fifty or

more of the cans of water, and Madame likes it quite full.
But the other maids are working too; one to bring out
Madame's collection of fans for approval; the other three on
tonight's coiffure.

In the style of all truly elegant ladies, Madame's head has
been shorn bald. She will wear a wig of regal proportions
and truly original design. No dowdy *Chien Couché* or out-
moded *Vénus* shall adorn her head; this headpiece,
bedecked with plumes and stuffed with horsehair, is fully
three feet high. Grey powder will give it a final touch of
elegance; but although it is strongly scented with musk
and attar, beneath the perfumes it still smells noticeably of
mice. I doubt whether Madame will notice this, however.
The combined stench of stale underthings, old sweat, fish-
glue, and the contents of the pisspot concealed inside the
panniers of her gown should already make for a pungent
mixture.

Still, angered now at Jeannette's lateness, she awaits the
bath. Saphir, too, is growing impatient, and yaps and growls
at the maids as they set about their business aiding Madame
in her selection of fans. She has a large collection, of ivory,
of plumes, or of cunningly painted chicken skin. These
smell particularly vile – the armoire in which Madame
keeps them stinks like a hen house. Madame seems not
to notice; on my advice, she selects a fan of crimson and
gold to match her gown, and dreams pleasantly of the
billets-doux she will receive at the ball. Perhaps young
Monseigneur de Rochefort will deliver one, in a nosegay or
a napkin; he has been so wilful of late, transferring his

attention from one lady to another, but tonight, Madame feels sure that she will conquer.

'Jeannette, the hot water!'

Such a bore; but it must be done. Once every six months is not such a terrible burden, and besides, in a few hours the young men will begin to call, and Madame must be ready to receive them. She considers her legs. The blisters have almost vanished from her last attempt at singeing, and the hairs, though dark, are few. Madame uses a pair of tweezers to remove them; it may well be that she will accept to stroll in the garden with Monseigneur de Rochefort, and everyone knows that a lady should never contemplate a gallantry with hairy legs.

'Madame? The bath?' Poor Jeannette is sweating. It has taken her more than forty minutes to drag the cans of water upstairs. The bath is still warm, though by now not hot, and I have already scented the water with stephanotis and chypre. It takes both of us some time to immobilize Saphir, who barks and struggles and tries to bite; but before long he is immersed in the lukewarm water and Jeannette can begin with the brush.

Meanwhile, Madame makes the finishing touches to her toilette, and sits rapt before her reflection in the mirror. Surely this time Monseigneur de Rochefort will be enamoured. Behind her, Jeannette and I struggle to envelop Saphir in a towel. A touch of violet essence seems to enhance, rather than mask, the reek of wet pug.

All the same, I think as I dust myself down, I must consider myself privileged to serve such a beautiful and fashionable lady. I am more than aware that my own sensibilities are somewhat bizarre; my sensitivity to smell verges on the monstrous, and that combined with my country upbringing means that I cannot – however much I may wish it – find the ladies (or gentlemen) of the Court to my taste. One day, God willing, I may find them so. For the moment, however, I have my duties to perform. I am Madame's *parfumier*: Monseigneur de Chanel, at your service.

Acknowledgements

Once more, as always, many thanks to the unsung heroes who have helped to bring these stories into print: to my agent Serafina Clarke, my foreign agent Jennifer Luithlen, my editor Francesca Liversidge and all my other friends at Transworld; to Louise Page, and to Anne Reeve, for keeping me in line, to Stuart Haygarth for his jacket designs, and to Kevin, Anouchka, Christopher and all those other people who have inspired me and kept me wriring, even when sometimes I didn't want to. Lastly, my heartfelt thanks to everyone who works to keep these books on the shelves – booksellers, sales representatives, distributors – and you, the readers, who have followed me this far.